Salvation

Also by
Mike Kirkpatrick

After Shocks

SALVATION

A Susan Solari Mystery

Mike Kirkpatrick
Author of *After Shocks*,
Finalist—Violet Crown Award

iUniverse, Inc.
New York Lincoln Shanghai

Salvation
A Susan Solari Mystery

Copyright © 2007 by Mike Kirkpatrick

All rights reserved. No part of this book may be used or reproduced by any means, graphic, electronic, or mechanical, including photocopying, recording, taping or by any information storage retrieval system without the written permission of the publisher except in the case of brief quotations embodied in critical articles and reviews.

iUniverse books may be ordered through booksellers or by contacting:

iUniverse
2021 Pine Lake Road, Suite 100
Lincoln, NE 68512
www.iuniverse.com
1-800-Authors (1-800-288-4677)

Because of the dynamic nature of the Internet, any Web addresses or links contained in this book may have changed since publication and may no longer be valid.

This is a work of fiction. All of the characters, names, incidents, organizations, and dialogue in this novel are either the products of the author's imagination or are used fictitiously.

ISBN: 978-0-595-47558-2 (pbk)
ISBN: 978-0-595-71205-2 (cloth)
ISBN: 978-0-595-91826-3 (ebk)

Printed in the United States of America

This novel is dedicated to my wife Leah, without whose love and support I would have never written a word.

Acknowledgments

Larry Shriner, Nikki Garza, and Karen Milton were always there for ideas, inspiration and support. I'm very much in their debt.

Prologue

▼

The rain glistens on the pavement, illuminated by the headlights of the medallion cabs rushing down Central Park West like an angry swarm of yellowjackets. A midnight blue Mercedes abandons the race, slows at 72nd street, and glides to a stop in front of the copper-clad gatehouse at the entrance to the Dakota.

The blonde twenty-something doorman steps forward, umbrella in hand, and opens the door of the sedan, greeting the woman in the back seat with a broad smile. The woman thanks her driver and starts to slide out of the car. Her skirt clings to the leather seat, exposing well-tanned, finely sculpted legs. She pauses just a moment longer than necessary as her eyes accept the doorman's admiring glance.

It's only moments until she's through the lobby and into the elevator. She puts her cardkey into the slot for the seventh floor penthouse, and the light to the left of the slot glows a welcoming green. The elevator takes her swiftly upward to her destination.

The doors open and she steps into the entry hall of her home and cuts off the alarm system. The sharp clicks of her Ferragamo spike heels reverberate off the terrazzo floor as she walks toward the bedroom. The echoes emphasize the loneliness she is feeling. Four days ago her husband left on a business trip to China, and already it seems he has been gone four months.

She reaches the bedroom and slips out of her gown, smiling as she thinks of the heads she turned upon her arrival at the opening of the new SoHo gallery. The green of the dress was the perfect complement to her red hair, and the cut of the skirt made a statement about her figure that no words could express.

The woman is tired and decides to go to bed immediately. She walks to the closet, meaning to pull out one of her husband's shirts. When he is gone she likes to sleep in them, relishing his smell. Suddenly a slap of a large hand covers her mouth and she feels the prick of a cold sharp point on the side of her neck. She tries to scream and pull away, but the strength of her attacker makes her efforts useless. Then she hears the muffled words, "If you scream, you die," and her assailant puts a blindfold over her eyes.

✳   ✳   ✳   ✳

When he's gone, she cannot get her breath and her heart seems to be trying to explode through her chest. One thought fills her mind: "I didn't scream. I didn't die."

Chapter 1

▼

They say a woman's work is never done. Well, mine sure as hell was, at least for today, anyway. I walked into the kitchen, where a narrow blade of afternoon sunlight cut through a window and illuminated a glass sitting on the counter. I filled that glass with a shitload of ice and looked around for the moving box marked "scotch". I spotted it in a stack of four in the corner of the room. Shit! Of *course* it was the one on the bottom. Give me a break.

I'd been schlepping crap around the apartment all day. I was tired, sweaty, and wanted a shower. But I needed a drink first, so I hauled the top three boxes to another corner and tore open the scotch box. Thank God the bottle hadn't broken. I filled the glass and quickly took a long sip. Hot damn, Johnnie Black never lets me down.

I carried the drink into the living room, pushed away a wad of packing paper, and collapsed on the couch. The bouquet of red carnations my sister Barbara had bought me as a housewarming present caught my eye. It was the only color in the place. My walls were still bare, my art still packed. Barbara had helped unpack for most of the day, but an hour ago she'd left for Greenwich to meet her husband and sons for dinner. I took a sip of the scotch and thought about the differences between us. She, meeting all the expectations of our parents. Me, two ex-husbands, ex-FBI, ex-Texas Female Executive of the Year. Ex, ex, ex. Did I detect a pattern? No shit, Sherlock.

But this wasn't the time to go down that road. Too much work left to do. I took another sip of the drink and let it linger in my mouth before it slid down my throat. Then I remembered one last chore I wanted to do. I left the couch and walked into the kitchen. I needed to clear off the kitchen counter so I'd have room for my coffee maker. The coffee from the deli just off Sheridan Square tasted like it was made from water straight out of the Hudson. Just as I picked up a stack of plates off the counter, I heard a loud knocking at my front door. It quickly became a pounding. Then I heard a male voice I didn't recognize bark out "Susan Solari? Susan Solari?"

I felt an emptiness in the pit of my stomach. *Terry disguising his voice? How had he found me so quickly? Had I locked the door after Barbara left?* The pounding continued.

I quietly approached the door and saw that the lock was open and that the safety chains were dangling toward the floor. And there was no damn peephole. Crap! I slowly slid the chains into their brackets on the doorjamb. But when I turned the lock, it responded with a loud thud.

"I heard that." He wasn't shouting, but there was an edge to his voice. Barely controlled. "I know you're in there."

"Who the hell are you?"

"Glenn Manion."

"That means squat to me."

"Fred Kirkland told me to get ahold of you. Said you'd be here unpacking. He was going to call."

"He didn't. How the hell do you know Fred?"

"We're both members of the CEO Roundtable."

"I haven't talked to Fred in a couple of days. Get the hell outta here or I'm calling 911."

"You'll regret that. Call Fred instead. He'll tell you I'm legit."

I wanted to get this asshole away from my front door. Maybe I could pacify him a little. "Tell you what. Come back tomorrow. I'll call Kirkland tonight. If you're okay, I'll see you tomorrow."

"Hell no, I need to see you now. Time's important." He pounded on the door again.

He wasn't going to go away. I looked for my purse and found it sitting in the corner of the couch. A couple of steps and I had it. I slipped my hand in the front pocket, took out my Glock 36, and walked back into the living room.

"If you'll shut up and stop pounding on the door, I'll try and reach Kirkland."

There was a pause. "Make it fast."

I almost yelled "Fuck you" but caught myself. No use in enraging him more than he was. I walked into the kitchen, Glock in hand, and picked up my cell phone off the counter. I returned to the living room and flipped the phone open. My thumb hit the speed dial number for Kirkland. He answered in two rings.

"Do you know some idiot named Glenn Manion?" I asked him.

"Damn. Sorry. I meant to call you. He's CEO of Medical Diagnostics, and he's no idiot. I ..." I cut him off and threw the phone on the couch. Fuck you, Kirkland. Sicing this jerk on me.

I walked to the door and released the lock, but not the safety chains. "Manion," I told him, "I'm going to let you in. But don't open the door until I tell you to. If you jump the gun, it'll be bad for your health."

"My health?"

"Just shut up and back away from the door." I silently released the two safety chains and then moved across the room, my back to the windows. I held the Glock in the two handed Weaver stance, aiming the pistol just to the right of the doorjamb, about chest high.

"You can come in. But open the door slowly."

He was a good boy. He slowly opened the door and stepped into the room. If he wasn't a CEO, he was dressed like one. Navy pinstriped suit, white shirt, and a red power tie. I saw his eyes widen when he saw the Glock. Without a word from me he raised his hands.

I kept the Glock pointed at his chest. "Leave the door open. Now, show me some ID." Manion lowered his hands. "With a picture," I added.

"Sure," Manion said. "But can you point that thing someplace else?"

"Not until I see the ID, and maybe not then."

He reached inside his coat pocket. "Take it out slowly," I said. "And slide it across the floor to me."

He pulled his hand out of his coat and slid a blue plastic card toward my feet. I kneeled down, keeping the Glock aimed at him, and picked up the card. When I flipped it over I saw it was a Medical Diagnostics company ID badge. Glenn Manion was printed in bold black lettering across the top. Below his name was a headshot of the man standing before me. The full head of short, black hair. The wide forehead and large jaws that created the impression that his head was almost square. The brown eyes set wide on his head under bushy eyebrows. The broad nose. If this guy wasn't Glenn Manion, he was his identical twin. Still, I wanted a cross check.

"You got a driver's license?" I asked.

"Yeah."

"Slide it over."

He reached into the back pocket of his trousers and produced his wallet. He pulled out the license and tossed it at my feet. I picked it up and compared it to the ID badge. Same name, same guy.

I handed the badge and license back to Manion, but kept the Glock pointed at him, snug against my stomach. Reaching for it would have been his death sentence. "Okay, I believe you're Glenn Manion. But that doesn't explain why you showed up at my door raising hell. By the way, how'd you get to my door? I sure as hell didn't buzz you in."

Manion returned the license to his wallet and put the ID badge back in his coat. "One of your neighbors left the entry door open a little too long. And I'll answer your question, but first put down that goddamned gun."

I lowered the Glock. "Sit over there," I said and pointed toward the couch. Manion took off his suit coat, threw it over the back of the couch and sat down. I sat in the wing chair a few feet away, then realized a stack of boxes partially blocked my view of Manion.

"Don't get too comfortable," I said and pointed at the boxes. "I need you to move those. Put them behind the couch." Manion glared at me. Apparently the CEO in him didn't like taking orders. Still, he did move the boxes and then returned to the couch.

"Put away the gun."

"Not just yet. Tell me why you're in my apartment."

Manion leaned toward me. "Two nights ago, my wife was raped."

And what the hell does that have to do with why you show up here beating on my door, I thought.

"I'm very sorry, but what does that have to do with me?" I said.

Manion closed his hands into fists, and the Glock came up. "I'll get to that," he said, too loud, tension seeming to wrack his entire body. "I was out of town. She called the police. They came, asked questions and left. Janet took a post rape exam."

"Sounds like they're on it," I said.

"They're not on crap. From what I can tell they've got nothing. The bastard was clever. Even used a condom so there's no semen."

I set the Glock on the table at the side of my chair. "Give them time. The New York Special Victims Unit is good."

"I'm not giving them shit. Here's what I know is going to happen. They'll investigate for a while. When nothing turns up, they'll lose interest. Go to another rape that they have a better chance of solving. Janet's case will wind up in some cold case file. And the bastard will get away. I'm not going to let that happen. He took something that's mine and I'm gonna get the asshole." His square face was red and he was breathing hard. I left the Glock where it was.

"I think you've got it all wrong, but you still haven't told me why you are here."

"I want to hire you to investigate Janet's rape."

"No way. That's just plain fucking crazy."

Manion stood up. "Look, I know what you're probably thinking. That I'm just some drunk-on-power CEO that wants special treatment for his ditzy trophy wife. That's not how it is. I love Janet. I want her rapist caught. With what little evidence the police have, they'll put this in the cold case file next week. I want more than that for Janet." He sat down, brown eyes watching me, sizing me up.

I just looked at Manion, trying to figure him out. I needed a couple of minutes to get my thoughts together. I left the chair, shoved the Glock in my jeans, and turned toward the kitchen. "I'm getting a glass of water. Do you want one?"

"Not now."

In the kitchen, it took just moments for me to fill a glass from the tap, but it gave me the time I needed. I returned to the chair and laid the gun on the side table again.

"Well?" Manion said.

I took a sip of the water. "Look, when I was with the FBI I ran undercover drug operations. I didn't investigate sex crimes. I'm starting a corporate security consulting practice, not a PI agency. Hire a PI. There are hundreds in Manhattan."

Manion shook his head and leaned toward me. "I want you."

"Why?"

"Francie Marcos and the other women."

I was stunned. "Fred told you about that?"

"Yeah. He said you were good with dealing with violated, vulnerable women."

"He had no right. Those women are owed more." I heard the edge in my voice.

"But he did." Manion's manner changed, the initiative passing to him. "And I know what you can do. And why you do it. That's why I want you on the case."

For a moment I envisioned Francie Marcos hanging from her closet door. Her face distorted and her blood collecting in her hands and feet. Finally Manion said, "So you'll take the case?"

"I want to talk to your wife first. Then we'll see." But I knew I was kidding myself. The past gave me no options.

Manion left the couch. "Fine, you can see Janet tomorrow at three." He had known the outcome of this discussion before it started. He put on his coat, reached into his breast pocket and offered me a business card. "This is our address. The Dakota. Seventh floor. Do you want me there?"

I stood and took the card. "In the apartment. But not in the room." I showed him to the door. There were no polite goodbyes. He just walked out. I was glad to see him go.

I noticed the ice had melted in my drink. I dumped it in the sink and refilled the glass. This time no ice. I threw the scotch to the back of my throat. Damn you, Francie Marcos.

Chapter 2

▼

I was still on the couch when there was another knock on my front door. *Jesus, he's back.* I glanced at the door. *I didn't lock up when he left!* I picked up the Glock, hurried across the room, threw the deadbolt into place, and called out "Who's there?"

"Well, it ain't some stud that's going to break in, ravish you and make all your fantasies come true, if that's what you want." It was the raspy voice of Cecelia Boldaccio I had first heard fifteen years ago.

"Cecil! Just a sec." I jammed the Glock between the cushions of the couch, hurried back to release the deadbolt and flung the door open. "Cecil!"

Before I could say another word, she enclosed me in a bear hug with my nose buried in her ample breasts. "God, it's great to see you," she said. "You look terrific."

I managed to free myself so I could get some air, "Liar. I'm dirty, I smell, and my hair looks like shit. But otherwise, I'm terrific. How about you?"

"Nothing wrong with me a little dinner won't fix."

Then I remembered. Last week Cecil and I had agreed to have dinner together tonight. The encounter with Manion had so addled my brain I'd forgotten. I tried to hide it. "Come on in, but dinner's going to have to wait a little bit. I'm running late. I've got to take a shower and put some decent clothes on. Where are we going to dinner?" We moved out of the hallway into my apartment. I closed the door and *this time* I threw the deadbolt.

"Home," Cecil said.

"I thought we were going out," I said. "Besides, if I remember correctly, you have only a passing acquaintance with that strange room called a kitchen."

"No, not at my apartment; at the restaurant, Home."

"Where's that?"

"Oh, yeah. I forgot you've been in the hinterlands for God knows how long. I'm going to have to retrain you."

Cecil was still Cecil. "Just tell me where the restaurant is."

"I picked a place close to you, so you wouldn't get lost in the big bad city. It's about a ten-minute walk from here on Cornelia Street. It's not expensive as Village restaurants go, and the food is great."

"Perfect," I said. "Sit down and I'll get you a glass of wine to sip on while I shower. Chardonnay okay?"

Cecil took a seat on the couch. "Sure. But only the best in the house."

"You got it," I said and walked into the kitchen. As I poured the wine, I observed Cecil. Her fashion sense hadn't improved since we'd shared an apartment at NYU. She wore a loose-fitting white cotton top and a pair of khaki slacks. She'd tried to dress up the outfit with a multi-colored scarf around her neck. But it looked like what it was, a cheap outfit with a scarf.

I went back into the living room and handed Cecil the wine. "Give me twenty minutes. I've got to wash a day of unpacking boxes off my body."

A broad smile spread across Cecil's face. "Honey, anything on my body, I'm gonna keep there."

I shook my head. "Well, I guess it's nice to know you haven't changed." With that I headed for the shower.

Fifteen minutes later I was all dressed except for putting on a pair of black, loose fitting slacks. The ones with the right side pocket cut out so I could reach through to get the NAA mini .32 in the holster I had strapped my thigh. Normally I'd be taking a big chance carrying a weapon in New York. The Sullivan law calls for a mandatory year in jail if you're caught. But celebrities and other VIP's can get a letter of courtesy from the mayor permitting them to carry. So before I came to Manhattan, I cashed in a marker. A few years ago, when I was in the FBI, I had done a favor for the current mayor's son. A big favor. So when I requested a letter, I had it within a week.

I slipped on the slacks and Cecil and I were on the way to Home in a matter of minutes. But before we started down the stairs, I taped one end of a slender translucent thread to the top of my apartment door and the other end to the doorjamb. No sign of Terry for six months. But I couldn't afford to relax. For me, to relax is to die.

* * * *

Cecil was true to her word; Home was just a few minutes away. We walked the two blocks to Bleecker Street and then south on Bleecker for a half block. Cornelia was just a block long, tucked in between Bleecker and Avenue of the Americas. As we walked up Cornelia, we stopped to admire a half dozen Siamese kittens playing in a pet shop window. After a couple of minutes of making baby talk with the kittens, Cecil suddenly turned to me. "Hey, where's Caesar?"

"He's still back in Dallas," I said. "My former next-door neighbor is taking care of him until I get settled in here. I'll go get him in a couple of weeks."

"Well, tell that one-eyed cat hello."

"Sure thing. I'm sure it won't take him a week to decide he's king of my new place."

Two doors down was the restaurant. We were greeted by the smell of coffee brewing at a serving station at the front of a narrow dining room. Small tables lined the left wall; three booths were on the right. I could see an open kitchen at the back of the dining room. The aromas of the food being prepared wafted in and made me hungrier than I had been in days. And it wasn't just food whetting my appetite. I was in an oasis of calm with a trusted friend. Safe, for a while.

In a couple of moments the hostess arrived. She was rail thin with shoulder-length blonde hair; her dark roots were showing. Four rhinestone studs sparkled at the edge of each of her ears and a larger silver stud nestled between her bottom lip and her chin. A small nametag on her straight black cotton dress said Brenda. Cecil asked for a table available on the patio. Brenda nodded and led us around the kitchen and down a narrow hallway. It spilled out onto a small square concrete patio. It was filled with small, closely spaced tables with faux green marble tops. About half the tables were occupied.

"Can we have the one over there, in the back corner?" I said.

"Sure," Brenda said, and showed us to the table. I slid into the chair that faced out onto the patio, putting my back to the wall.

Cecil smiled and shook her head. "Still protecting your backside, Special Agent Solari?"

"Old habits die hard."

At that moment a waiter with GQ model looks arrived at the table. His smile was as beautiful as he was. "Hi, I'm Wayne and I'll be taking care of you this evening."

"God, I hope so," Cecil said. "What time are we leaving this joint?"

A practiced smile spread across Wayne's face. "Unfortunately, I'm otherwise engaged tonight. Something I know I'll regret forever."

"Oh, you're good," Cecil said. "You've got a great future ahead of you. Now bring me an Old Fashioned, and one for my friend."

I shook my head. "Just a scotch and soda, Johnnie Walker Black." Wayne made a note on his order pad and left to get the drinks.

I unrolled the napkin in front of me and nudged the silverware around the table. "So how's the world of pottery treating you? Last time we talked you were hoping to get big a showing."

"I got it, girlfriend. In a couple of months at a gallery in SoHo. Almost didn't happen, though. It was all set, then the owner, a guy named Bill Watson, started making noises that we might have to reschedule. I always thought Bill was gay, but I found out a certain little chippie was proving me wrong. Seems like she did watercolors and wanted a show in his gallery. I got a look at her. She brought things to the table this body couldn't serve up ..."

"So what happened?"

"She must have been working both sides of the street. In January, a gallery with twice the clientele of Watson's announced a major show for her in April. She dumped Watson faster than Fritz Schumer can get in front of a camera. I was back on the schedule."

I smiled and shook my head. "A pure heart will win out every time."

Cecil let out a whoop. "Honey, if that were the case, the only place my pottery would be is Big Lots."

Wayne returned with our drinks and brought us dinner menus. "We've got a roasted lamb special tonight," he said. "I recommend it. It comes with glazed carrots and spinach in a lemon sauce. I'll give you some time to look over the menu."

We spent a little time looking over the choices and sipping our drinks. As Cecil wrapped her hand around her glass, I noticed the toll her potter's work took on her hands. Her skin was dry and her cuticles were cracked and irregular.

She noticed me looking. "Damn clay sucks all the moisture out." Then she laid her menu on the table and leaned toward me. "Okay, out with it."

"Out with what?"

"Why you moved back to Manhattan. I'm not buying that crap about being close so you can take care of your parents. They're in Mount Vernon. Your sister's in Greenwich, about, let's see ... a whole thirty minutes away?"

I didn't answer for a few seconds. I took a long swig of my scotch. "I'm starting a corporate security consulting practice. This is where corporate headquarters are."

Cecil took a very long sip of her Old Fashion. "Bullshit. You can do that from anywhere. Anyway, I thought you had something going with that reporter."

A little too quickly I said, "He's not a reporter. He's the business editor of the *Dallas Morning News*. And he writes a nationally syndicated column."

A little smile appeared on Cecil's face. "Uh-huh. What's his name?"

"Dom. Dominick Shapiro. But I'm not ready to get involved. The thing with Terry is just too raw."

"Baby," Cecil said, "don't let the memories of that asshole drive you away from a good thing."

I started to tell Cecil it was other memories that were coming between Dom and me, but I just let it go. "He's not happy I moved. He's coming here in a couple of days to 'help get me settled,' as they say. We'll see …"

Wayne was back. "Ready to order? And I'll refresh those drinks too."

"I'll have the lamb," I said. "And I'm switching to wine. A glass of your house Shiraz."

Cecil ordered veal chops and a glass of Chardonnay, and then turned her attention back to me. "I never quite understood what came down in Dallas."

I told her the story of the most recent year of my life, ending with the confrontation at Tee Pee Hill.

When I finished Cecil almost shouted, "Holy Shit!" Several of the other restaurant patrons jerked their eyes toward our table.

"Let me see if I've got this straight. You and Terry separate and you file for divorce. Terry thinks you're having an affair with your boss … what's his name again?"

"Tom Grant."

"Yeah. Tom Grant. Then old Tom's murdered. Then Terry tries to kill you. Right?"

I just nodded, afraid my voice would betray me.

"You set a trap for Grant's killer but it goes bad. The killer's about put one in your gut, but Terry offs him just in time. So Terry saved your butt?"

I drank the last of my scotch. "You might say that. I guess his Special Forces training was good for *something*. But then again, not really. He didn't want someone else to kill me. He wanted to do it himself. I have to live my life like he still does and will try again."

She put her hand over her mouth, the full impact registering. "Sorry, I didn't know."

"I don't like to talk about it. I was just lucky that one of my guys wounded him. Bad thing is he's still at large. And I'm paying him alimony."

"What? How the hell can that happen?"

"I'd signed the divorce settlement before he tried to put a bullet in my head. He hasn't been convicted of anything yet, so the court won't vacate the order."

"Fucking lawyers," Cecil said. "Do you have any idea where he is?"

"Not a clue. My alimony check goes to a bank in Grand Cayman and the trail ends there. Those bankers are tighter than the Swiss."

"I think," Cecil said, "there's more to this than you're telling me."

"Yeah, get me drunk some night and I'll give you the whole story."

"No time like the present, sweetheart."

I felt the weight of the mini .32 on my thigh. "Believe me, I'd like nothing better. But I've got to be at the top of my game tomorrow."

Cecil looked like she wanted to ask another question, but said nothing. Wayne brought our wine and then went to a nearby table that was signaling for their check.

Cecil's eyes engaged mine and would not let go. "You haven't answered my first question."

"And that was?"

"Why did you move back to Manhattan?"

I thought a long minute about that. "Let's just say that I needed to come home."

Chapter 3

Cecil didn't push me any further. I considered telling her about my encounter with Glenn Manion, but thought better of it. I wasn't sure how that was going to play out.

We spent the rest of the meal recalling our time at NYU. Cecil was far better than I at networking. She had kept in touch with a number of our classmates who lived in the city and promised that after her show, she'd host a reunion party at her apartment. By the end of the evening, whether because of the wine or Cecil's good humor, I was feeling better about myself and my decision to return to Manhattan.

* * * *

The following afternoon, I was at the round, brass gatehouse of the Dakota about ten minutes before my three o'clock appointment. I showed the doorman some ID. He made a phone call. While I waited, I realized I was standing within a foot or two of where John Lennon was shot, and for some, the world was changed forever. My reverie was broken when the doorman waved me through the large iron gates that guarded the entrance to the building.

It was a quick ride to the seventh floor. There was only one apartment door opening off the small elevator lobby. I punched the doorbell and heard a chorus of Westminster chimes sound inside the apartment.

In a few moments, a stunningly beautiful woman opened the door.

"Janet?" I said.

"Yes." Her dark red hair, worn shoulder length, framed an oval face that featured eyes the color of emeralds. But there was no life in those eyes. Just a vacant stare as if she didn't recognize I was standing in front of her. She stood at least two inches taller than me, but the slump in her shoulders almost equalized our height. Her figure suggested that she could have spent some time on high fashion runways, but if she had ever had the proud carriage of a model, the rapist had ripped it away.

She wore a short-sleeved green cashmere sweater and a pair of white linen slacks. A pair of green sandals, perfectly matched to the sweater, completed the ensemble. It was if she had decided that if she picked the perfect outfit, her life would be okay, like it was before the rape.

Without another word she turned and walked away from the door. As I followed her from the entry hall into the living room of the penthouse, I reminded myself that I needed to avoid my usual bull-like rush to the point and handle her more like a cracked vessel. Otherwise, I'd probably do more harm than good.

She stopped in front of a large window that overlooked Central Park. I walked up beside her and took in the view. The late spring foliage on the trees blanketed the park in bright green, punctuated by red and yellow color beds. I could see park visitors sitting on the benches that encircled the Imagine mosaic in the heart of Strawberry Fields.

"Can I get you something to drink?" she asked.

I don't usually drink on the job, and I *was* on the job, but I thought a glass of wine might break the ice, and if she joined me, relax her a bit. "A glass of Chardonnay, perhaps?"

"We have a Chateau Chandon, or if you want something domestic, a J. Lohr. Glenn has become quite the wine expert and takes a lot of pride in his selections, so I'm sure you will like either."

"The J. Lohr," I said.

Janet hadn't yet made full eye contact with me. Instead, she just walked to a bar beside the window, opened a small wine cellar, withdrew a previously opened bottle, and filled two glasses. She returned and set the glasses on a coffee table that separated a light blue loveseat and a rose wing chair. I took the wing chair, she the loveseat.

"I appreciate your time," I said.

Janet took a sip of her wine and finally looked me in the eye. "I really didn't want to talk to you. But Glenn thinks the police will treat this as just another rape and won't give my case the attention it deserves. He's determined that my rapist …" She stopped speaking, shook her head, and her eyes became moist.

"*My rapist, my rapist* ... curious phrase, that. It suggests that every woman has one, and in some form we all do, don't we?"

I thought about Terry. "Yes, in some form." I resisted my urge to get past this small talk and charge right into an interrogation. Better to have her guide the conversation for a few minutes and become more comfortable with me.

She set her wine glass on the coffee table. "What's your agreement with Glenn?"

"I'm to investigate your rape. Find the perp if I can. Of course, I'll turn over any information I uncover to the police, who will ultimately make the arrest."

Janet furrowed her brow, "How much do you have to tell Glenn?"

I leaned toward her. "Beg pardon?"

"About the details of the rape ... if I tell you."

"How much have *you* told him?" I asked.

"Very little."

"Do you want to keep it that way?"

"Yes."

"Then that's the way it'll be."

She picked up her wine glass and drained it. "But he's paying your fee. He'll insist."

I sat back in my chair. "He may be paying my fee, but I consider you my client. I always observe client confidentiality when requested."

"Thank you," she said, almost in a whisper. She paused a few seconds and said, "Glenn is here, you know ... in the study. He said you were to meet with him after we talked."

"That's the arrangement we made. I'll want you at that meeting as well," I said.

"That's not necessary. I trust you to keep any confidences."

"I appreciate that," I replied. "But I'd like to have you there. Shall we begin?"

"I'd like another glass of Chardonnay," Janet said. "How about you?"

"No, I'm fine."

She went to the bar, filled her glass, and returned to the loveseat. She ran her hand through her hair. "What do you want to know?"

I reached into my purse and pulled out a note pad and a pen. "For starters, just tell me about the evening you were raped."

Janet diverted her eyes from mine and stared at the coffee table. "A friend I volunteer with at the Metropolitan Museum was opening a new gallery in SoHo. Glenn and I were invited to a preview party. He had a conflict, a trip to China, but I wanted to support my friend so I went to the party alone."

"How'd you get to the gallery?" I asked.

"I had a limousine take me there and bring me back. A service Glenn and I use all the time."

"Go on."

"I got back home about eleven-thirty. I was tired and meant to go directly to bed."

"Was your security system armed while you were at the party?"

Janet took more than a sip from her wine glass. "Yes, I remember disarming it when I got home."

I made a note on my pad. "Did you rearm it immediately after you got in the apartment?"

Janet slowly shook her head. "I meant to but didn't. I remember thinking that I had to do that before I went to bed."

I could see Janet's hands beginning to shake, and she slid them between her slacks and the couch. "Oh God," she said, "That makes what happened my fault. If I had reset the alarm and locked the door, it never would have happened. Please don't tell Glenn."

I put my pen and note pad on the coffee table. "Janet," I said, raising my voice slightly, "Look at me and remember this, internalize it. Rape is *never*, I repeat *never*, the victim's fault."

Janet was crying softly. "Okay."

I pulled a tissue out of my purse and offered it to her. She took it and dabbed at her eyes.

"Are you ready to go on?"

"Yes," she said and took another sip of her wine. "I remember taking off my dress and walking to Glenn's closet. I like to sleep in his shirts when he's gone. I had my back to the room, looking in the closet. That's when he grabbed me."

She described feeling a knife at her throat, her losing struggle to free herself, and finally being blindfolded.

"Tell me about the blindfold," I said.

"It was more of a mask, really, with no holes for the eyes. You know, like people wear to help them sleep. He just slipped it over the top of my head and over my eyes. He told me that if I took it off he'd slit my throat."

I flipped over the page in my note pad. "Did you get any kind of look at him before he blindfolded you?"

"No."

Janet began to cry again and reached for her wine. I leaned across the coffee table and put my hand on her wrist. "Janet," I said, "let's slow down on that till we're finished. I need you to have a clear head."

She blushed and released the glass. "You're right. It's just so hard to talk about."

"I know," I said. "But that's going to help us get the bad guy."

She nodded and took a deep breath. "Okay. After he blindfolded me, he put his right hand on my shoulder and backed me away from the closet. He kept the knifepoint on my neck. I think we stopped in the middle of the room.

"He took his hand off my shoulder and again told me he'd kill me if I tried to take off the blindfold. Then he took the knife away. I could hear him walking around the room. I could see a little light at the edges of the blindfold, and it kept getting brighter and brighter as he walked around. I think he was turning on all the lights in the room."

I stopped taking notes. I knew I would remember what she was going to tell me in the next few minutes. I could write it down later.

"Finally he said, 'Let's have a look at you.' He made me take off my bra, and then I heard him walk in a circle around me. Then he said 'Very nice.'"

Janet turned her head slightly so she was looking directly into my eyes. "Please, just a little more wine?"

I nodded. She took two long sips from the glass and returned it to the coffee table.

"Janet," I said, "go on."

"He told me to take off my panties. I heard him walking around me again and then the words 'Even better.' Then he told me to stand very still, that if I tried to escape, he'd kill me. He didn't say anything for a few minutes. I thought I could hear him moving, but the sound came from the same spot in the room.

"When he spoke again, I could tell he was directly in front of me. He told me to kneel down and bow my head. I followed his directions."

When Janet said this, she lowered her head, as if she was acting out the experience.

"He told me that he was going to remove the blindfold, but if I looked at anything other than the floor, he's slash my face. Then he took the blindfold off."

I hadn't realized that I was leaning toward Janet until my pen and note pad slid off my lap and landed on the floor. "Sorry," I said, but Janet didn't seem to notice.

"When the blindfold was gone, I saw his feet. Just his feet, no shoes, no socks."

"What color was his skin?" I asked

"White."

"What was he wearing?"

Janet shifted on the loveseat, "All I saw were his jeans. They were black."

"It's strange he took off his shoes and socks, but kept his pants on, I said. "But Go on."

"He told me to raise my head to the level of his waist, and again threatened to slash me if I looked any higher. I slowly raised my head. Before I got to his waist, I saw that his fly was open and I saw his erection. Then his hand came down in front of my face. He wore a surgical glove and held a condom between his thumb and index finger. 'Put it on me,' he said. I unrolled the condom on his penis."

Janet stopped talking. "Just a little more," I said.

She picked up her wine glass and drained it. "He told me to lower my head. He put the blindfold back on. He put his hands under my armpits and raised me to my feet. Then he shoved me onto the bed, forced me to spread my legs, and raped me."

"I know this is difficult," I said. "But I do have a few more questions. Are you up to it?"

Janet nodded.

"Think for just a moment. Anything unusual you haven't told me?"

"No, nothing I can remember ... Wait, there was one thing. When I put the condom on him, I noticed he had no pubic hair."

Yeah, I thought, no pubic hair. I bet he shaved his entire body, including under his arms. Nothing to leave for DNA matching.

"His voice," I said. "Was there anything distinctive to it, an accent or something?"

"No accent, but he seemed to be angry. And I don't think I did anything to provoke him. He was that way from the beginning." Janet's voice was becoming stronger. The tears had stopped.

"One other thing I remember now." She left the loveseat and began to pace around the room. "When we were on the bed, when he was raping me, his head touched my cheek. But I didn't feel his skin. It was some sort of fabric, like he was wearing something over his head."

"Like a stocking?" I asked.

Janet picked up her wine glass and set it on the bar. "No it was thicker, rougher."

I got out of my chair and joined Janet at the bar. "Like maybe a ski mask?"

"Perhaps. But why would he wear a mask? He blindfolded me."

"Insurance," I said, "in case you sneaked a look."
"Are we done now?" Janet asked.
"Almost," I said. "What happened after he raped you?"
"He told me to stay on the bed and keep the blindfold on. He left the bed and in a few seconds, I heard the toilet flush in the bathroom. Then I heard him come back into the room, and he didn't say anything for a few minutes. Then he said he was leaving. That I had been a good girl. That I had saved my life. He told me to stay on the bed with the blindfold on until I had counted to one hundred. I heard him start to walk out of the room, but he stopped. Before he left he said, 'Give my regards to Glenn.'"

Chapter 4

▼

Janet Manion's statement hit me like a slap in the face. If true, the circumstances surrounding her rape were far more sinister than I had imagined. "He did what?" I said. "He used Glenn's name?"

The tone of my voice or my face must have told her more than I intended. Her eyes darted from side to side and she took two steps back away from me. "Yes."

"Did you tell that to the police?"

"I think so ... but I don't remember."

I walked over to the coffee table, picked up my note pad and pen, and put them in my purse. "It's important that we talk to Glenn. Now."

"He said that you could meet him in the study."

Before we left the living room, I asked Janet if she had told Glenn about the rapist calling his name. She shook her head.

"He has to be told," I said. "I'm sure the police said something ... if you told *them*. But if not, we have to tell him now."

Janet didn't comment directly. After a few seconds, she said, "I'll show you to the study."

We walked out of the living room down a short hallway that ended at the entrance to a brightly lit room. As I walked down the hallway, I could hear a man's loud and angry voice coming from the study. Janet stopped about three feet from the entrance and did not move. I brushed past her and went to the doorway of the room. Glenn Manion was on his cell phone. He had a microphone hooked over his ear and paced around the room as he talked. He spoke in short, direct sentences and punctuated his remarks by waving his arms.

"No, damn it. That won't cut it ... that's no excuse. You have the revised schedule on my desk Wednesday or you'll be our new vice president in charge of five Chinamen and a goat. And the goat might be the smartest one. And I want all the players to sign off on this: engineering, software, and manufacturing. Everybody. Understand?"

He saw me, signaled for us to come into the room, and continued his conversation. "And you better make sure Pearson knows he's exhausted his quota of fuck-ups. One more missed milestone and he's out on his ass ... well, make sure, damn it."

He hit a button on the phone and yanked out the earpiece. "Fucking product development," he said as he put the phone on a writing desk.

He turned to face us. "I'm sorry, these bastards make me crazy."

He wore a white dress shirt with gold cufflinks and no tie. His blue pinstriped trousers and black wing tips suggested that a suit coat hung in a nearby closet. He walked across the room and extended a beefy hand to me. "Are you and Janet through?"

"Not quite. I need to talk to you before we finish."

"Okay," he said. "Come in and have a seat."

Glenn Manion's study was a man's room, done in hunter green and deep reds. The furniture was large and overstuffed. Built-in bookcases occupied one wall. Across from the hallway door, a series of windows provided a view of 72nd street.

Manion took a seat on a rust-colored leather couch that looked crinkled enough to be comfortable. I sat in a green leather wing chair separated from the couch by a low table with a chessboard built into the top. A full complement of chessmen was set for battle on the board. Janet joined her husband on the couch ... at the opposite end.

I was barely seated when Manion said, "Why do you need to see me?" The question was put directly to me, as if his wife were not in the room.

"There's been a significant development," I said.

"What?" Manion said as he leaned across the table toward me.

"I believe there's a strong possibility that Janet was targeted for this rape." I explained how the rapist had mentioned Glenn's name as the left the apartment.

Manion looked back and forth between Janet and me. "Why didn't the damn police tell me this? Incompetent son'bitches."

He looked over at Janet. "See, that's why I hired Susan here."

She shuffled deeper into the couch. "I ... I don't think I told them. I didn't remember until I talked to Susan. I'm sorry."

Manion turned away from Janet. "How the hell can someone forget something like that?"

I was tired of Manion's bullying manner. "It's not Janet's fault that she didn't mention it to the police ... if she didn't. A terrifying experience like a rape does awful things to a mind. It tries to block out the worst parts of what happened. Janet will probably remember other details as time goes by. It's normal and very common among victims of violent crimes."

Before Manion could respond to my remark, we were interrupted by the shrill ring of his cell phone. He went to the desk and picked up. "This is Glenn."

He listened to the caller for a short time and then said, "No, Ray, we won't be making it this month. I'll explain later ... No, nothing permanent, I imagine we'll be there in June, maybe July."

He walked the length of the couch as he talked. As Manion reached where Janet was seated, she turned and looked up at him. I saw her eyes widen, the color drain from her face, and tears roll down her cheeks. It was as if she were silently pleading with him.

Manion finished the call and returned to his end of the couch. "I was about to say I think your point about Janet being targeted is a lot of horseshit. There are a lot of ways he could have found out who lives in this apartment."

"That's my point exactly," I said. "Rapists aren't normally concerned about the names of their victims. Rape is usually a crime of opportunity. This is the Dakota, for God's sake, Glenn. This guy had to plan how to get into the building and then into the apartment."

Manion sat back on the couch, silent for a few seconds. "I guess it's worth checking out, but why the hell would he target Janet?"

"If we can answer that," I said, "we're a long way down the road to getting the guy." I looked at Janet. Some color had returned to her face and she was using a tissue to dry her tears.

"Have you been getting any strange phone calls ... hang ups, nobody on the line, obscene?" I asked.

Janet sat straighter on the couch. "No, nothing."

"And has there been a situation recently where you thought someone might be hitting on you? Even just flirting with you at a party."

"I'll answer that," Manion said. "The only parties we've been to recently have been Medical Diagnostics company parties. You think some ignorant son'bitch is going to be stupid enough to think he could get in my wife's pants?"

"For certain men," I said, "the fact that Janet *is* the wife of the CEO would make her more attractive."

Janet buried her face in her hands. She made no sound.

Manion turned around on the couch to face her. "Some asshole hitting on you? I'll tear him a new one."

Janet raised her head from her hands. Tears again streamed down her face. "No ... nothing like that ... really. It's just that ... this has just ... been, too much, that's all."

Manion stood up and walked around the couch, put his hands on its back and leaned forward toward me, "We're not getting any damned place with this."

"Not necessarily," I said. "Let's focus on you."

Manion pulled his hands off the couch. "Me? I wasn't the one raped." Janet quickly turned her head and looked away from both of us. Manion didn't notice.

I just stared at him, then slowly moved my eyes to Janet. He finally got it. "I'm sorry, hon. I'm as upset about this as you are."

When Janet turned around, her face was red and the look of sorrow had been replaced by one of anger. "Hardly."

I left the wing chair. "Glenn, have you been getting any threats? Anyone in particular have it in for you?"

He shook his square head, brown eyes cold. "No specific threats. But I'm a CEO. My job *is* to make decisions that piss people off. But I don't think any of them would be crazy enough to rape my wife." He walked to the windows and looked down on 72nd street.

"Never say never," I said.

Manion walked from the windows and leafed through the papers scattered on the desk "There might be one guy."

"Go on," I said.

"Couple of months ago, the company discovered the design of one of our new products was leaked to a competitor. We narrowed it down to three people, but couldn't determine which one. So I fired all three. We gave them generous packages; two went away quietly, one raised holy hell."

"Do you remember the names?"

"You bet your ass I do. Alex Watson, Alice Nixon, Errol Sanregret."

"Which one raised hell?"

"Sanregret. He told his boss he'd make my life miserable as long as I lived. For a couple of weeks he tried to get back into the building. Security kept him out. We haven't heard from him in several weeks."

"Why'd he focus on you? I'd think it'd be his boss."

Manion stabbed his index finger at me. "The loss of that fucking design may kill our company. I had to make an example. I made a company-wide address on our satellite network. I announced the firings, named names."

I returned to the wing chair. "I expect your human resources people will have a current address for him. After all, he didn't reject the settlement checks, did he?"

"Hell no, the son'bitch."

"One more thing, and then we're done for today," I said. "What was the reason for your trip to China?"

"I was part of the mayor's trade delegation."

"Did the trip get a lot of publicity?"

"Hell, yes. You know the mayor; he doesn't miss an opportunity to get his name or his mug in the press. The *New York Times* did a big article on the trip. And I know WNBC did a story; I was interviewed."

"So it would have been fairly easy for someone who was paying attention to know you were out of the city?"

"Yeah, I guess so," Manion said, staring at me.

"Well, I've got work to do," I said. As I stood to leave, I glanced at Janet. Her shoulders were slumped. There was no light in her eyes. She did not rise from the couch to tell me goodbye. I put my hand on her shoulder and she raised her head to look at me.

"We're on our way," I said. "We'll get him."

"Thank you," she whispered.

I looked at Manion. "You'll hear from me," I said, and walked out of the room.

Chapter 5

▼

As I left the Dakota and made the short walk down 72nd Street to Central Park West, the symphony that was the sounds of Manhattan filled my ears. The traffic roared and impatient cabbies blasted away on their horns. I heard the siren of an emergency vehicle fading away as it headed south toward Columbus Circle. Friday afternoon rush hour was underway.

I hailed a cab, gave the driver my address and settled in for what I anticipated would be an agonizingly slow and expensive trip back to my apartment. The cabby's badge hung over the passenger side visor and identified him as Lazlo Valdic; birthplace, Budapest, Hungary. The man in the picture was clean-shaven, but my driver sported a heavy beard. His prominent nose, however, was the same one visible on the ID photo. Next to the ID was a picture of the bearded one with a brunette woman and two small girls. We all have family pictures in our office.

Lazlo hit a button on the dashboard and a recorded message from Bernadette Peters reminded me to fasten my seat belt. Before I could buckle up, I heard my cell phone's irritating ring. I fumbled around in my purse for the damned thing, but by the time I grabbed it, the ringing had stopped. I took a chance and hit the answer button, but the caller was long gone.

As I was putting the phone back in my purse, it started beeping and a message on the screen announced that I had one missed call. "Shit," I said under my breath. "Cell phones are like men," I thought. "I'd just as soon do without them, but when I need one, I *really* need one … and the alternative ain't nearly as good."

I displayed the caller ID and Dom Shapiro's number appeared. "Jesus," I thought, "he'll be here tomorrow." Before I could work up a good case of guilt for almost forgetting about his visit, the cell phone beeped again and the screen announced I had a voice mail message. Just as I keyed in my password, I heard Lazlo shout out a long string of what must have been Hungarian expletives and then hit the brake hard.

Because I hadn't taken Bernadette's advice, I was hurled forward into the plastic divider separating me from the driver. My cell phone flew out of my hand and landed on top of my purse that had been thrown onto the floor of the cab.

"Jesus Christ," I screamed. "What the hell was that?" While I was taking inventory to see if I still had all my body parts, Lazlo let loose with another string of words I couldn't understand. But somewhere in the middle, I did catch "fucking" and "cutoff." It was all the explanation I needed … and all the explanation I got.

I picked up my phone and reentered my password. When I played the message, there was urgency in Dom's voice. "Susan, it's Dom. My flight tomorrow morning's been canceled, but I can catch one tonight. It doesn't get into Newark till eleven. Don't know what you've got planned, but could you stand some late night or early morning company? Call me back on my cell as soon as you can."

Damn it! I'd planned to use tomorrow morning to think through my feelings about Dom and decide how to handle his visit. He had insisted on coming to Manhattan to help with any heavy lifting I needed to get settled. At the time, I was ready to put anything or anybody associated with Dallas behind me. But the news of my move had been such a blow to him, I hadn't had the heart to say no. I thought it was a mistake at the time, and was sure it was now.

But it was too late to chicken out. I called him back and told him that a late arrival was fine. That I'd have a midnight snack ready for him. As I hung up I thought, "That's all you'll be getting tonight."

* * * *

My kitchen was in no shape to whip up a late night snack. That was a good excuse, but not the real reason I found myself in the Blue Fox deli buying a couple of turkey on focaccia bread sandwiches and a quart of coleslaw. I was there because I remembered the feelings I used to have when I prepared food for Dom, and I didn't want to get anywhere close to them tonight.

The guy behind the counter bagged up my purchases, and I was leaving the deli when a woman barged through the door and plowed directly into me. The blow knocked me off balance, and I stumbled and fell to the floor. The coleslaw container burst open and splattered the slaw all over my jeans.

"Why don't you watch where the hell you're going?" I snarled as I struggled to my feet.

Then I heard, "Oh shit! I'm sorry. Are you hurt?"

"Why the hell would I be hurt?" I snapped. "I only got knocked down and covered with fucking coleslaw. No problem here."

The woman moved away from me and watched while the deli clerk, towel in hand, rushed from behind the counter and tried to wipe the coleslaw off my jeans. Maybe at the start he *was* trying to be helpful. But he soon proved that all men are pigs, when the towel began lingering a little too long on my butt.

Just before I jerked it out of his hand, he felt the .32 on my thigh and his eyes got real wide real fast. "That's all the help I need, boy scout," I said. "Go feel up some salami, start with your own." He quickly retreated back behind the counter.

As I finished what cleanup I could do, I glared at the woman across the room. She was about my height, short blonde hair, and blue eyes. She wore jeans, a white cropped-top, and sneakers. Her face was flushed and her eyes were moist. "I'm really, really sorry," she said. "I'm late to meet my boyfriend, and I wanted to rush in and out."

Then I saw her expression change and she said, "He's gonna really be mad now. I gotta go. Are you sure you're okay?"

I sensed she had bigger problems than knocking down a stranger in a deli. My butt hurt, but I didn't think anything was broken. "Best I can tell, I'll survive," I said. "But in case something turns up later, give me your name, phone number, and address."

She looked hesitant, but finally said, "Sure."

I borrowed a pen from the clerk, grabbed a napkin off the counter and said, "Shoot." This seemed to really upset the clerk.

"It's Lynette, Lynette Mason. And I'm going to give you my business number. It's the Raven bookstore in the East Village. I work there."

She gave me the number and her address. I didn't recognize the street and made a mental note to check it out. I took another napkin, wrote my name and cell phone number on it, and handed it to Mason. "Just for the record."

"Now I really gotta leave," she said. "I'll pick up something when I meet my boyfriend." With that she was out the door and jogging down the sidewalk.

Me? I bought some more coleslaw.

* * * *

The sound of my doorbell startled me. I was making up the guest room bed and had lost track of time. A quick glance at the clock on the bedside table revealed it was twelve-thirty. "Well, here we go," I said to myself.

When I opened the door, Dom smiled broadly and said, "Welcome to New York." Then he put his right arm around my waist and pulled me to him. He put his left hand under my chin and gently tilted my head upward. I closed my eyes and felt his lips on mine. I let them linger for a moment and then turned my head away.

I stepped back, put my hands on my hips, and cocked my head. "Come on in. And by the way, whatta you mean, 'welcome'? I'm the one who lives here."

Dom just stood in the hallway for a moment, saying nothing. He ignored the signal I had sent him and continued the conversation in a light-hearted manner. "Yeah, but I'm the one who grew up here. Once a New Yorker, always a New Yorker." Then he grabbed the handle of a small rolling suitcase that sat in the hall behind him and walked into my apartment.

"Fair enough," I said. "Here, give me your jacket. We can put your suitcase away after we eat. I've got some sandwiches in the refrigerator."

As he took off his navy blazer, I studied him closely. Something had changed since we were last together in Dallas. His black hair was still cropped close to his head. And his silver wire framed round glasses were perched precariously on his long nose. It didn't appear that he had gained weight; his tall frame was still angular. But something *was* different; I just couldn't put my finger on it.

I must have been staring at him because as he handed me the blazer, he frowned. "What?"

"Nothing," I said. "Let me show you the place and then we'll tackle the sandwiches." I took him on a quick tour of the apartment and then we settled in at the kitchen table. I opened the refrigerator and took out the sandwiches and coleslaw.

Dom smiled. "I see you've already found your neighborhood deli."

"You bet your ass. And there's a story about this food." I opened a kitchen cabinet and reached for a couple of bowls for the slaw.

"Don't bother with that," Dom protested. "Just get a couple of forks and we'll share the container. It'll save some cleanup."

I ignored him and pulled out the bowls, set them in the middle of the table, and filled each one. "We're in the big city now." I pushed a bowl down the table toward Dom, took my seat and pulled over the remaining bowl.

I told him the story about the Blue Fox deli and Lynette Mason. We sat there and ate, he and I, and made small talk. He, telling me about friends in Dallas, the wonderful new restaurants downtown, the new companies moving into the Mid Cities, who he knew would be excellent candidates for my consulting services, and, of course, I'd have to see the new performance hall for the Dallas Opera when it opened in September.

Me, telling him about the great deal I got on the apartment lease because I'd signed up for four years, about how nice it was to be close to my parents and my sister, and to Cecil, my best friend in college, and how, because of the money I got from my InterTrans termination package, I had the resources to get by, if I was careful, until I got the consulting practice started.

He asked me about Terry. I told him Terry had been too quiet lately, and I was worried. He asked if I still carried my Glock, and I said of course.

In truth I heard little of it, not even what I said ... because I knew what was coming. I heard my grandfather clock strike two. I said it was late and we'd better get to bed. He agreed. I walked down the hall and stood in front of my bedroom door. He went into the living room, got his bag and started down the hall. When he was even with me, he stopped. I shook my head. He stared at me for a long time. I prayed I wouldn't divert my eyes. I didn't. He said nothing, leaned toward me and lightly brushed my cheek with his lips. Then he took his bag into the guest room and closed the door.

Chapter 6

The next morning, over a late breakfast in my kitchen, I told Dom this was going to be a day off from moving chores. Today I wanted to play. First, a stroll in Central Park, and then a late lunch in Midtown. We'd stop by the TKTS booth in Times Square and try to score some tickets for one of the shows tonight, but only for a musical, no heavy dramas allowed. After the theater, a late dinner at La Bonne Soupe on 55th.

He read the signal sent by my perky demeanor and readily agreed to the plans I had laid for the day. There was no discussion of the events of the previous evening, though I knew his questions were inevitable.

Before we left I strapped the .32 on my thigh. Just in case we might have to go through some museum's metal detector, I put the mayor's letter in my back pocket.

Twenty minutes later we stepped from the platform of the Houston Street station into a number 1 train and headed for Columbus Circle. When we emerged from the subway, my senses told me I had picked a perfect day to explore Central Park. The sun was bright, but it was still spring, so its rays didn't bring the searing heat of noontime in July or August.

Then I saw them. All the smoking refugees from surrounding office buildings, gathered around the monument to the battleship *Maine*, puffing away. It was impossible not to smell all the secondhand smoke. We hurried past them and through the Merchants Gate entrance to the park. After a few steps, the smell of the smoke was replaced by the sweet scent of a bed of lavender blooming at the side of the walkway.

Dom took my hand, and I permitted it, but I was careful not to look him in the eye as he intertwined his fingers with mine. We decided to head to the park's information center, housed in a structure known as The Dairy. We walked slowly north along a meandering sidewalk that led to the 65th Street transverse road. Through the trees I could see several softball games in progress on the diamonds cut into the playgrounds on the south end of the park. We had just crossed a small bridge over a dry creek, when from behind I heard a voice call out, "Susan, Susan."

Fear swept over me. I recognized the angry voice that had cursed me so often as my marriage fell apart. I jerked my hand from Dom's grasp and turned around. All but the figure of Terry McCauley melted from my vision. He stood holding a bright silver revolver. I instinctively jammed my hand into my pocket, going for the .32. But I knew it was too late.

I heard him say "Goodbye, bitch," and I thought Central Park was as good a place as any to die. Then someone suddenly slammed into me, knocking me to the ground. Two shots shattered the peacefulness of the park, followed immediately by a cry of pain. I didn't expect to hear more shots, only to feel their impact as they penetrated my body.

But there were no more shots. I realized it was Dom who was on top of me, and I struggled to free myself. He rolled off me, and as I scrambled to my feet, I saw Terry running toward Columbus Circle. I pulled the .32 and considered a shot. Too many people in the park, too risky.

Then I looked down at Dom. He was lying on his back, not moving. His eyes were fluttering, his right arm extended, his left arm across his stomach. Blood stained his shirt on his left shoulder, just above his armpit. Blood was also flowing from what looked like a gash on his left temple.

I knelt down beside him and put two fingers on the carotid artery on the right side of his neck. There was a strong pulse and I could see he was breathing. Blood continued to flow from the shoulder wound, and I had to get it stopped.

A crowd had gathered around, and I spotted a man wearing a white shirt. I pointed at him and shouted, "You ... Give me your shirt."

"Fuck you," he said, and ran deeper into the park.

The closet thing I had to a bandage was my white polo shirt, so I pulled it out of my pants and over my head, all the while regretting that the bra I had chosen for the day was named "Uplifting Angels."

I tore Dom's shirt away and discovered the source of the blood was a wound on the back of his shoulder. As I rolled him on his side, he moaned, "Oh God."

I touched his cheek and said, "Stay with me, baby ."I pressed my wadded-up polo against the wound. As I held my shirt against his shoulder, I looked at the gash on his temple. It appeared one of the two shots had grazed his skull. Despite his current condition, he was one lucky guy.

The crowd around us continued to grow. A huge black man stepped forward and walked to within a couple of feet us. I swore I was looking at Shaquille O'Neal's twin. "I called 911," he said as he pointed to a cell phone in his hand.

"Thank you," I said.

A woman standing at Dom's feet suddenly punched the shoulder of the man next to her. "Hey, butthead," she said. "Give her your shirt." There was no argument. The man immediately started unbuttoning his shirt.

Then the woman turned toward me; "I'll hold the bandage while you put it on." She knelt next to me and put her hand on the bandage. I noticed the pressure seemed to be working. The blood flow was slowing down.

I stood up, put on the shirt, and then knelt back down and resumed holding the polo on Dom's shoulder. "Thank you," I said.

The woman stood up and said, "Honey, we broads gotta stick together. Men are such assholes … mainly."

An elderly man whose appearance suggested the park was his home walked out of the crowd toward me. He was pointing at the man who had called 911."That feller saved you ass." Then he pointed at Dom, "His too."

The sound of a siren getting louder by the second distracted me, "Beg pardon?" I said.

"Knocked that bastard that shot him clear to Jersey, messed his noggin up pretty good too."

I must have had a confused look on my face because another man left the crowd and joined the conversation. "Perhaps I can help. I saw it all. After the first shots, this gentleman," he pointed to the black man, "tackled the man with the gun. Hit him squarely in the small of the back and propelled him forward onto the ground. The gunman hit face first and the impact knocked the gun out of his hand. I guess without his gun, he knew he was in a fight he was going to lose, because when he got up, he took off running."

I started to thank the black man, but before I could get the words out, the EMS van arrived, siren still blaring. It was followed in short order by a blue-and-white NYPD patrol car.

Two paramedics rushed out of the van and began to work on Dom. Two uniformed officers left the patrol car and walked toward the paramedics. As they moved through the crowd, I could see some of the bystanders pointing toward me. The scene was all wrapped up in about forty-five minutes. The paramedics stabilized Dom, put him in the van, and left for Bellevue Hospital. The cops questioned me and others who had seen the shooting. They also collected Terry's gun that was still lying on the pavement. The detectives arrived about fifteen minutes after the uniforms, and I told my story again. I told them I was sure it was Terry and that they should contact Dallas because they had warrants out on him. I waited for them to ask me about the .32, but apparently none of the witnesses mentioned it, because it never came up.

The crowd slowly drifted away. I looked for the black man that had saved my life, but he was gone. I realized that I had never thanked him and that I didn't even know his name. I did find Butthead, though. I needed to get his name and address. I was going to have to mail him his shirt.

* * * *

Bellevue Hospital was located at E. 28th Street and First Avenue, separated from the banks of the East River by FDR Drive. The cab ride from the park took fifteen minutes and I had to wait another twenty minutes in the line for the information desk, where an indifferent clerk gave me a small map of the hospital. I immediately headed to the emergency room. A volunteer there told me Dom was in surgery and gave me directions to the surgical waiting room on the lower level of the hospital.

The path from the emergency room to the elevators was convoluted; the directional arrows led me down more false paths than New Jersey highway signs. When I finally burst through the waiting room door, the smell of scorched coffee greeted me.

Small knots of people were scattered around the room, whispering among themselves, not seeming to be aware of other little gatherings just feet away. Halfway down the right side of the room, a matronly, gray-headed woman sat behind a blonde oak desk. Above her head, a sign proclaimed "Surgical Waiting Registration."

I approached the desk and said, "I'm here for Dom Shapiro."

On her gray-and-white striped uniform, the woman wore a badge that said "Sara" on the first line, and "Surgery Volunteer" on the second. She checked a list on her desk and then said, "Please sign in." She rotated a large loose-leaf book around so that it faced me. "Here's a pen," she said, a warm smile spreading across her face.

I started filling in the columns, "Time, Name, Patient, Relationship." At the last column, I paused a few seconds and finally wrote "Friend."

"I'd like to talk to the doctor as soon as Dom is out of surgery," I said as I rotated the book back.

"You're his friend?"

"Yes."

"Has he signed a HIPPA agreement naming you as someone that can have access to his medical information?' she said, the smile disappearing.

"No. He wasn't planning to be shot."

She drew herself up in her chair. "Unless we have a HIPPA agreement we can't release any information to you, and the doctor can't reveal anything either."

"But he was visiting me here in New York. He's from Dallas. There's no one else here for him."

Her face seemed to soften. "I understand, but it's the law. No release agreement, no information."

"Who can get information?" I said.

The woman sighed. "Is he married?"

I felt my face flush. "No."

"Are his parents alive?"

"His father is dead, and his mother is very elderly. She's in a progressive care institution in Connecticut. The news would just upset her."

"But unless we have a HIPPA, she's the only one we can release information to."

I wanted to scream, but instead just stared at her.

After a few moments she said, "I'll tell you what I can do. I'll get word to the recovery room nurses that you're here. After he's awake, perhaps you can see him for a few minutes there. No promises, but maybe."

"Thank you," I said. I walked across the room to where scorched coffee sat on a two-burner hot plate. I picked up the pot and poured the dark, syrupy brew into a small Styrofoam cup that I had taken from a stack sitting next to the hot plate.

I walked to a chair that gave me a good view of Sara and settled in for a long wait.

* * * *

Ninety minutes later Sara motioned for me to come to her desk. She glanced down at an 8 ½ x 11 sheet of pink paper. "Mr. Shapiro is in recovery and would like to see you."

A small, dark woman in blue scrubs walked up to the desk and took the pink paper. "I'll show you the way," she said. We arrived at the entry to the recovery room in less than a minute. A woman in a volunteer's uniform guarded access to the patients from behind a breast-high counter. My escort laid the pink paper on the counter. "She's here for Mr. Shapiro," she said and walked away.

The volunteer carefully examined the paper. "Ms. Solari?" she said.

"Yes."

"Could I see some ID?"

I felt the blood rush to my face as I spit out, "What is this, a hospital or a friggin' prison?"

The woman's face flushed and she leaned across the counter toward me. "Look, lady, it's not my rule, but I need ID. It's the hospital rules. No ID, no entrance."

We stared at each other until I backed down. "Fine," I said. I dug around in my purse and produced my driver's license.

"Do you have a cell phone with you?" she asked.

"Yes."

"You'll have to turn it off before you can go into the recovery suite."

Once again I fumbled around in my purse. I produced the cell phone and cut it off as the volunteer watched my every move.

"Follow me," she said and pushed open the recovery room doors. As I walked into the room, it could have been noon, midnight, dawn, or sunset. There were no windows, and the sterile blue fluorescent lighting provided no connection to the rhythm of life taking place beyond the hospital walls. I could see beds lined up along the walls to my left and right, separated by white curtains. In most of the little cubicles, one or two people were gathered around patients, softly talking. Occasionally one of the patients was fully surrounded by a curtain pulled across the foot of their bed. Lights threw shadows on the curtains.

The volunteer led me about two-thirds of the way down the room, turned to her right, and said, "Here he is."

Dom had his eyes closed. His left arm was bound across his chest, and bandages made his left shoulder appear twice as big as his right. There was a dressing on his left temple. I leaned over and whispered his name.

He opened his eyes and turned his head to face me. His lips moved and I heard a faint question ... "Why?" Then he drifted back to sleep. I didn't know if the question was about the shooting or the events of the previous evening. There was a simple explanation for the former; I wasn't sure I knew the answer to the latter.

Chapter 7

▼

I stood by Dom's bedside for a few more minutes, and then my escort said, "I'm afraid that's all the time I can give you. He'll be here for about an hour and then we'll transfer him to a room. You can see him there. Besides, he's going to be sleeping for quite a while. The pain medication does that."

"How can I find out what room he's in?"

"Once the transfer is made, the information desk in the lobby will know."

"God, isn't there any other way?" I said, "You've seen those lines at that desk."

The volunteer started walking toward the exit door of the recovery suite, and I followed along behind her. "I'm afraid not … Oh, maybe there is one other way. Call the hospital and ask for his room. The operator won't give you the number, but she will connect you. Mr. Shapiro probably won't be alert enough to answer, but maybe his roommate will. He'll most likely be in a semi-private room."

"Thanks," I said. "Great idea."

I had an hour to kill and was hungry. I figured it wouldn't be hard to find a good, cheap place to eat since the NYU medical school was only two blocks north, and med students were notorious for rooting out such joints. I didn't want any fine dining places because I was still wearing Butthead's hideous chartreuse and aqua checkered shirt and looked like hell.

Sure enough, at the corner of West 30th and Second Avenue, I found Sid's Diner. At three in the afternoon, the little restaurant was packed. The majority of the diners wore scrubs.

I ordered a tuna salad sandwich on whole wheat and a cup of real coffee. The adrenaline of the morning was fading fast and I needed the caffeine. I heard a cell phone ring at the next table. It reminded me that my cell was still powered down. When I hit my On button, the phone responded with two beeps and a notice that I had voice mail.

I played the message and was surprised to hear Glenn Manion's voice. "Susan, this is Glenn Manion. I've got the information on Errol Sanregret. I want you to talk to him on Monday. He lives at 451 Candlewick in Red Bank, on the Jersey shore. Phone number is 732-876-5210. You can get to Red Bank from Penn Station on the North Jersey Coast line. There's a Hertz agency at the Red Bank station. I've sent you an e-mail with the directions to Sanregret's house. Call me immediately after you've talked to him."

Arrogant bastard, I thought. *Fuck him, I'll see Sanregret on my own timetable.*

I finished my sandwich and started back toward Bellevue. Between First and Second Avenues I spotted a women's clothing shop with a banner in the window that screamed "CLEARANCE" in large red letters. I scooted across 30th and went into the shop. In fifteen minutes I was wearing a new blouse and Butthead's shirt was stuffed in a bag. I almost felt human again.

I called the hospital, and as luck would have it, Dom's roommate did answer the phone. When I got to the room Dom was still pretty much knocked out. We talked a bit as he slid in and out of consciousness, but at five-thirty I gave it up and went back to my apartment, ever alert for Terry. I spent the evening being comforted first by Robert Mondovi and then later by Johnnie Walker. By nine o'clock the lights were out.

*   *   *   *

I woke up Saturday morning with a throbbing pain that felt like my head was in a vice. A couple of aspirin helped a little.

I scrambled around and got the home number for Dom's boss at the *Morning News*. She said someone from the paper would be in Manhattan first thing Monday morning. I gave her my cell phone number as a contact point. When I hung up, a sense of guilt swept over me. At first I didn't understand why. Then I realized I was glad that someone else was soon to accept the responsibility for Dom's welfare. Not a lot of thanks for someone who just saved your life.

About noon, I went to Bellevue and spent some time with Dom. He was lucid, but I kept the conversation light, avoiding all the unanswered questions between us. He seemed particularly grateful that I had called the *News*. That he was a torch I needed to pass took away any pleasure I might have taken from his gratitude. By two o'clock he was tiring. I told him I'd call in the morning, kissed his cheek, and fled.

On the way back from the hospital I stopped by a hardware store and bought two heavy-duty door security chains, and a special item that I hoped I would never have to use. When I got back to my apartment, I spent the next hour replacing the smaller security chains on my door. After completing that job, I grabbed one of the last unpacked moving boxes sitting in my closet. I opened the box and took out a Taurus 651 titanium .357, a Smith and Wesson 642 and its holster, and a new addition to my arsenal: a Derringer Model 1 .45/. 410 that Mike Riley had given me as a going-away present. I also retrieved the Glock and the .32 that I had brought with me in checked luggage.

For the next hour, I cleaned and loaded the weapons. Then I took the Taurus and hid it behind the orange juice carton in the refrigerator. I put the Smith and Wesson in its holster and hooked the holster to a bracket that was attached to the back of the nightstand on the right-hand side of my bed. The .32 went on the top shelf of the closet, and its holster in my underwear drawer. Just as necessary as panties and bras. The Glock went in the concealed, easy access pocket of my purse.

Next, I pulled a plastic simulated brick out of hardware store bag. The words "Save-A-Flush" were embossed across its top. I slit the underside of the brick, shook out the gravel used to weigh it down, and shoved the Derringer inside. I sealed the slit with three strips of duct tape and dropped the brick into the tank of the toilet in my hallway bathroom. All set.

I hadn't yet set up my personal computer, so I spent about an hour getting the printer, monitor, and PC connected. When I logged on to the Internet, my e-mail icon told me I had one message. It was the message from Manion giving me directions to Errol Sanregret's home. Whether it was from my lack of any other clues to Janet Manion's rapist, or some other reason, I decided to pay a surprise call on Mr. Sanregret Monday morning. I could take an early train, interview Sanregret, and be back in Manhattan early afternoon to meet Dom's visitor from the *Morning News*. If I missed Sanregret, I could at least enjoy a brunch at the shore.

Sunday went by quickly. A morning visit with Dom, during which he told me he would be released from Bellevue sometime Monday afternoon. A phone call from Bill Harris of the *Morning News* informing me of his arrival plans. He agreed to stay with Dom at Bellevue until I got back from my interview with Sanregret. My afternoon was spent unpacking my final few boxes.

Monday morning I caught the eight o'clock train out of Penn Station. I was in Red Bank by nine-twenty. In ten minutes I had my rental car and started the drive to Sanregret's home.

He lived about two miles south of the Navesink River in a community of acreage lots and tall oak and hickory trees. The Tudor home sat well back from the street and was partially obscured by a small berm that ran across the entire front of the yard. I turned into a gravel driveway on the right side of the property and heard my tires crunching the small stones covering its surface. If he was at home, Errol Sanregret now knew someone was approaching.

I got out of my car and walked up an artfully curved, washed pebble sidewalk to a shallow front porch. I punched the doorbell and heard three chimes announce my arrival. There was no response, so I hit the doorbell again. This time I heard footsteps and saw a blurred image approach the frosted glass panel in the door.

The door opened and a tall, thin man in a white tee shirt and baggy jeans confronted me. "Yeah?" His thin mustache curled up in a sneer when he spoke.

"Errol Sanregret?"

"Yeah."

"I'm Susan Solari." I handed him a business card. "I'm an investigator and have been retained by a law firm representing Alex Watson and Alice Nixon."

"So?"

"They're suing Medical Diagnostics for unfair dismissal."

The right corner of his upper lip curled up. "About time the bitch and that bastard got some backbone."

"I'd like to talk with you for a few minutes, if that's possible."

"Why should I do that?" Sanregret said. "When I tried to fight that asshole Manion, they just took their checks and ran. Screw 'em."

"Are you going to court over this?" I said.

Sanregret shook his head, "Haven't decided yet. All it'd do is fill some lawyer's pocket."

"If they win their case, it would make yours stronger, if you do decide to sue. Besides, I'd like to hear your side of the story."

Sanregret stared at me for a few seconds, then stepped back from the door. "Come on in. But I've only got a few minutes." He abruptly turned and walked away, leaving me to close the front door and follow him through the house.

There was no furniture in the living or dining rooms except for a single table lamp sitting on the living room floor. As I walked through the kitchen to a den at the back of the house, I noticed several empty frozen dinner cartons sitting on a counter. If Sanregret wore a sign around his neck that said "I'm Divorced" the message would not be any clearer.

He had taken a seat in an overstuffed recliner and motioned for me to sit in a tub chair across from a low wooden table near the recliner. Several white rings were prominent on the table. "So, what do you want to know?"

"Let me tell you what I know about this case, and you can correct any bad information I have."

"Okay, but make it quick."

I went through what Manion had told me. As I talked, I saw Sanregret's face redden. He suddenly got up out of his chair. "That's all bullshit. The company line. Makes me one of the bad guys. I'm not the villain in all this."

"Then maybe you can tell me who is," I said.

He sat back down in his recliner. "Maybe Nixon, maybe Watson, but for sure that bastard Glenn Manion."

"Manion?" I said. "It was his company's designs that were stolen."

"Yeah, and that cheap asshole wouldn't spend the money to find out who did it. Narrows it down to three people he *suspects* did it, and fires all three. Say one of us did do it, two innocent people's lives are ruined." He got out of his chair and started pacing.

"It wasn't me," he said, his voice getting louder. "My life is ruined. Nobody will hire me. All because Manion took the easy way out. And that asshole sits in his big corner office and doesn't give a shit. Bastard!" He hit the wall with his right fist and the sheet rock shattered, creating a large hole.

I quickly left the tub chair, "Mr. Sanregret, I ..."

He was grimacing and shaking his right hand, "Enough! I don't want to talk about this anymore. Get out."

"But ..."

He cut me off again. "I said get out."

He followed me to the front of the house. Before I opened the door to leave, I turned and faced him. "Before I go, answer me this. Where were you last Friday evening?"

His eyes darted from side to side and he took a step backwards, rubbing his right hand. "What the hell has that got to do with anything?"

"I'm not at liberty to say," I said.

He leaned forward, his voice almost a growl. "But I'm at liberty to tell you to go fuck yourself." He walked around me and flung the door open. I had learned enough. I walked out the door without comment. Mr. Errol Sanregret would stay on a very short list.

Chapter 8

I made the short drive back to Red Bank. It was about an hour until the next train into Manhattan, so when I turned in my rental car, I asked the agent if there was a nearby place to grab a quick lunch. "Sure," she said, "Jersey Joe's Clams and Cannolis. It's just around the corner." She handed me my receipt.

"Thanks," I said. "With a name like that, the food's gotta be great." I was out the door and at Jersey Joe's place in less than five minutes. Even though it was just after eleven, the restaurant was crowded. The sound of the diners' conversations and the clatter of plates being served bounced off the dining room's walls. The room was small with maybe ten tables that were all occupied. A counter offered a half a dozen stools. I took one of the stools and ordered a bowl of steamers and a glass of white wine.

While I waited for the clams, I made a phone call to a number in Dallas. A woman's voice answered, "Federal Bureau of Investigation."

"Special Agent Sherman, please."

"One moment," she said, then I heard ringing, followed by, "Sherman."

"Jack, its Susan Solari."

"Susan, how are you? I thought you moved to New York."

"I did; matter of fact, I'm calling you from New Jersey." For the next few minutes we caught up with each other's lives. Jack Sherman had been my mentor in the Dallas FBI office. He had been there five years when I arrived from the San Antonio office. He knew the lay of the land in the city, and more than once he kept me from stubbing my toe in an investigation.

At the time, he was recently divorced and had custody of his daughter, Amy. As my friendship with Jack developed, there were times when I played surrogate mom to her, helping with things that dads don't do so well. After I went to Inter-Trans, Jack and I stayed close for a while, but our contact had gradually diminished.

As we talked, a large, fat man appeared across the counter in front of me. A stained white apron stretched across his massive belly. A bowl in his right hand was piled high with steamers. The bowl in his left hand was empty. "I'll bring the water," he said as he set both bowls on the counter.

"Can you hold a second, Jack?" I said.

"Sure."

I reached into my purse and took out a small combination earpiece and microphone, hooked it over my ear and plugged it into my cell phone, which I laid on the counter. The fat man returned with a bowl of water for rinsing the clams, and my Chardonnay. Now I was all set.

"Okay," I said. "My food just came and I'll have to eat while we talk. I have a train to catch."

"Same old Susan," Jack replied. "Still multitasking. So, what are you up to, professionally, I mean?" This was the opening I was hoping for. I explained my plans for corporate consulting and then said, "But I'm working on something that I could use your help on."

"Shoot."

Before I started, I made sure no one was close enough to hear our conversation. Nearest to me was a woman at the end of the counter also talking into a cell phone. What with the other noise in the café, she wouldn't hear a thing. So I told Jack about the Manion rape and about my suspicion that Janet Manion had been targeted. "I don't think this is a simple rape case. But I don't have a handle on what's going on. That's where you can help."

"How?"

"If I give you the facts of the case, will you run it through VICAP for me?"

"Whoa, Susan! You know VICAP analysis is for police departments only. Why don't you ask the New York detectives to do this?"

"I don't have any connections up here yet, and besides, they don't know I'm investigating the rape."

There was a long silence on the other end of the line. I opened a steamer, swished it around in the water and popped it into my mouth. It was delicious, sweet and juicy. Finally Jack said, "I don't know, Susan, this is getting pretty deep."

"You don't have to give me the full analysis. Just tell me if you get a hit."

"And then what'll you do with it?"

"Depends," I said. "Anyway, it's better you don't know."

"Damn it, Susan, you're asking an awful lot."

"I know, but I wouldn't ask if I didn't need it."

There was another long silence, and then, "Okay, but only because it's you, Susan."

"You're a friend, Jack," I said. "I'll get you details on the case tomorrow morning. What's your e-mail?"

"No e-mails. Just give me a call. I'll be in the office."

"Fine. Listen, I hate to talk and run, but I've got to finish these clams and get to the train station."

"Okay," Jack said. "Oh, before you go, Garrett Nelson was in the office last week. He asked about you."

It had been twelve years, and still the sound of his name caused my breath to become shallow and a rush of memories to fill my head. I didn't say anything for a moment, hoping my voice wouldn't betray me. Finally I said, "Is he still in San Antonio?"

"Yeah, for now, but maybe not for long. He wants to transfer to the Dallas office. Some personal matter. He wants a new start."

He had a chance at that before! Then the words came out before I could stop them, "Well, let me know if the transfer comes through."

"Will do. Maybe you two could get together if you are ever in Dallas."

"Maybe."

"Finish your clams. I've got to get to a meeting. Talk to you this afternoon."

"Yes, and thanks, Jack."

We said our goodbyes and I unhooked the earpiece. I paid the bill and left the restaurant. But I didn't finish the clams. I was no longer hungry.

Chapter 9

I was back at Penn Station by one o'clock. During the trip back to Manhattan, I got a call from Cecil inviting me over for dinner the next evening. I immediately accepted and took a few minutes to briefly fill her in on the events of the last couple of days. As usual, she made me promise to provide her all the dirt when we got together. I promised, but without much enthusiasm. Thoughts of Garrett Nelson still swirled in my mind.

When I got to Bellevue, Dom was agitated. He was supposed to be discharged at one o'clock, but now it was almost two and there was no word. While Bellevue's medical care was world class, it suffered from the bureaucracy inherent in any municipal health care system.

While we waited, I met Bill Wilson from the *Morning News*. He assured me he'd take good care of Dom on the trip back to Dallas tomorrow. Finally, after many phone calls, Dom was discharged at four o'clock.

A large Latino orderly arrived at Dom's room and helped him into a wheelchair. This proved to be no simple matter. Dom was in a foul mood and insisted that he was going to walk out of the hospital. The orderly tried to explain this was against hospital rules, but his English was limited and he couldn't get his point across. Eventually, I played interpreter and Dom agreed to be wheeled out the front entrance.

Bill took Dom's suitcase and went ahead to hail a cab on First Avenue. In just moments, Dom and I went past the crowds in the lobby and into the courtyard in front of the hospital. The orderly pushed the wheelchair rapidly down the sidewalk, underneath the canopy of trees, seeming to want to spend as little time in the late spring heat as possible. I trailed behind, my mind unsettled, knowing the cab ride would be far too short and the evening far too long.

Bill had a cab waiting when we arrived at the curb. We loaded up and started what should have been a fifteen-minute trip to my apartment. Luck was not with us. On 29th Street, at Park Avenue, a florist's delivery van and a box truck tried to occupy the right hand lane at the same time. The noise of metal meeting metal bounced off the surrounding buildings. The drivers jumped out of their vehicles and started yelling at each other in the middle of the intersection. I couldn't hear the exact words, but between the arm waving and finger pointing I imagined references to each other's paternity. I got on my cell phone and reported the accident to 911. Amazingly the cops arrived in about five minutes.

Dom, Bill and I sat and waited in the cab while New York's finest took charge of the scene. Our cab's air conditioner couldn't cope with the afternoon heat, so the driver lowered the windows to get some ventilation. The noise of the traffic on Park made any meaningful conversation impossible. I counted my blessings.

An over-weight cop who was sweating heavily came over to our cab and got all our names, addresses, and phone numbers, for his report, he said. I remember thinking that I'd probably hear from the lawyers on both sides of the accident. *Shit!*

Finally, the wreckers arrived, the vehicles were towed off, and we were permitted to go on our way. We reached my apartment in about ten minutes, but not before the heat had sweat rolling down our faces and soaking our clothes. Bill said he'd carry Dom's suitcase up the stairs, and he asked the cabbie to wait so the taxi could take him to his hotel in Midtown.

Dom moved to the right side of the staircase as we began the climb, his good arm grasping the rail. I put my arm around his waist in support, hoping he didn't interpret the close contact for more than it was.

There are some moments we wish could go on forever because of their sheer pleasure. There are others we hope will never end because of what we know will follow. The climbing of the stairs to my apartment was the latter. But too soon we reached my apartment door. Bill said his goodbyes, retreated to his taxi, and was gone. Dom and I were alone.

I checked the translucent thread I had taped to the top of the door and the doorjamb. Still in place. No intruders this afternoon. I unlocked the door, picked up Dom's suitcase, and we went into the apartment.

"Grab a spot on the couch," I said to Dom. "I'll just put this suitcase back in the bedroom."

"Sure," Dom said as he sat down. "Damn. Those stairs wore me out. I guess this has taken more out of me than I realized."

I was back in the living room in just moments. "Yeah, taking a bullet in the shoulder'll do that to you. But I have the cure. It'll just take a couple of minutes."

I went into the kitchen, rattled around in a cabinet and produced a bottle of Gray Goose vodka. I loaded two double old fashion glasses with ice, poured in the vodka and some Rose's lime juice. "Violá," I said. "Gimlets."

I took the drinks into the living room and handed one to Dom. "Gimlets will fix anything." I settled in at the opposite end of the couch from him. "Your flight home is, what, around noon tomorrow?"

Dom took a sip of his drink and then set it on the coffee table in front of the couch. "Yeah. Bill said he'd be here at eight-thirty and we'll grab a cab to Newark about nine." There was no life in his voice. I waited for the inevitable. It came quickly.

Dom closed his eyes, took a deep breath and tilted his head upward. "In the hospital, I had a lot of time to think. To try to figure out things. I guess it was the drugs. I never got an answer."

Time to deal with it now. "Let's define the question."

Dom opened his eyes and looked directly into mine, his voice hard. "Don't play games with me, Susan. I'm not in the mood and don't have the time."

I set my gimlet on the coffee table. "I'm not playing games. I'm too old for games."

"Then what the hell are you doing? I thought we had something going on in Dallas. Then with no discussion, no warning, you tell me you're moving to New York. What changed so suddenly?"

"It wasn't sudden."

Dom slowly shook his head. His voice had softened. "I don't understand."

"I've got too many ghosts in Texas."

Dom reached for his drink, but winced and put his good hand on his wounded shoulder. "Ghosts don't go away when you move. They follow."

"I'm not naïve about that," I said. "But at least I'm away from the things and places that trigger the memories. I need to find some peace. I can build a new life here."

"I could have helped you build a new life in Dallas."

I got off the couch and moved to the wing chair across the coffee table, taking my drink with me. "No, Dom, you couldn't. There'd always be the reminders, the people. Most of all the people."

"And I'm one of the people that remind you of …"

I cut him off. "Yes."

Dom left the couch and stared out my living room window. The sun streamed through the blinds and painted stripes across his face. "How the hell can that be? I led you to what was going on at InterTrans. I sent you to Rachel Grant. I was there for you, damn it."

I made an effort to keep my voice strong. "That's true. But still, you were a part of something that I want to be far away from."

He stepped away from the window, picked up his gimlet, swirled the ice around with his finger, took a drink and set the glass back on the coffee table. I realized I hadn't touched mine. "Don't try to spare my feelings!" he said. "It's not like you. Ms. full-steam-ahead. Doesn't it come down to the fact that you're just tired of me?"

I reached for my gimlet. The sharp taste fit the words that hung in the air. "No, Dom, not just you. I'm bad for men. When they get close to me, they get killed. Dave, Tom Grant, Jim O'Brien. Look what almost happened to you."

"That's ridiculous, Susan. Not one of those deaths was your fault."

I could hear my voice rising. "The hell they weren't. It was my mistake that got Dave killed. If Tom Grant had trusted me more, the corruption at InterTrans might not have cost him his life. And it was my brilliant plan at Tee Pee Hill that got Jim O'Brien a knife in the chest. And if not for a little bit of luck, I'd be making your funeral arrangements today."

"If you want to use that as an excuse to run away, I guess you can, but it's still bullshit."

I got in his face. "You call three deaths bullshit? Then fuck you. Fuck you!" I sat back down in the wing chair and crossed my arms across my chest. Dom returned to the couch.

We sat and stared at each other, neither of us wishing to be the first to speak. The noise of Greenwich Village traffic on the street below was the only sound filling the room. Finally, Dom quietly said, "This is it then?"

"This is it."

That evening I brought in some sandwiches from a deli a couple of blocks away. The conversation was sparse. The next morning Bill Harris showed up at precisely eight-thirty. Dom was ready to go by nine. I didn't walk them to the cab.

Chapter 10

I watched Dom's cab depart from the window of my apartment. I knew I had to stay busy to keep from falling apart. Our separation was the right thing to do, but it hurt like hell.

I made a fresh pot of coffee and then called the Dallas FBI Field Office. I gave Jack Sherman the details on the Janet Manion rape. With a little more nudging on my part he agreed to expedite the VICAP search.

Then I called Glenn Manion at his office. He picked up immediately.

"Glenn, it's Susan Solari."

"I know. I saw your caller ID. Why the hell didn't you call me yesterday?"

"I had personal things to take care of. Now, do you want me to tell you about my talk with Sanregret or do you just want to abuse me some more?"

"Go ahead." I briefed him on my interview.

"So when are you going to the cops?"

I really needed some coffee, but I was talking to Manion and couldn't reach it. I regretted that I had called Manion on my landline.

"Glenn, can you hold a minute? Someone's at the door."

"Yeah, but make it quick."

I laid the handset down on the counter and filled my coffee mug to the brim.

"Okay, just someone with the wrong apartment."

"So what about the police?"

"Not yet. Sanregret's a possibility, but not a sure thing."

"Damn it, maybe I've hired the wrong PI."

"I'm not a PI, and maybe you've hired someone who can keep your ass out of a lawsuit."

There was a long silence, "Keep me posted," and then dial tone.
God I hate asshole CEO's. Is there any other kind?

* * * *

My cab pulled up in front of Cecil's building on Spring Street in the heart of SoHo. I paid the cabbie and paused a moment on the sidewalk to admire the façade of the building. It's a beautiful example of late 1800's cast-iron architecture. The windows are framed by arches set on columns flanked by taller columns. The mass-produced sections repeat the pattern over and over. The building is gorgeous.

I pushed open a glass-and-steel door and went into the lobby. Dead ahead of me was an elevator that could only be described as "early freight." I raised the gate, walked onto its rough wooden floor and hit the button for three. Nothing happened. I hit the button again and then realized I'd left the gate up. I grabbed the gate and pulled it down. As soon as the gate touched the floor, the elevator made a loud creaking noise and lurched upward, almost throwing me against the back wall. When it reached the third floor, it stopped as abruptly as it had started. I made a vow to take the stairs when I left.

I stepped out of the elevator into a narrow, dimly lit corridor, found Cecil's loft and gave the door three hard raps. In moments I heard the clicking of footsteps.

The door burst open and Cecil greeted me with "Get your way-too-small butt in here." She wore what in the seventies would have been called a caftan or a muumuu. It was vaguely Hawaiian, with light green, blue, and orange blobs splashed over the fabric in no coherent manner. The sleeves were three-quarter length, and the collar of the garment was huge. It ended in long points that lay on her breasts and pointed to her feet, which were clad in raffia sandals.

"Jesus," I said, "I didn't know we were going to have a friggin' luau."

Cecil laughed and twirled around in a circle. "I wore it just for you. I figured, after the last couple of days, you needed a little brightness in your life."

"You got that right." I carefully set my purse down on Cecil's couch. You don't throw around purses containing pistols like they're beanbags. "You've made some changes in this place since I was last here."

"Yeah, take a look around."

Cecil's loft was two rooms and a bathroom. The larger of the rooms she had split in half with a multi-section Chinese screen that extended two thirds of the way across the width of the room. She used the back half of the room as her studio. A bright red kiln sat in one corner. Large cylindrical stone containers for her clay sat on each side of the kiln.

A potter's wheel stood against the back wall. The tools of her trade-glazes, brushes, and several things that I didn't recognize-jammed several shelves on the wall. A small gas range, refrigerator, and a cabinet with a sink were tucked into the corner opposite the kiln and served as a rudimentary kitchen.

She used the front half of the space as her living room. It reflected her eclectic tastes. A dark brown, wide whale corduroy couch dominated the room. A round coffee table sat between the couch and two low-slung, ochre leather chairs. The light brown and soft orange tiles of its mosaic top complemented the couch and chairs. A round red-orange and white oriental rug under the table provided the exclamation point for the grouping.

"Nice touch," I said, pointing at the oriental.

"I just got that last week. Bought it from a friend of mine. In the middle of a divorce. Seems her husband was not too enamored of her, how shall I put this … her artistic attachment to her painting instructor."

"How often was she attached to her instructor?"

"At least once a week." Cecil walked to the refrigerator, "Want a Mai Tai?"

"Oh! We're keeping up the theme. Yeah, but just one. You know I'm not much on sweet concoctions. Scotch, Irish whiskey, that'll do just fine for me."

Cecil took a pitcher out of the refrigerator and poured out the Mai Tai's. We relaxed in the living room, she on the couch and me in one of the leather chairs. I filled her in on the events of the last week. When I finished she cocked her head and looked me in the eye. "So you cut him loose."

"Yeah," I said. "But I don't want to talk about it."

I took a sip of my Mai Tai and made a face. "Can you get me a scotch? This tastes like Willy Wonka spilled a whole bag of sugar in it."

Cecil started to walk toward the kitchen, but stopped. "My, my. Affairs of the heart making us cranky, eh? Okay, I'll get your scotch, but first I have a little surprise about dinner."

"What's that?"

"There isn't any. The damn stove quit working this afternoon. But in keeping with my exotic theme for the evening, I thought we could go to the Chinese take-out around the corner and bring something back. I'm buying. Okay?"

I couldn't help but laugh. "Cecil you're amazing. Only you can think of Chinese take-out as exotic, but it sounds great. Nobody has to cook."

"Fine. I'll get your scotch. It's in the cabinet over the sink." She walked around the screen, picked up a small footstool and placed it in front of the sink.

When she climbed up on the stool and reached upward into the cabinet, the sleeves of her caftan slid toward her shoulders, revealing two large blue-black bruises on the upper part of her left arm. I felt prickles on the back of my neck and lost my appetite for Chinese food.

"Cecil, what the hell happened?"

She stepped off the stool, scotch in hand. The sleeves of the garment slid back down her arms, covering the bruises. "Whatta you mean?"

I walked across the room to her and pulled up her sleeve. "This."

"Oh, that. Last week I wasn't paying attention and tripped over my new rug and fell into the coffee table. Really pissed me off."

I just looked at her. "Yeah, and you must have bounced, seeing as you have two bruises."

Cecil looked away from me and pulled her sleeve back down her arm. "That *is* funny, but I did hit my head on the edge of the table and got a little woozy, so I'm not exactly sure how it happened."

"Bullshit. I know when a woman's been beaten. Those bruises are fist size. Now again, what the hell happened?"

She still would not look at me. "It's not important."

I got in her face. "It sure as hell is important. Now once more, what happened?"

Her voice was soft. "Nothing I can't handle."

"Yeah, it looks like you handled it real well." There was more sarcasm in my voice than Cecil deserved.

She took a double old-fashioned glass out of the kitchen cabinet, filled it with ice, and poured in the scotch. "Here," she said as she handed me the drink. "Let's just enjoy the evening. You've got enough on your plate."

I started to tell her I wasn't going to let this go when I heard my cell phone ringing. I went into the living area and dug it out of my purse. I was going to let the call go to voice mail, but I saw it was from Glenn Manion.

I hit the answer button. "This is Susan Solari." Manion started speaking immediately, his voice angry and loud. His message to me was punctuated by expletives. The conversation couldn't have taken three minutes. When I hung up I looked at Cecil. "Sorry, Chinese is going to have to wait. A messenger just delivered a package to Glenn Manion. It's a video tape of his wife's rape."

Chapter 11

The prime minister of Israel was in Manhattan visiting the United Nations. Tight security had traffic at an absolute standstill between 32nd and 50th streets from Second Avenue all the way across the island to Eighth Avenue. Cops stood in the middle of the streets waving their arms and blowing their whistles. But their efforts were to no avail. The intersections were completely grid locked. The smell of exhaust fumes from idling cars and trucks filled the air.

After sitting stuck for twenty minutes, I pulled my cell phone out of my purse and left a voicemail message for Manion telling him I was delayed. Then I bailed out of my cab and went down into the subway. I took the B train to the 72nd street station, just a half block from the Dakota.

Apparently Manion had notified the doorman I was on the way, because after I showed some ID, he let me through the gate without calling Manion's condominium. All told, it had taken me an hour to get from Cecil's loft to Manion's door.

The doorman must have called after I went into the lobby, because before I could ring the doorbell, Manion flung the door open. His face was red and he glared at me. "Where the hell have you been? A little ole lady from Jersey could have gotten here faster."

I wasn't in any mood to take his crap. After what I had just learned about Cecil, I hated all men. "Know how to access voicemail, big guy?"

He looked puzzled and cocked his head. "Yes."

"Then do it. You'll get your answer to your fucking question. "I brushed past him and moved into his entry hall. Manion slammed the door shut and whirled around to face me.

"I've had enough of your smart mouth. I ought to fire your ass."

"Fire away. Then you can let New York's finest find your wife's rapist. It ought to be easy. Him being such a thoughtful guy. Sending you a memento of the occasion and all."

We stood in the entry hall, staring each other down. After several seconds, which seemed like half an hour, I said, "Look. This isn't doing anything for Janet. She deserves better."

Manion didn't say anything immediately. It was as if the mention of his wife's name surprised him. He never acknowledged that we owed her anything. He only said, "Okay," then turned and walked down the hall to his study.

In a few moments I followed him down the hall. When I reached the study, Manion was standing by the wide-screen TV on the north wall of the room. He was holding a videotape cassette.

"That's it?" I said.

"Yes."

"Does Janet know what it is?"

"She doesn't even know it was delivered. She's out for the evening at one of her *very important* charity dinners. I don't expect her back until almost eleven." Manion's voice was lifeless; the only inflection was to denigrate his wife's charity work. "There were two of them, filthy bastards, perverts."

"Maybe, maybe not. He could have put the camera on a tripod."

Manion shook his head. "No, the camera was moving around. Shooting different angles."

"You've watched it, then."

"Only the first minute or so. A messenger delivered the box. It was addressed to me with 'Personal' stamped in red. I opened the box and found the cassette. A small sticky note attached to it said 'For Immediate Viewing.' I was curious, so I put it in the VCR. When I realized what it was, I cut the damned thing off." Manion's eyes were devoid of expression. It was as if he had erected a wall between what he had seen on the tape and his emotions.

I sat in a blue wing chair that faced the TV. Manion did not move. He just stood beside the TV, holding the videotape.

"Have you told the police?" I said.

"No."

"You need to do that. But first I want to make a copy. Once it gets in police hands, we'll never see it again."

My statement jarred some life back into Manion. There was anger in his eyes. "Why the hell would I ever want to watch this piece of garbage again?"

"You, no. Me, yes. This guy is arrogant as hell. Arrogant people make mistakes. Maybe he made one on the tape. I might not catch it the first time, but on the third or fourth time, maybe."

"All right."

"I have to watch it, Glenn. Now, before Janet comes home."

He sighed heavily, walked to a component cabinet sitting next to the TV and slid the cassette into a VCR. "I'll watch the first minute or so. Then I'll leave the room. I'm not watching some bastard rape my wife." He picked up a remote control, turned on the TV, and then started the VCR. He didn't sit down, but remained standing, his brown eyes staring at the screen.

I don't know what I expected, maybe some grainy, badly lit tape like you find on an amateur porn flick. I did not expect what I was seeing and hearing. The music came first, symphonic and very melodic. Then the title appeared, "Rape at the Dakota," in bold red script on a pink background. The graphics were professional grade. The title faded and "Starring Janet Manion" appeared, same red script and pink background. Janet's name stayed on the screen a long time, maybe fifteen or twenty seconds.

Then it too faded away and a headshot of a man in a ski mask appeared. He began talking, his voice disguised, metallic, sounding as if he were speaking through a kazoo. "Hi, Glenn. I hear you've been working too hard, screwing over Medical Diagnostic customers. No time to do fun things, like go to the movies. That's not good, and I'm worried about you. So I made a movie just for you. You've seen the credits. It stars your wife. I'm in it too. Here's the plot. I do to your wife what you've been doing to your shareholders.

"Oh, and Glenn, you must have been too busy to take care of business at home. Because when I finished, I swear she whispered, 'Thank you.'" Then he let out a long, sinister laugh.

Out of the corner of my eye, I saw Manion flick his finger on the remote control and the TV screen went blank. He put the remote in the component cabinet and turned to face me. His face was red and he was breathing heavily. "That bastard can't do this to me. You find him. Tell me who he is. Then I'm gonna kill him." He turned away and walked out of the room.

Chapter 12

The sound of Manion's footsteps faded. I heard a door slam in another part of the apartment. Good. I hoped he'd stay away while I watched the rest of the tape. I didn't need his histrionics distracting me from some important detail.

I picked up the remote and restarted the VCR. The image of the man in the ski mask faded from the screen as the tape resumed playing. In its place was Janet Manion, standing in the middle of her bedroom, blindfolded and wearing only panties and a bra.

About three feet away, a man in a ski mask stood facing her. He wore a tight, long sleeve, black polo shirt and black jeans. He was barefoot. I saw his lips move and then Janet removed her bra. There was no sound on the tape. *Curious.*

The man walked around Janet, looking her up and down. Then he stepped aside and the video came in for a close-up of Janet's chest, spending some time focusing on each of her breasts.

The camera pulled away and the man again appeared in front of Janet. I saw her lips move. It was not hard to lip read *please, please!* The man spoke again and Janet removed her panties. Again he walked around her. Then the video did a long close-up of her pubic area.

Then suddenly the scene shifted. Janet was on her knees, still blindfolded, head bowed. The man stood in front of her. His erection protruded from the fly of his jeans. He said something and then bent down, removed the blindfold, and handed Janet what looked like a translucent round circle. Janet slowly raised her head to the level of his waist and unrolled the condom on his penis.

Again the scene abruptly changed. Janet was on her back on the bed, the man between her legs, moving in an obscene rhythm. And suddenly there was sound.

Loud violent sound. Janet's pleading cries, *No! Please! Stop! Please! Oh God, stop him, please!* The man's guttural *Uh, uh, uh,* and then a shout of pleasure as he completed his work.

Then another sound. A scream. Not on the tape. In the study. I whirled around to see Janet Manion standing in the door. Her hand at her mouth, her face ashen. Her eyes rolled back into her head as she crumpled to the floor.

Twenty minutes later, I was standing with my hands on the back of a small straight chair as Glenn Manion paced around the room shouting at me. Janet lay on the study's couch. "How could you have let this happen? It's like she was raped twice. You stupid bi-"

Janet cut him off. "Glenn, it's not her fault. I got home early. I was looking for you. I didn't hear the TV, not until the end. I didn't know Susan was even *in* the apartment."

Manion glared at me. "God damned thing should have never been played here in the first place. But you had to watch it, *now,* you said. Before Janet gets home." The corner of his upper lip curled. "Well, you didn't quite make it. Did you?"

He was right. In my zeal to find a clue, any clue, I had pushed to watch the tape. What the hell would it have hurt to take it back to my place and look at it, what, thirty minutes later? I sighed and tried to put some positive spin on the incident. "You're right, Glenn. But at least we've eliminated at least one suspect. No way was that Errol Sanregret on that video."

"Big fucking deal."

I looked at Janet just as she sat up on the couch and said, "I'm sorry. I wasn't thinking."

She reached for a glass of water sitting on the coffee table and took a sip. "I know you meant me no harm, but will you get that tape out of the apartment? It was so real. I could almost smell the aftershave."

It seemed like I asked the question before she was finished speaking. "What aftershave?"

Janet looked confused. "I didn't mention it?"

I shook my head. "No."

"I kept catching a whiff of aftershave or cologne, or something. I had the impression of flowers."

"Could you identify it if you smelled it again?"

Janet looked me in the eye. "For the rest of my life. But there was one unusual thing. When he was ra ... when he was on top of me, when his face was next to mine, I didn't smell it."

"Could have been on the camera guy," Glenn said.

I had almost forgotten he was in the room. "Possible." I looked at Janet. She was still pale and was leaning into the corner of the couch. Time to go.

I turned to Manion. "I'm going to take the tape for duplication. I'll get it back to you tomorrow. Give it to the police."

"Sure. Lotta good it'll do with those bozos."

I picked up the cassette and started toward the hallway. "Give it to them anyway, Glenn. They might surprise you."

* * * *

The next morning I took a short walk to the A line station on 14th street. From there it was just a short ride to the station at the Port Authority Bus Terminal at Eighth and 42nd. I remembered Eighth Avenue in the eighties. You could get anything you wanted in the four blocks between 42nd and 46th. Need a bargain on a watch? The windows of small electronic shops promised undreamed of savings. Hungry? Narrow bodegas with their produce stands spilling out on the sidewalks could satisfy you. But most of the merchants in this small section of Manhattan catered to other appetites.

It started with the pocket theatres offering live shows, then moved on to the stores offering numerous implements to increase your and your partner's pleasure. Boy-girl, boy-boy, girl-girl ... any combination of the above, it didn't matter.

Finally, it ended with New Jersey executives trolling the sidewalks, looking for the right glance, making a quick duck into a doorway, emerging a desperate twenty minutes later thanking God that they had made a connection. They'd be back the next week, maybe the next night.

Giuliani had cleaned up much of it in the nineties, but a few small video shops stubbornly hung on. I found Empire Videos at Eighth and 43rd. The big sign in the window promised HOT XXX VIDEOS, but a small sign in the corner of the window said, "Your tapes duped." I chose a place like this to copy the tape because I thought there would be fewer questions about the content than there would be in a more legitimate video services store. And I didn't have the equipment to dupe it myself.

Ten minutes and $100 later, I had a promise that a copy would be available in a couple of hours. I grabbed a cab and killed the time doing a little shopping on Fifth Avenue. I found a pair of black pumps at Ferragamo that just cried to come home with me. What's a girl to do?

A little after noon I picked up my tapes, copy and original. I delivered the original to Manion at his office in Rockefeller Center, with strict instructions to make the police aware of its existence that afternoon. After a round of his epithets about the cops, he said he would make the call.

After a quick lunch at La Bonne Soupe, I was back at my apartment by two o'clock. As I opened the door, I heard the last few words of my outgoing message on my answering machine, a beep tone, and then, "Susan, it's Jack Sherman." I rushed into my apartment and grabbed the wireless extension in the living room.

"Hi Jack, it's Susan."

"Still screening calls, I see."

I set my bag with the Ferragamos on the floor. "Not really. I just got back home. Almost missed you."

"Well, you'll be glad you didn't. I got a hit on VICAP. Same MO. The victim was blindfolded. The guy used a condom. And he told her to say hello to her husband. Used his name."

"And that name is?"

"Matt Thompson. His wife's name is Felicia."

My mind was racing. "When did it happen?"

"A month ago."

"This is going to sound like a strange question, but did Matt Thompson receive a video tape of the rape?"

"What the hell, Susan?"

"I'll explain later. Did he?"

"No."

"Shit! Where'd this happen?"

I could see Jack's smile as he answered. "You're going to love this. One of your favorite places. Right here in big D."

Favorite place, my ass. I'd just spent the last two weeks trying to cut all my ties there. "Who caught the case for DPD?"

"That's another thing. You know the guy. Mike Riley."

"Know him? Hell, yes, I know him. He saved my life." But for a bullet in his shoulder from Mike Riley, Terry would have put one in my head at Tee Pee Hill. I owed him everything.

I heard a muffled conversation through the phone. I could tell Jack had his hand over his mouthpiece. Then I heard, "Susan, I've got to go. Boss needs me. Call Riley. He can fill you in. See ya."

I made the call and caught Mike at the station. It was great to hear his voice and we spent a little time catching up on each other's lives. Then he gave me the details of the case. "It sounds like the same guy to me, but I want to interview your victim," I said as he wound up his summation.

Mike's response was immediate. "No way, Susan. The department won't go for that. I just rejoined the force; I don't have a lot of chits to play with. Word gets out I put you into the middle of this, it's my ass."

"But Mike, you didn't, Jack Sherman did. All I'm asking is that you talk to the Thompsons before I contact them. How could I hang you out? Not after what you did."

Mike hesitated. "Okay, but just a phone call. Nothing else."

"Sure. Matter of fact, why don't I get off the line so you can call Felicia Thompson now. I'd like to see her as soon as possible. I can fly to Dallas tomorrow and interview her Friday. And thanks, Mike. I owe you ... again."

Throughout the afternoon calls flew back and forth between Dallas and Manhattan. First to arrange the interview with Felicia Thompson, and then to make my travel arrangements.

The last part bothered me. Because of Terry, I always tried to keep my travel plans close to the vest. But because this was short notice, I knew I had been a little careless, even booking what he knew was my favorite hotel.

But when all the calls were done, the arrangements were made. I was to fly to Dallas Thursday afternoon and interview Felicia and Matt Thompson first thing Friday morning. Then brief Jack Sherman and Mike Riley at noon.

Friday afternoon was mine. But not really. It was Tom Grant's.

Chapter 13

▼

I woke early Thursday morning to a rising sun streaming through my bedroom window. *Damn, I didn't close the blinds!* I checked under my sheet and sure enough, I was in my usual state of dress for sleeping. Nude. The neighboring apartments had a direct line of sight into my window, so I pulled the sheet around me before I left the bed.

The bright sun offered the promise of a glorious day. I tucked the sheet tight around me, raised the blinds and threw open the window. A cool late spring breeze rushed into the room. Time to get some much-neglected exercise before my evening flight to Dallas. It took just a few moments to slip into panties, a sports bra, red jogging shorts and a blue tee shirt that said WOMEN: THE FAIRER SEX, EVERY TIME.

I put the .32 in the pocket of my shorts. I didn't think Terry would be up this early, put I couldn't take a chance. One slip and I was toast. In moments I was out on Morton Street. I jogged the few blocks to Washington Square and took ten turns around the park.

The area was quiet; NYU students were not out and about yet. A couple of homeless people were curled up under the Sanford White arch in the center of the park. As I ran, I scanned for something out of place, but I spotted no obvious threats. I thought I had a line on Terry. He didn't get up to stalk early in the day. Except for three terrifying sniper shots in Dallas. He attacked only when he knew the terrain. Except for the morning in Central Park. *Yeah, you really got a line on him ... dumbass!*

I made the corner off Washington Square South and headed north along the west side of the park. An NYU flag flew over the entrance of a red brick building ahead. I saw a tall figure emerge from the glass doors of the building and pause under an archway that covered the entrance. An open trench coat hung off his broad shoulders. The wide brim of a straw hat shaded his face.

Why the hell a trench coat on a morning like this? Who knew about college students? Especially NYU students. Still, I wasn't comfortable and there was an escape route. I increased my pace and took it. West Washington Place to Seventh Avenue and on to Morton.

As I approached my building, I noticed a beige sedan parked in a fire zone in front of the entrance. I glanced in as I passed. A dark-haired woman sat in the passenger seat. I couldn't tell who was behind the wheel.

I went into the entryway and punched in my code. The door made its usual 'thunk.' I pushed it open and quickly slipped through. No movement from the car. Up the stairs, a quick check of the doorjamb, and I was in my apartment. As I put the .32 on a shelf in the fridge, I heard the buzz of my intercom. I hit the button. "Yes?"

A deep male voice with a slight Irish accent said, "Susan Solari?"

"Yes."

"I'm Detective Sergeant Collin Fitzgerald with the NYPD Special Victims Unit. I have Officer Aurora Garza with me. We need to talk to you. Buzz us in, please."

Shit! Manion must have spouted off. But I wasn't really surprised. I knew if I pursued the case, I'd cross paths with New York's finest at some point. But how'd I know this guy was legit? "Buzz you in? Just like that? No way."

A woman's voice over the intercom. "This is Officer Garza. I don't blame you. But we do need to talk to you. Maybe this will help. We got your name from Glenn Manion when he gave us the tape."

Better. But still ... who *for sure* knew about the existence of the tape? Me, the Manions, and *the rapist and his partner*. Not good enough. "I'll tell you what. Stay put. I'll come down and you can show me some ID through the door. If it's okay, I'll let you in."

The woman again. "Fine." But before I went down, I took my Glock out of my purse and slipped it under the cushion of the living room wing chair.

He was black Irish. Tall, about six-six, I thought. Black hair, blue eyes. The inevitable detective moustache. His belly hung over his belt, offering evidence that he spent more than his share of time in cop bars. I looked at his cheap suit. There was a high probability he spent more on drinks than on his wardrobe.

She was about my height, five-seven or so. Olive skin. Her eyes matched the color of her dark brown hair. She looked all business in a charcoal pantsuit and plain white blouse. But a striking face and trim figure also suggested that if the girl just wanted to have fun, she'd have no problem finding someone to help her.

They pressed their ID's to the glass door without saying a word. I studied them for a moment and nodded. "Okay." I hit the buzzer and they followed me up the stairs. When we reached my apartment, I motioned for them to sit on the couch. As I took my place in the wing chair, I felt the Glock beneath the cushion.

"Glenn Manion mentioned my name?" I directed my question at Aurora Garza, but it was Collin Fitzgerald who responded.

"Yeah. He said he'd hired someone who gave a shit about his wife's rape. As opposed to us, of course."

Oh boy! "Of course, Sergeant Fitzgerald, you *do* know that Glenn Manion doesn't represent my opinion of the NYPD."

Fitzgerald's voice was flat. "Of course." Officer Garza removed a notepad and pen from the inside pocket of her suit jacket. Fitzgerald continued, "For the record, just how are you involved with the Manions?"

I explained my arrangement with Glenn Manion. Sarcasm dripped from Fitzgerald's response. "So you're a 'security consultant'? And you're going to catch the rapist? And what qualifies you for that?"

Time to play a little dumb and find out what they knew about me. "Well, I was security director for a phone company."

A loud laugh burst from Fitzgerald's mouth. Garza didn't crack a smile. Finally, Fitzgerald said, "And how'd you get that job?"

"Worked my way up."

The smile on Fitzgerald's lips said everything. "Yeah. I bet you did."

Garza squirmed in the corner of the couch, looking uncomfortable. "And the job with Manion?"

"Through a business contact," I replied. I waited for the other questions I knew were coming. About the FBI. About the InterTrans investigation. About Tom's murder case. Nothing.

Fitzgerald leaned toward me. "And what has your *intensive* investigation revealed so far?"

"Well, I've really just gotten started."

Fitzgerald leaned toward me. "Look, I'm gonna talk straight. Stay away from this. You're just some fucking amateur trying to make a few bucks playing to the ego of some over-the-top CEO. All you can do is screw things up."

"Well, I certainly wouldn't want to do that," I said meekly. Garza shot me a look, pulled a small card from her jacket and wrote something on it.

"So we understand each other," Fitzgerald said. "You do what you need to do to so Manion will keep the checks coming. But stay away from the heart of this investigation. We'll get along just fine. Understand?" He stood up and walked toward my front door, followed by Garza.

I left my chair and opened the door. "Understood." Fitzgerald started down the stairs. Garza remained for a few minutes, staring at me. She slipped a card into the pocket of my shorts, then turned and followed Fitzgerald down the stairs.

As they left I heard him say, "Hell, I thought this might be trouble. But shit, what a ditz."

Back inside the apartment I retrieved Garza's business card from my pocket. On the back, handwritten in blue ink, was "CALL ME."

Chapter 14

Mid-afternoon I called Aurora Garza. I left a voice message with my travel plans and cell phone number. I asked her to call me any time over the weekend. In the back of my mind I wondered how she dealt with the Irish buffoon. A first impression, but I was sure she could run rings around him. We all had to deal with it, seniority and the good old boys club.

I also called Mike Riley's cell phone. He picked up on the first ring.

"Mike, I need one more favor."

"Shoot."

"You still have that spare .38?"

"Yep."

"Will you load it, box it up, and leave it at the Melrose desk for me this evening? I'll pick it up when I arrive."

I could hear the smile in his voice. "What's the matter? You don't think airport security would take too kindly to your Glock?"

"Not so much. I could get it through in checked luggage, but security would probably search through my bags, and I don't want that."

"Consider it done. I'll put it in a steel box I've got. It has a combination lock. Want some extra ammo?"

"Yeah. Just in case. What's the combination?"

"I can set it. Something you'll remember. How about 8-1-1?"

My turn to smile. "My birthday."

"Didn't think you'd forget that. See you tomorrow."

A couple of hours later, I was about to walk out the door and grab a cab for LaGuardia when my cell phone rang. I checked the caller ID. The number was vaguely familiar, so I took the call.

"Ms. Solari, I'm so glad I caught you. It's Lynette Mason. You know, the woman who knocked you down in the deli last week."

I couldn't tell if she was out of breath, or just nervous. "What can I do for you, Lynette?"

"You gave me your number, so I figured I could call. I just wanted to see if you're okay and apologize again for what I did. I was so flustered; I didn't even offer to replace the food I ruined. I'm sorry."

I'd cut it close leaving for the airport and I didn't know how long it would take to flag down a cab this time of day. "I'm fine. Listen, I've got to go. I'm on my way the airport."

"Please don't hang up. I want to do something to make up for what I did."

I pulled my carry-on through my front door and set it in the hallway. "That's not necessary, Lynette."

"Oh, yes it is. Someone gave my boyfriend two tickets to *The Producers* next Tuesday night. He can't go. I want to take you."

"Like I said, not necessary." I locked my front door and put my security tape on the doorjamb.

"Oh, but it is. It'll make me feel so much better. Please?"

"Isn't there someone else you'd rather take? Girlfriend, someone at work?"

"No. I want to take you. If nothing else, do a good deed and let me relieve my conscience."

I *had* to get this woman off the phone. And I'd never seen *The Producers*. "Okay. But I *have* to go. I gotta be on a plane to Dallas in an hour and American Airlines wouldn't hold a plane for the fucking king of Siam. Call me Monday and we'll talk details." We finished the conversation and I grabbed my carry-on and dashed down the stairs. Sure enough, it took me fifteen minutes to hail a cab. I promised the cabbie an extra ten if he got me to the plane on time. A harrowing twenty-five minutes later, I was at LaGuardia. I made the plane moments before they closed the cabin door.

* * * *

Thunderstorms at DFW delayed my arrival almost an hour. We made the gate a little after midnight. Thirty minutes later I was in my rental car and on my way out of the airport. Getting in late had an advantage. All the rental agency had left was a Cadillac CRX. I got it for the price of a compact.

Traffic was light. It looked like a quick trip to the Melrose Hotel in the Cedar Springs area of Dallas. I got on the LBJ freeway, but then decided to take a short cut on Walnut Hill Lane. Getting to sleep even just fifteen minutes earlier sounded great.

Walnut Hill was a two-lane road that had not yet been developed like many of the roads around DFW. Cattle pastures, mesquite trees, and Johnson grass flanked the road. For about six or seven miles I might as well have been on a remote West Texas highway.

As I took the exit, I glanced in my rearview mirror and saw a black SUV follow me on to the road. I sped up to put some distance between us. After a mile or so, the headlamps behind me were tiny pinpoints of light.

I felt a little drowsy, so I tuned the radio to a classic rock station and started to think about my interview with Janet Manion. I tried to mentally catalogue the commonalities with the rape of Felicia Thompson. I remembered something about …

Suddenly my car was flooded with light. I looked in my rearview mirror and saw the headlights and grill of the SUV just a few feet behind me. I pushed hard on the accelerator, but it was too late. The SUV struck the left side of my rear bumper. My car lurched forward toward the ditch that ran along the right side of the road.

I got control just as my tires spun on the narrow gravel shoulder. The SUV pulled alongside and tried to force me into the ditch. I took a chance and hit my brakes … hard.

The SUV shot up the road in front of me. I felt my car lean toward the ditch and I thought I was going to flip. I hit the accelerator and my rear tires dug into the gravel and pulled me back onto the road. I made a spinning one-eighty and raced back toward LBJ. Out of my side mirror, I saw the SUV turn and come after me. A three-mile race back to the freeway! I had a head start and was sure I could outrun the bastard.

That was until I came to the top of a rise in the road and almost rear ended a pickup that had to be going no more than thirty miles an hour. On the other side of the highway I could see the headlights of three vehicles coming toward us. In my rearview mirror, the headlights of the SUV grew larger and larger.

I pulled into the opposite lane and hit the gas. The CSX downshifted and roared forward. The oncoming headlights almost blinded me. I heard the squeal of tires on pavement and the uninterrupted blaring of a horn. As I cut back in front of the pickup, the headlights coming at me swerved away. The explosion of metal colliding with metal never came. In front of me, I could see a clear road. Behind, the pickup truck receded in my rearview mirror.

I sped toward LBJ, opening a clear advantage on the SUV. It finally passed the pick up and took up the chase. In less than a minute I was at the entrance to the freeway and merged into traffic. I checked my rear view mirrors. There was no sign of the SUV. Suddenly, I couldn't control the shaking of my hands on the steering wheel. I didn't remember the rest of the drive to the hotel.

But there I was, at the corner of Cedar Springs and Oak Lawn. Tonight the Melrose would be my shelter. I went through the revolving doors and on to the front desk. Despite the late hour, the desk clerk greeted me with a smile. I presented my credit card and passport. "Thank you, Ms. Solari," the clerk said.

I asked if Joyce Abbott, the assistant manager of the hotel, was on duty tonight. Joyce and I had become acquainted when I was with InterTrans. Tom liked to entertain at Imperial, the Melrose's restaurant. I had worked with Joyce on security issues for several high-ranking U. S. government officials he was wining and dining.

"No," the clerk replied. "But she'll be in tomorrow. I'll leave her a note you're staying in the hotel."

"Thank you. And one more thing. There should have been a package delivered to me this afternoon."

The clerk said he'd check and disappeared through a door behind the desk. When he returned he held a box wrapped in plain brown paper. "Here it is."

I took the package. Now I felt complete. What's a girl without her gun?

The bellman was waiting with my luggage when I arrived at my room. It seemed an eternity as he busied about putting my bags on the luggage racks, getting ice in the bucket, making sure I knew the hours of the dining rooms. Finally, I tipped him and he was gone.

A sense of absolute loneliness overcame me and I said to myself. "Stupid bitch. You got careless and you almost got dead. But how the hell could he have known where I was?" But there was no one to answer. David was dead, Tom was dead, Jim was dead. I had sent Dom away.

I got a bucket of ice, broke out the scotch, and tried not to think about the answer.

Chapter 15

Matt and Felicia Thompson lived in what was referred to as Far North Dallas. The streets approaching their home wound around the eighteen holes of the Bent Tree Country Club. The developer had done his best to make sure every house backed up to the course, or at least had an unobstructed view of a tee or green. It's called maximizing value ... for the developer.

A little before eight-thirty, I pulled up in the gray stone circular drive of their two-story Tudor-style home. The Dallas sun was already promising a typical high-nineties day in May, so I was grateful the drive was completely shaded by a large live oak tree.

I rang the bell and was greeted by a twenty-something blonde in a tailored camel skirt and a dark green silk blouse. "Welcome, Ms. Solari. Please come in. I'm Lucy Whitethorn, Ms. Thompson's personal assistant. She's running a little late from her riding lesson. She's asked that you wait in Mr. Thompson's study. He phoned and said he'd be joining you and Ms. Thompson a bit later. Can I get you something to drink?"

Jesus! She sounds like she's welcoming me to a ladies' tea party, not a rape investigation.

"Yes, I'll have some coffee, but not until Ms. Thompson arrives."

"Yes, ma'am."

"When Mr. Thompson gets here, ask him not to disturb Ms. Thompson and me until I call for him."

Lucy frowned. "I'm not sure I can do that, Ms. Solari."

I patted her on the shoulder. "Sure you can, Lucy. Just blame the bitch PI."

Her eyes darted around, as if she were trying to think of something, anything to say to end this conversation. Finally she said, "Please follow me."

Lucy led me through the entry hall and into Matt Thompson's study. "Make yourself comfortable. I'm sure Ms. Thompson will be here momentarily." She backed out of the room and closed the door.

There was no mistaking that this was a man's lair. The furniture was large and overstuffed. Hundreds of books were jammed into built-in shelves on the wall to my right. To my left, papers lay scattered across a large writing desk. The scent of tobacco lingered in the air. The entire back wall was a series of windows that looked out on a broad green fairway.

My natural curiosity drew me to the papers on the desk. I was about to glance through them when a slim blonde woman burst through the door and strode into the room. She wore a green jacket, camel jodhpurs, and chocolate-brown riding boots. I thought about Lucy's attire. *What the hell is this? The Thompson corporate colors?*

She walked directly to me and held out her hand. "I'm Felicia Thompson. You're Susan?"

"Yes." I shook her hand.

"Matt said you were a private investigator from New York. That you were investigating a similar rape in Manhattan. But how could something in New York have anything to do with my rape?" As she spoke, she took a seat on a deep red leather couch that looked crinkled enough to be very comfortable. She motioned for me to sit in a green leather chair across a coffee table from the couch.

"The similarities suggest it might be the same man."

She cocked her head. "What similarities?"

"I'd rather just have you recount what happened to you," I said. "I don't want to influence your recollection. Are you up for that?"

"It can't be any worse than when I went through it with the police."

There was a knock on the study door. "Come on in, Lucy," Felicia said.

The door opened and Lucy pushed in a teacart. On the top shelf was a teapot, a teacup with a silver tea ball draped over its edge, a small stainless coffee carafe, a coffee cup, and two scones.

"I like a cup of tea after riding," Felicia said. "Lucy said you wanted coffee." Lucy moved each of the items from the cart to the coffee table and left the room. Felicia put the tea ball in her cup and added the hot water. I poured myself a cup of coffee.

"Tell me about that evening," I said.

Felicia did not reply but diverted her eyes to the tea set on the coffee table. She picked up the small chain on her tea ball and bobbed the tea up and down in the hot water, then set it on the tray. After several seconds, she sighed heavily and began to speak. "Matt was in California. I spent the early part of the evening at a YWCA board meeting. I do the community work; Matt's not good at that sort of thing."

I put down my pad and took a sip of my coffee. "What time did you get back home?"

"About eight-thirty."

"So it was just about dark?"

"Yes."

"Did you notice anything unusual when you arrived home? Strange car on the street, anything like that?"

Felicia took a bite of her scone before she answered. "No, nothing. But I really wasn't on the lookout for trouble. I drove right into the garage and closed the door before I got out of the car."

"Was the security system armed while ..."

Felicia cut me off. "Look, this is hard enough. Let me tell this my way."

"Of course," I said. "I'm just trying to make sure I get every detail."

Felicia's back straightened. "Don't worry, I remember 'every detail,' as you put it."

"Go on."

"In answer to your question, yes, the security system was armed. I remember cutting it off. But didn't you read that in the police report?"

"I haven't seen the police report," I said. Felicia rolled her eyes. I ignored the insult. "Did you rearm it after you got in the house?"

"No. Matt usually sets it. But when he's gone I don't usually arm it until just before I go to bed."

I picked up my pen. "Go on."

"After I got into the house I went into the bedroom, kicked off my shoes, and went into the bathroom to remove my makeup. That's when I heard what sounded like the garage door going up. I thought maybe something had happened and Matt didn't make the California trip. I went to see what was going on. As I walked into the den, I saw a man standing there, dressed all in black. He had a ski mask on and was carrying a knife. But his eyes frightened me more than the knife."

I could see Felicia's hands beginning to shake. She slid them between her jodhpurs and the couch. "They were ice blue, with the intensity of an animal about to kill. I tried to run into the bedroom and lock the door. But he grabbed me and pulled me back into the den. He pushed me to the floor, put the knife to my throat and said, 'If you scream, you die.'"

* * * *

Felicia had been softly crying for several minutes. I reached in my purse and handed her a tissue. "Can we go on?"

She took a deep breath. "Yes," she said, and began to recount the rape. Most of what I expected was there. The blindfold, lights on, condom, no pubic hair, the mention of her husband's name. She told the story with an air of detachment, as if she was describing a scene in someone's home movie.

Finally, she said, "I did like he told me. I counted to one hundred before I took the blindfold off." She picked up the tea ball, set it in the cup and added more hot water. There was no light in her eyes and they seemed focused on someplace far away from the room and me.

"When you were blindfolded, at any time did you have a sense that there might be a third person in the room?"

"Somebody else in the room? No. Why?"

I considered how much to reveal. But something might jog her memory of a detail she had left out. "The other rape I am investigating was videotaped by a third person."

Felicia's hands flew to her face. "Oh, my God. Please, God. Please don't let it be."

I leaned across the coffee table and patted her knee. "Felicia, listen. Several things lead me to believe he didn't tape you. First, your rape happened before the one in New York and no tape has appeared. And tell me one more thing. During the time the rapist was in your home, did you smell any fragrance?"

Felicia's hands returned to her lap. "Do you mean like perfume?"

"Yes, or aftershave."

"No."

"I don't think there's a videotape."

Felicia sighed and she sat back on the couch. "Thank God. I don't think I could take that. Knowing the police would look at the tape. They would, wouldn't they?"

I took a sip of my coffee and nodded.

Felicia couldn't seem to drop the subject of the videotape. "Knowing that strangers would watch her rape. That must have been awful for, for ... you haven't told me her name."

I paused a moment before revealing the name. But then I said, "Janet. Janet Manion."

Felicia's voice became as cold as the look in her eyes. "Is this some cruel joke? Because if it is, you can go straight to hell and get out of my house."

"I don't understand," I said.

"I know Janet Manion."

"How?"

"Through Matt. He knows her husband, Glenn."

I leaned toward Felicia. "It's true. The other victim was Janet Manion. Get Matt in here ... now."

Matt Thompson was seated on the couch, next to Felicia. "I find it hard to believe that Janet Manion is also a rape victim! Are you sure you have the correct Janet Manion? Her husband's name is Glenn? He's chief executive officer of Medical Diagnostics?" His hand jabbed at me as he spoke.

"Yes, Mr. Thompson. The same Janet Manion," I said. "How do you know Glenn Manion?"

"We are both members of the CEO Roundtable."

The answer surprised me. Thompson didn't look like a typical chief executive officer. He was at least an inch shorter than me, his build was slight, and his blonde hair was prematurely thinning. A pair of round, gold-rimmed glasses sat on his thin, upturned nose. He had a precise way of speaking.

"CEO Roundtable," I said. "Tom Grant, my boss at InterTrans Telecom, was a member. As I understand it, it's basically a lobbying organization for the Fortune 100."

Thompson shifted around on the couch. "Well, it is certainly more than that, but you do have to be the CEO of a Fortune 100 company to be a member." His tone was thin and had no warmth. He pulled a pack of cigarettes from his sport jacket. "You mind if I smoke?"

"I know it's your house," I said. "But since you asked, yeah, I do."

He glared at me through his gold-rimmed glasses and put the cigarettes back in his jacket. "You're CEO for what company?" I asked.

Thompson gave a long sigh, obviously meant to signal his impatience with my lack of knowledge. "I am chief executive officer of American Healthcare. The largest operator of for-profit hospitals in the country."

"And Glenn Manion's largest customer?"

"Yes."

The thought struck me that the bully Manion and the pristine Thompson made an odd twosome.

"Any other connections between you?" I asked.

"Yes, we have the same financial planner. Scott Barnes from Asset Management. Glenn introduced me. I liked Scott's approach. Very research oriented. You may have heard of him. He's based in Manhattan."

"I wish." I turned and looked at Felicia. "How much time have you spent with Janet Manion?"

"We're not close," she said. "We knew each other through our husbands. Did the 'spouse activities' things together when Matt and Glenn were at conferences."

"Then you have no thoughts about why the same man might want to rape both of you?"

Matt spoke before Felicia could answer. "Then you believe it is the same man?"

"High probability," I said. "I want you to think through your association with Glenn Manion. Any reason someone might have it in for both of you? Business or social. The slightest thing. Felicia, same thing with you. Even the tiniest detail about someone that would feel slighted or dismissed by you and Janet. It's important."

I stood to leave. "Matt, I need the phone number for Scott Barnes. I want you to give him a call. Tell him I'm going to contact him."

He pulled a business card from his jacket, wrote a number on the back with a Mont Blanc pen, and handed it to me. "Of course. I'll call him tomorrow."

The goodbyes were brief. I was in my car in five minutes. As I pulled away from the house and headed for the FBI field office, I called Glenn Manion. His assistant put me through to him immediately, and I filled him in on what I had learned from Matt Thompson.

"So I want you to think hard about anyone that might want revenge on you and Thompson."

Unlike Thompson, who was cooperative, Manion was incredulous. "That's the biggest bunch of bullshit I've heard in a long time. Sounds like a re-run of your Errol Sanregret theory. That didn't work out so well, did it?"

I kept my temper. "Glenn, this is something solid. What do you think the odds are that a guy with the same MO would rape both Janet and Felicia? One in Dallas and one in New York. Think about it."

There was silence on the line for a few seconds. Then Manion grudgingly said, "Okay, I'll think about it."

"You do that." I hung up on him.

Just before I reached the FBI offices, my cell phone rang. Aurora Garza's name came up on the caller ID.

When I answered, she didn't waste words. "You're back in Manhattan on Monday? Do you know Charlie's at 39th and Lex?"

"The place that looks like a diner. Yeah, never been in there, but I know where it is."

"Meet me there Tuesday morning. Seven o'clock."

"What about your partner?"

"He's a drunken asshole. I've gotta deal with him. You don't. I'm gonna do you a favor and keep it that way."

Chapter 16

▼

Three years ago the FBI field office moved into a new building in Northwest Dallas, at One Justice Way. Cynics said that Justice Way should be a one-way street with railroad tracks down the middle. I appreciated the black humor now more than I would have a few years ago.

I signed in at security. I'd locked Mike's .38 in the trunk of my car before I came into the building, knowing that I'd never get it through the metal detector. In a few minutes Jack Sherman stepped off the elevator, a wide smile on his face. He shook my hand and said, "Great to see you, Susan. You finished here?" The beefy man behind the counter who gave me my visitor's badge nodded.

"Looks like I passed muster," I said as I followed Sherman toward the elevators.

He winked at me. "So far ..." Then his demeanor turned more somber. "But keep your badge visible. We're pretty serious about that sort of thing these days."

"I understand."

"Mike Riley's waiting for us in my office. You get anything from the Thompsons?"

"Yeah. Plenty."

When we reached Sherman's office, Mike sprang from his chair and wrapped his huge arms around me in an affectionate bear hug. "New York must be good for you. You look terrific."

I escaped his grasp so I could keep breathing. "Save that malarkey for your girlfriends, big man. How many currently?"

The corners of his mouth turned up. In his best Irish lilt he said, "Only one, Susan. As always. You know I'm a monogamous man."

I took a seat in one of Sherman's side chairs. "Yeah, and St. Patrick was Italian."

Sherman settled in the chair behind his desk as Mike returned to the other side chair. Apparently he had had enough of the repartee between Mike and me."Okay, let's get started. What'cha got, Susan?"

I filled them in on my interviews with the Thompsons. When I finished Sherman said, "So you're pretty sure this is the same guy that raped Janet Manion?"

"Absolutely. It's the identical MO."

Sherman massaged his temple. "Not quite, Susan. There's no videotape in the Thompson case."

I'd thought this out. "Given what I've told you, do you agree we have a serial rapist?"

Riley nodded. Sherman shook his head. "I'm not sure. Most serial rapists operate in a very restricted locality. Same city or same metro area."

"I'll give you that," I said. "But the similarities in MO are too strong here. Look, what do we know about serial rapists and killers … the time between incidents decreases and the violence, case to case, increases. Right?"

They waited.

"The women are the victims," I said. "But their husbands are the real targets. I think this guy, in his own mind, was punishing Matt Thompson and Glenn Manion. He raped their wives as some sort of revenge. And in Manion's case he increased the punishment by sending the videotape."

Sherman leaned across his desk. "Revenge for what?"

Riley ran his hand through his curly red hair. "Let's look at the connections between Thompson and Manion."

"Here they are," I said. "Glenn Manion and Matt Thompson are both CEO's of Fortune 100 companies. Their wives know each other and they're both very attractive. Both Manion and Thompson belong to the CEO Roundtable. And they have the same financial advisor. They're both in health care and Thompson is Manion's best customer."

Sherman was writing on a yellow pad as I spoke. "I'm interested in the health care angle. Any lawsuits against Thompson and Manion? I'm thinking of possible malpractice at one of Thompson's hospitals caused by use of Manion's diagnostic devices?"

"You gotta be shitting me," I said. "I've got the resources to check that out?"

Sherman looked toward Riley. "Okay, I'll put some people on it," Mike said. He jotted something down on small leather note pad.

"We're gonna have to really bear down into this," I said. "Get the details on Thompson and Manion's business relationships."

Sherman cocked his head and looked at me. "Who's 'we,' Susan?"

"Mike, you, and me."

"Not me, Susan. You know better than that. I'll keep monitoring VICAP, but the rapes are under the jurisdiction of the Dallas and New York City police departments. My boss would never authorize any resources on this."

I fired back at Sherman. "Let me translate what you just said. 'Susan, the same perp probably did both rapes. But there's shit for forensic evidence. With what we know now, the chances of getting this guy are zilch. The Bureau ain't touching this with a ten-foot pole.' Did I get it right?"

Sherman smiled. "Right now I hate it that you were once one of us."

"Fair enough," I said. "But if I can connect some dots, you'll revisit?"

"No harm in that."

I looked at Mike. "I'm going to talk to Scott Barnes, the financial advisor. He's in Manhattan. You're going to work the medical connection?"

"Yeah, and anything else that comes up on the Thompson rape."

The meeting was over and I was disheartened. I followed Mike into the hallway outside Sherman's office. "Why the long face?" he said.

"Shit, Mike. We both know the same guy did this. But I can't do all the spadework to make the connections. This is going to wind up as two isolated, unsolved rape cases. Tell me I'm wrong."

"Wish I could. I'll check for malpractice suits while you connect with the financial advisor. Maybe something'll turn up."

Mike and I said our goodbyes. I turned to walk to the elevator, fumbling in my purse for my car keys, not watching where I was going. Just before I reached the elevator, I collided with someone and my purse fell on the floor of the hallway.

"I'm sorry," I said. Then I looked up and saw the face of Garrett Nelson.

He bent down, picked up my purse, and handed it to me. "Susan, I've wanted to tell you that every day for five years."

I took the purse and moved a couple of steps away from him. "Seems like I heard those words five years ago. 'I'm sorry, Susan. I love you but I just can't leave her. It'd be the end of her world.' Did I get that right?"

An elevator door opened and I stepped toward it. I didn't care if was going up or down. I just wanted to get away.

Garrett put his hand on my arm. "Don't go, Susan. Just give me a few minutes, please. There's a visitor's office I'm using. Please."

I pushed his hand off my arm. "What's the point? You just wanna be my friend. I got lots of friends."

"Things are different now. Deborah left me."

"Ah, so all of a sudden I'm number one on your hit parade? You gotta be kidding me."

"I still love you, Susan. I won't give up easily."

Another elevator door opened. "Fuck off!" I said as I stepped into the car.

Chapter 17

When I reached my car, I took the .38 out of the trunk and slipped it back into the compartment on the side of my purse. As I drove away from the offices, I cursed myself for letting Garrett Nelson upset me. *Shit, Susan, there are some things we just never get over. Grow up.* I'd moved away from Dallas to start a new chapter in my life, and I wasn't going to let some asshole resurrect memories and feelings that I'd thought were long dead.

I just wanted get back to the Melrose, change, relax, and have a quiet dinner in my room. I had to remember to call my former next-door neighbor, Andrea Thompson, no relation to Felicia and Matt, and make arrangements to pick up Caesar the next day. He'd probably give me the cold shoulder, having been farmed out for two weeks.

Joyce Abbott was behind the front desk when I walked into the lobby. She looked up from some papers she was studying and called out, "Hi, Susan. I got the note you were in the hotel."

I walked across the lobby toward the front desk. Joyce was wearing the standard assistant manager garb: tailored blue skirt and jacket, white blouse with a short red tie peeping out from the edges of her collar. Very corporate, but her blonde good looks made any outfit look special. "Hi, yourself," I said as I reached the desk. "What's up?"

"Just checking occupancy numbers. Are you settled in New York?"

"Barely."

Joyce winked at me and an impish smile appeared on her face. "Well, someone must be glad you're back."

"Beg pardon?"

"Just wait 'till you get to your room. It'll be obvious."

"Come on, Joyce, this isn't funny. What do you mean?"

I saw my concern reflected in her eyes. "Susan, what's going on here?"

"Joyce, just tell me what you're talking about."

"Flowers. Delivered to your room. Lots of red roses."

"When?"

Joyce turned and looked at the clock on the wall behind the front desk. "A couple of hours ago. I know I was back from lunch. I'm having to cover for a desk clerk that called in sick."

My mind raced ahead. Trying to put together the scenario. "You were here then, when the roses arrived?"

Joyce's eyes were wide now. "Yes."

"How'd they get delivered to my room?"

"Well, the florist's delivery guy brought them to the front desk. I had a bellman take them to your room. Did I do something wrong?"

I realized I had unconsciously slipped my hand inside the front compartment of my purse and was gripping the .38. "Of course you didn't. But try to remember something for me. Before the flowers were delivered, did you notice anyone hanging around the lobby, especially a man?"

She paused. "Well, there was this one guy. He came up to the desk and asked where Star Publications was meeting. I gave him the meeting room, but told him he was an hour and a half early. He said he'd just wait. He went over there to the couch, pulled a piece of paper out of his briefcase and started reading."

"The briefcase ... big, little? Thick or thin?"

"It was leather, hard sided, and yeah, sorta thin. Regular size, I'd say."

Well, probably not a bomb, but ... "Can you describe the guy?"

"Sure." It took her maybe twenty seconds. Terry to a T.

"Did you notice if he had a serpent tattooed on the back of his right hand?"

Before Joyce could answer, a tall brunette in a tailored navy suit approached the front desk. A younger man with fashion model looks followed a couple of steps behind her.

"Miss, I'm just dropping off my key ... express checkout," she said. By her voice and manner, I guessed she was at least executive vice-president material. "I arranged for late checkout," she said as she laid the key on the desk.

"Do you need help with your luggage?" Joyce asked.

"Thank you. That won't be necessary."

I glanced again at the younger man. I hoped they'd had a pleasant afternoon.

Joyce turned her attention back to me. "Sorry. About the serpent, I can't be sure. But I did notice when he took the paper out of the briefcase, there was *something* on the back of his hand."

Bingo! "Do you remember seeing him after the bellman took the flowers to my room?"

"Not right away, no. Just after I gave the bellman the flowers, the desk got very busy. I wasn't paying attention to what was going on out in the lobby. But I did see him later. I thought it sort of strange."

"How so?"

"He was coming out of the elevator, but his meeting was on the first floor. Also, he was leaving an hour before the meeting was supposed to wrap up."

"Did he have the briefcase?"

"Yes."

Good! The probability of a bomb goes down a little. But what the hell else is in that room? "You saw him leave the hotel?"

Joyce nodded her head. "Yes."

I looked her in the eye. "You sure?"

"Yes."

"And he didn't come back?"

"Not that I know of. Susan, I know something's wrong. What is it?"

I didn't want to alarm her more than I already had. "Residue of a divorce. Probably a process server. Missed me again. Do me a favor, though, let me know if you see the guy again."

Some of the tension left her. "You sure, Susan? I can call securi ... Oh, yeah! Probably not needed. Right?"

I was still on full alert, but managed to wink at her. "Right. But there is something you can do. Do you have anything available on the concierge floor? If I remember correctly it's card key access. And you have someone on the desk there all day?"

Joyce went to a keyboard and began typing. "Yes. Let me check to see if we have anything." She watched the monitor for a few moments. "Yeah. Something's available."

"Great," I said. "I'm gonna have dinner in the Imperial room at seven this evening. I'll pack up. Will you have a bellman move me while I'm out of the room? I'll stop by for the key."

Joyce added, "And we'll keep your current rate."

"Thanks," I said. "Now I think I'll go enjoy my roses."

As I rode up the elevator, I considered the possibility of a bomb. I was certain Terry had been in my room this afternoon. But a bomb wasn't his style. He'd shot two men who were trying to kill me. Wounded one, killed the other. He wanted my death to be between him and me. He wanted to look me in the eye as I died.

The elevator opened on the fifth floor. I stepped out and scanned the hallway. A housekeeping cart was to my right. The sound of a novella on TV spilled out of an open door. Entertainment for a housekeeper doing a tough job.

My room was just four doors away from the elevator. I put my ear to the door and listened for a few moments. Nothing. I made another scan of the hallway and saw no one, so I eased the .38 out of my purse, which I placed on the floor. I quickly slipped my cardkey in and out of the lock. The little green open signal began flashing and I slowly cracked the door open.

I could see the roses sitting on a work desk. I entered the room, gripping the .38 in both hands. I put my back to the wall that faced the closet and eased my way forward. As I passed the bathroom, I could see it was empty. I checked the closet; nothing but my clothes. Then I saw them. Lying on the bed. Four pictures of me. Nudes in various poses. Taken in better times with Terry. But the pictures weren't complete. In each of them, my head had been cut out and a dab of crimson placed at the top of my neck. He was playing mind games again.

I put the .38 on the bed and began examining the pictures. No worry about messing up evidence. No fingerprint technician was ever going to dust these babies. There was no message written on any of the pictures. But I knew I would find one somewhere in the room. It was Terry's way.

Just then I heard knocking on my door and a female voice saying, "Susan, Susan. Are you all right?" I hid the .38 and the pictures under the pillows at the head of the bed and went to the door. When I opened it, Joyce Abbott stood there holding my purse. "Susan, you scared me to death. I came to tell you the room move is all set and I find your purse out in the hall by your room. I thought something happened to you."

She handed me the purse and waited for an explanation. "Just a dumbass move on my part," I said. "I was having trouble getting the lock open, so I set my purse down while I fiddled with the key. Just forgot it." I could tell by the look on her face she wasn't buying it.

She looked over my shoulder into the room for a few moments, and then let it go. "Okay, but don't go scaring me again. And the room move *is* set. Just drop by for the key this evening."

I was anxious to look for Terry's message. "Thanks, Joyce. Thanks for looking out for me." I glanced at my watch. "But I have to go. I'm expecting a conference call any second."

"Sure," she said. "Just watch yourself." She turned and walked toward the elevators.

I closed the door and glanced around the room. My eyes fell on the roses. I had to admit they were gorgeous. Deep red interspersed with delicate greenery, they fanned out of the top of a translucent pink vase. For the first time I realized their fragrance filled the room. Then I saw an envelope lying at the foot of the vase. "To Susan" was written in a woman's hand across its front.

I tore open the envelope. The message was in Terry's handwriting. "This was so easy. The stupid bellhop believed I was your husband. I was, but you started fucking around. Enjoy your next screw because it will be your last."

As I studied the note, I noticed a green ballpoint pen lying on the carpet beneath the desk. I picked up the pen and rotated it between thumb and index finger. The words "DalTex Inn" appeared. A smile spread across my face.

I put the pen on the desk and called Mike Riley. It took me a few minutes to tell him of Terry's latest threat. When I finished, he said, "I'm sorry, Susan, but there's not much we can do now."

"Oh, but there is. This time the dumb son-of-a-bitch left his address."

Chapter 18

It pissed me off that Mike Riley wouldn't be part of the raid on the DalTex Inn. He was in sex crimes, and this would be one for the homicide boys and girls. If he had been involved, I'd have hounded him unmercifully to let me be part of the team. But even he probably wouldn't have allowed it. Ex-FBI or not, I was still just a civilian. There'd be hell to pay if something went wrong. All I could do was wait. And pray for Terry's capture. It would mean my first good night's sleep in months.

The afternoon wore on. I called Scott Barnes, Thompson's and Manion's financial advisor. Thompson had called and greased the wheels, so Barnes gave me no grief. I set up the interview for nine o'clock Monday morning. Barnes' office was in the Trinity building in the heart of lower Manhattan. It'd be a short cab ride from my place.

I'd told Mike to call me on my cell phone the minute he heard anything about Terry. As I talked to Barnes, I kept glancing at the cell lying in front of me on the work desk. The damn thing didn't ring; it just sat there.

I called Andrea and made arrangements to pick up Caesar tomorrow. As I hung up, the cell phone sprang to life.

"Susan Solari."

A raspy Yeeee Haaaa blasted into my ear. "And greetings to you too, Cecil," I said.

"I thought I'd give you a proper Texas greeting. Being that's where you are."

I wanted to get her off the line. "What's up?"

"I'm throwing together a party Monday night at my place. You need to come. Cleanse yourself of any bad Texas habits you may have reverted to. You in?"

"I'm in. What time?"

"Nine. And don't bother to ..."

I cut her off. "Cecil, I gotta get off this line. Talk to you Sunday."

There was a short pause. "Uh, you all right?"

"Yeah. See ya Sunday."

I hit the off button and dialed Mike Riley's cell phone. No answer. I tried his home. Same result. *Where the hell was he? And what was going on with Terry?*

Six o'clock, six-thirty. By the time I had packed for the bellman, it was seven. I went down to the front desk, got my new key, and then went into the Imperial room. I had no appetite, but ordered brook trout out of habit. I poked at the fish for about a half hour and decided it was a losing battle. I'd just been given the check when the call came through.

"Where the hell you been, Mike?"

"Susan, what room are you in?" His voice was all business.

"Right now I'm in the restaurant. But what the hell difference does that make? What happened?"

"I'm about ten minutes away from the Melrose. I'll tell you all of it when I get there, but for now, just know we missed him. Now what room are you in?"

"Fifteen ten. The concierge floor."

"See you in a few minutes. Got my .38 with you?"

"Of course."

"Keep it handy. No telling what his next move may be."

Mike was true to his word and in my room less than fifteen minutes later. "So tell me," I demanded.

He walked across the room and stared out the window before turning to face me. "They asked me to go on the raid. Since I knew him when you were married, they thought I might help if we got in a barricade situation. But it was no use. He was playing with us.

"When we hit the room, he was gone. But he left this." Mike pulled a picture out of the breast pocket of his coat and handed it to me. It was of my apartment building in the Village. Across the bottom of the picture he had scrawled "She has only days."

So much for a good night's sleep.

* * * *

Saturday morning dawned bright and beautiful. The drive to Cochran Gardens at the northern edge of the city took thirty minutes. I checked in at the gatehouse and got the location of Tom Grant's grave. The attendant, Sunday school perfect in her pastel dress, consulted a laptop computer. From beneath the counter she produced a map and highlighted a small square at the western edge of the cemetery.

"That's it. There's a road that circles the property," she said. "You can drive close to the grave."

"No, I'd rather walk."

"Suit yourself."

I left the gatehouse and started down a narrow, winding path. Massive, one-hundred-year-old live oaks spread their branches over gravesites and headstones, sheltering me from the relentless Texas sun. I carried a single long-stemmed yellow rose surrounded by the delicate white blossoms of babies' breath. In the branches above me, mockingbirds sang endless variations of their songs. Small squirrels chased each other across the lawn, nature's testimony that life renews itself even in a place dedicated to the dead.

As I moved along the path, I was not sure I had the strength to complete my journey. Tom Grant's graveside service had been private, attended only by family members. In the months that followed I didn't have the heart, or the courage, to visit his final resting place. But now other places, other people, were pulling me to a new life. Time had numbed the pain. I needed closure.

I'm not at ease in large public spaces. The attack in Central Park still haunted me. The safest thing would have been to make the drive to the gravesite. But today I needed time for reflection. I felt secure. I had the .38. The sightlines in the cemetery were good enough to spot any threat in plenty of time for action.

I found Tom's grave tucked under a large live oak. The sun filtered through the leaves of the tree and reflected off the polished granite of the headstone. "GRANT" was deeply chiseled into the center of the stone. Tom's Christian name was carved into the lower-left hand corner, the dates of his birth and death below his name. The lower right-hand corner was blank. Room for Rachel's name when her time came.

But I wondered if the name of Tom's widow would ever occupy that space. Perhaps she would choose to rest alongside some future love she encountered as she rebuilt her life. Time corrodes bonds we think are strong as steel. Never forgotten, but no longer real.

I thought of what might have been, and then knew it was time to leave. I bowed my head for a few moments, then knelt down and placed the rose on the ground below Tom's name. I stood and walked away, briefly looking back at the headstone. I would never return to this place. Whatever the outcome, the pain would be overwhelming should I learn the fate of the space in the lower right-hand corner of the headstone.

Chapter 19

Monday morning the metallic "bang-bang" of a sanitation truck emptying a dumpster into its hopper jarred me awake. I hugged the pillow lying at my side. Hell of a substitute for a man.

I stretched my legs and felt Caesar at the foot of the bed. He had tolerated the flight home well and he spent Sunday exploring the apartment. Checking out cabinets, closets. Finding hiding places. His single eye discovering a new world.

When he felt my touch, he uncurled and walked up the bed. It was only moments before he was poking on my chest. I pulled my hand from under the sheet and stroked the top of his head. "Okay, big guy. I get the hint. Time for treats."

I threw back the covers and looked at the clock on the bedside table. Ten minutes after eight. *Holy shit!* The fucking alarm didn't go off. I was due at Scott Barnes' office in less than an hour.

I hit the bathroom and threw the shower fixture to hot. Maybe three minutes to brush my teeth and do a piss-poor job of flossing. In and out of the shower, towel off, blow-dry the hair, do the makeup, get the clothes just right. *Fuck! It's not fair. All guys have to do is shit, shower, and shave.*

* * * *

My taxi pulled to the curb where Wall Street meets Broadway. I shoved a ten-dollar bill through the slot in the Plexiglas and joined the crowd rushing along the sidewalk. The gothic tower of Trinity Church loomed on my left. A few yards of grass separated the church from the building in which Scott Barnes kept his offices.

Asset Management occupied the entire seventeenth floor. In less than five minutes a receptionist ushered me into Scott Barnes' office. He walked from behind his desk. "Ms. Solari. Welcome," he said as we shook hands. He was tall, well over six feet. Curly blonde hair and blue eyes. Slim waist and broad shoulders. About my age, early thirties. I checked for a wedding ring. None. But an indention circled his finger where one would be. If I were in the market for a man, this one would be well worth exploring.

He must have caught me checking him out because there was a twinkle in his eye when he said, "Have a seat, Susan ... May I call you Susan?"

I felt the blush spread across my face as I sat in a red leather chair in front of his desk. "Of course ... Scott."

He closed his office door and settled in the large black executive chair behind his desk. Through the window behind his back I could see Trinity Church, its magnificent rose sandstone bathed in mid-morning sunlight. Barnes leaned across the desk. "Matt Thompson's phone call shocked the hell out of me. Felicia *and* Janet Manion. That's hard to believe. And Matt said you believe there's a connection."

I took a small note pad and pen out of my purse. "Right now, I'm exploring all possibilities, but, yes, I'm pretty sure the same man raped both women. That's why I'm here."

"I don't understand."

"I'm checking out all possible connections between the two men. I'm looking for some incident that might prompt somebody to take revenge on them. Maybe a business deal gone bad ... something like that. As their financial advisor, you're in a good position to know."

Barnes picked up a pen off his desk and slowly rotated it between his fingers. "I am. But there are difficulties."

"What kind of difficulties?"

"Asset Management provides executive financial planning for almost one third of the Fortune 500. One of the most important reasons we're given such responsibility is our confidentiality policy. In the vernacular, 'we don't tell nothing to nobody.'"

I felt my face getting red again, for a far different reason. "You gotta be shitting me. If you knew something that might lead to the capture of these women's rapist, you wouldn't tell me because of your sacred confidentiality policies?"

Barnes looked me right in the eye. "Not without permission of the client."

I left the chair, picked up the receiver of the phone on Barnes' desk, and shoved it in his face. "Then I suggest you get it ... now. I don't think you want me telling Manion and Thompson you were uncooperative."

Barnes glared at me, took the phone out of my hand and hit a single digit on the dial. After a couple of seconds he said, "Doris, I have a couple of private calls to make. Will you see that Ms. Solari gets some coffee while I get that done?"

Almost immediately an attractive redhead opened the door. "Just follow me, Ms. Solari." We went down a short hallway and turned in to what I could best describe as a concierge lounge for executives. There was a short buffet of fresh fruit, yogurt, and juices. Five coffee containers stood on a counter at the end of the buffet: regular, decaf, and three specialty flavors. Large overstuffed leather chairs were scattered about, as were small, round, marble-topped tables to snack on.

Doris noticed me checking the place out. "We take good care of our account executives. They're the ones bringing in the big bucks. Help yourself. I'll be just around the corner if you need anything. I'm sure Mr. Barnes won't be long."

He better not be, I thought. I got a cup of the leaded and picked up a banana from the buffet. No time for breakfast this morning. Caesar was lucky to be fed.

I'd just found a seat at one of the tables when my cell phone rang. I checked the ID. Aurora Garza. "Susan Solari."

"You still okay for tomorrow morning?"

"Yeah, Charlie's at seven."

"Okay, don't be late." And then she was gone. If she was this abrupt in the morning, I better order a short stack.

I had started peeling the banana when my cell phone rang again. Lynette Mason's number appeared on the screen. Then I remembered I had promised to go to the theatre with her tomorrow night.

"This is Susan."

"Oh great! I got you. You said we'd settle on details for *The Producers* today. Now here's what I have planned ..."

I cut her off. "I don't mean to be rude, Lynette, but I may have to cut this short at any moment. I know it's playing at the St. James Theater. Let's meet at the will-call window thirty minutes before curtain."

"But I wanted to buy you dinner before the show. Nothing fancy, but another way to sooth my conscience."

"I'm booked early in the evening," I lied.

"Well, I'm disappointed. But I'll see you at seven-thirty at the will-call window."

"Perfect," I said. "See you there."

A few minutes later, I'd just finished my banana when I felt a touch on the back of my shoulder. Then Doris' voice. "Mr. Barnes is free now."

I followed her back to Barnes' office, closing the door as I went in. "So?" Barnes motioned for me to return to the red leather chair.

I talked to both clients. You've got carte blanche. Fire away." He didn't look at me. There was a sharp, clipped tone to his voice. *So much for possibilities down the line. Men seemed to be something I was not destined to enjoy any time soon.*

"So was there a bad business deal? Something that made enemies for Thompson and Manion?"

"Yeah, a venture capital fund. Some of the investments went sour. Thompson and Manion cashed out early. Some of the investors lost everything. Felt Matt and Glenn hung them out to dry. In reality, Matt and Glenn were just sharper. Did their research better. But these things aren't settled by raping someone's wife. Everyone knows it's high risk, high reward. Go to court if you think you've been screwed."

"First time for everything," I said. "Any potential kooks in the group?"

Barnes let out a big sigh. "I can't even tell you who else was in the investor group, Susan. You'll have to get that from Matt and Glenn."

I didn't have much, but maybe it was a start. Time to go. But one last shot. "Anything else you can think of?"

Barnes swiveled his chair and looked at Trinity Church. Then he turned back to me. "Don't assume I know everything about their business dealings. They're into a lot of things. Tremendously competitive. Hell, they even bet each other where they'll wind up on the Fortune 100 each year."

"Say again?"

"Yeah, every year there's a hundred thousand dollar bet as to whose company will be ranked higher. This year Matt lost. American Healthcare was number ten. Medical Diagnostics was number nine. Glenn wouldn't let him forget it."

I tried to keep my voice calm." And who was number eight?"

Barnes took the mouse connected to the PC on his desk, moved it around on its pad, and clicked a few times. "Continental Communications."

"Who's the CEO?"

"Hillary Swift."

"Where's headquarters?"

"New York City"

"Scott, excuse me. I have to leave. I have to make a phone call."

* * * *

Eleven hours later I was in a taxi headed for Cecil's place and on the phone with Mike Riley. "Okay, I was a good girl. I went through channels. So did you talk to Hillary Swift?"

"You know I can't do that, Susan. It's NYPD's jurisdiction. I contacted their Special Victims Unit."

I was afraid of what was coming next. "Who'd you talk to?"

"Good Irish Detective named Collin Fitzgerald."

"Good, my ass! Sexist pig, more like it."

"You *know* him."

"Yeah. He tried to warn me off the Janet Manion case." The taxi pulled up in front of Cecil's building. The driver shut off the meter and looked over his shoulder, ready for his fare and tip.

"Mike, I gotta go. I'll fill you in on the details about Fitzgerald later. But please tell me he said he'd warn her."

"Yeah, he did. But he wasn't very enthusiastic. I don't think he bought into your theory."

"That buffoon wouldn't buy into a theory if it came up and bit him on the ass."

"Well, I do, Susan, so I took this one step further. I called Jack Sherman at the FBI and asked him to contact the police in the cities of CEOs one through seven. Put them on alert. Five are in New York, one near Dallas, and one near Seattle."

"Fucking brilliant, Riley."

I paid the fare and bailed out of the cab. "And don't worry about Swift. If Fitzgerald didn't put the fear of God into her, I will."

Chapter 20

I paid the cabbie and walked quickly into Cecil's building. One glance at the elevator reminded me of the bumps, jolts, and squeals of my last ride and I decided to take the stairs to the third floor.

The small, yellow light bulb on each landing fought a losing battle with the gloom that enveloped the stairwell. As I climbed, I heard the sound of heavy footsteps on the stairs. I wasn't alone. *Were they above or below me?* I stopped; listened. Silence. *Someone mimicking my movements?* Then a shaft of light penetrated the stairwell above me. A door slammed. Someone coming in or going out? I didn't move for a few more heartbeats. Nothing.

I started my climb again. *Even though I walk through the valley of the shadow of death I fear no evil, for thou art with me. Thy rod and thy staff, they comfort me. But not as much as my Glock and my .32. Paranoia reigns. Get it together, Susan.*

"Come in, come in. And who might you be?" An elderly elf sporting a thin gray mustache and a neatly trimmed goatee answered my knock on Cecil's door.

"I'm Susan Solari."

"Oh, yes, Cecelia said to keep an eye out for you. I'll tell her you're here." With that, he scampered away and disappeared into the crowd that filled the loft.

The screen that normally separated Cecil's kitchen and living area was folded against the wall, creating one large room. It was the kind of crowd I had expected. Young, artsy. A lot of pierced body parts. Body parts never meant to be pierced, much less displayed. A small knot of guests congregated around a makeshift serve-yourself wine bar in the kitchen. On the opposite side of the room, a blonde young man, perched on a chrome barstool, strummed his acoustic guitar.

I made my way to the bar and poured a glass of Chardonnay. Suddenly, I heard someone shout, "Hey you guys! Hey you guys! Listen up! I want you to meet someone!" Cecil. Just behind me. When I turned, all eyes were on me. *Jesus, didn't she realize? It was a large crowd. Easy access. He could be hiding in the second tier. I was on display. One step sideways. A clear shot.* I scanned the room and slid my hand to the .32.

"This is Susan Solari. She's come to her senses and moved back to New York. From Texas." Loud boos from the crowd. "She's a good NYU grad. Just a little misguided. Introduce yourself to her this evening."

No one tried to kill me, and Cecil's guests went back to cocktail conversation. She turned to face me. I couldn't miss the large purple blotch on the left side of her face.

There was controlled fury in my voice. "What the hell is that?"

Cecil touched her cheek. "Nothing. A can of glaze fell off a shelf and hit me."

"Yeah, sure. And is Mr. Glaze Can here this evening?"

"I can handle it, Susan."

"That's what you said last time. Looks like he's more than 'handling' you."

"I'll be okay."

"When you get your fill of him, let me know. I'll take care of it."

Cecil didn't reply, but turned and went to greet other arriving guests.

I picked up my Chardonnay and went to work the crowd.

A few minutes later, I was talking to one of the more conventionally dressed guests. She had approached me and introduced herself as Sara Grahm, Cecil's neighbor. As we were making small talk, the little man who had greeted me scooted past us. I remarked that he intrigued me.

"Actually, that's my father, Victor Prieb," Sara said. "He just retired from Hunter College. Mom passed away about a year ago and he's sort of at loose ends. So when it's right, he comes to an occasional party with me. He really enjoys it. He's a great conversationalist."

"Well, he certainly made me feel right at home when I arrived," I said.

"He's a very unconventional computer scientist. Loves to be around people, *and* is an absolute genius with computers and anything electronic. And he can find anything on the Internet. I'm finishing up my doctorate, and I don't know what I would have done without him."

An idea jumped up and bit me on the ass. "Think he'd like some part-time work?"

"He'd snap it right up."

I pulled a card from my blazer pocket and gave it to Sara. "I'd give this to him, but I see he's enjoying a conversation with a very lovely blonde. I wouldn't want to ruin that."

Sara laughed. "You *do* have him figured out. He'd never forgive you. Listen, we're going to have to leave in a minute. But I'll give him your card and make sure he calls you."

"Thanks. One favor before you go?"

"Shoot."

"Can you point out Cecil's boyfriend to me before you leave?"

"Sure." She looked around the room for a few moments and then pointed out a slim, brown-haired man across the room. He was whispering in the ear of a brunette who had obviously forgotten her bra when she left the house, but did remember to put the silver stud through her lower lip.

"Thanks," I said.

"No problem. Now, I think I'd better rescue Dad from the blonde goddess and hit the road. I'll make sure he calls you."

"Excellent," I said. "I've got an interesting proposal for him."

I circulated for about another forty-five minutes. It seemed like every time I turned around I saw Cecil's boyfriend hustling a blonde, brunette, or redhead. I was headed to the kitchen to refill my Chardonnay when I felt a hand on the back of my shoulder. When I turned around, I saw the fury in Cecil's face.

"Did you mean what you said earlier?" she said.

"About the asshole? Sure."

"Then take care of it. The little bastard hasn't talked to me in an hour. In the meantime he's been trying to feel up anything that's got a skirt on. That, and every time I walk by a mirror, I see you're right about him."

I felt a surge of excitement, almost pleasure. "The asshole bring anything with him tonight?" I asked.

"Just a jacket."

"Find it and put it on the chair by the front door. Does he have a key?"

"Yes."

"First thing in the morning, call a locksmith and change the lock. And make sure your safety chains are on tonight. I don't think he'll have the guts to come back, but just in case."

I left Cecil and scanned the room for the boyfriend. I spotted him in a corner, feeling up the butt of the braless brunette. He didn't see me coming, but the brunette did. "Uh, Waddell. I think the guest of honor is here."

When he turned around, his face was inches from mine. The acne scars that pitted his cheeks were so deep that the track lighting cast shadows into the small craters.

I gave him my best come-hither look and said, "Waddell, I need a little time with you."

He took a couple of steps back and played to the brunette. "Well, it's the little gal from Texas. Yes, ma'am, I'd be honored to have a pow-wow with you."

I gave him a wink. "That's terrific. You won't regret it. Let's go outside."

The brunette got her back up. "He's mine, bitch."

"Apparently not." I grabbed his elbow and guided him out the door into the hallway. He seemed to find the whole scene amusing. *Dumb fuck.*

"Be gentle with me, Calamity Jane," he said as we went through the door.

"This is going to be something you've prayed for your entire life," I said. I moved close to him, slid my left arm around his neck and took his right hand in mine. I licked my lips and stroked the back of his hair.

His pupils filled his eyes. "Oh! Baby!"

In one quick movement, I twisted his right arm behind his back. He let out a yelp of pain. I cut his legs out from under with one swift kick, and I slammed his face into the concrete floor.

Blood gushed from his nose and spilled across the concrete. I released him and he rolled over, his hands on his face. The blood flowed out around his fingers. "Shit! You broke my nose, you crazy bitch."

"That ain't all that's gonna be broken." I drew my beautiful Ferragamo boot back and delivered a blow between his legs.

The sound of his scream bounced up and down the hallway, and he curled up in a fetal position. I opened the door to the loft, grabbed his jacket and threw it at him.

"How do you like the rough stuff now, lover boy? Not so much fun when you're on the receiving end, is it?"

He was still writhing on the floor, his breath coming in big gulps.

"Get up and run, not walk, out of here. And if I catch you near Cecil again, you'll think this was one of the best days of your life."

The sound of his Doc Martens limping down the hallway faded as I opened the door to the loft. Apparently Cecil had spread the word about what was coming down, because as I walked into the room, the crowd burst into applause. Sometimes it's fun to be a bitch.

Chapter 21

▼

Sunlight streamed though my bathroom window, illuminating swirls of steam escaping from my shower stall. I stepped out, toweled off and flipped on the blow dryer. After a couple of minutes, I gave up. Manhattan humidity won. I ran my fingers through my hair and tossed my head from side to side. It'd have to do.

I picked up the baby powder that always sat on my basin counter, shook a little into my hand, and smoothed it over my body. This was usually a source of comfort. This morning it was to help my white silk shell and light blue linen trousers and blazer slide on.

Glock in purse, .32 in thigh holster, treats for Caesar, and I was out on Morton Street. Six-thirty. A half hour before I was due to meet Aurora Garza at Charlie's. I hailed a cab that the driver took north on Eighth Avenue. The morning rush hour was already building to its peak, but no gridlock ... yet. The driver turned right at 40th Street, another right at Lex, and then one block down to 39th. I saw Charlie's neon sign flashing at the southwest corner of Lex and 39th.

I'd arrived about ten minutes early. That'd give me a chance to pick the table. Something away from the windows that overlooked the sidewalk and where I could put my back to a wall.

The moment I went through the door, I knew Aurora Garza was good at picking diners. The aromas of bacon frying, coffee brewing, and hash browns on the grill melded together and reminded me of the little diner my father took me to on the Jersey shore. Good times ... good food ... good memories.

A little bit of negotiating with the hostess and a ten-dollar bill got me the perfect table, away from the windows and in a corner. As I waited for Garza, bright slashes of color on the wall to my left caught my attention. Dozens of ceramic clocks were hung over the entire length of the wall. Clocks in almost every shape and color imaginable. A red dog, a blue cat, a yellow house, Mickey Mouse, Donald Duck and on and on. All set for four o'clock and none of them running.

"What'll it be, honey?" A waitress that looked like one tough grandma stood by my table. A chipped nametag pinned on her faded blue uniform said "MABEL."

"Just a cup of coffee. I'm waiting for someone. When she gets here, we'll order."

She made a note on her order pad and started to move away. "One more thing," I said. "What's the story with all the clocks?"

"Only some of us old timers know. When I'm serving customers, I can see them looking at the clocks. They're curious, but most don't ask."

"I'm asking."

"They're for his wife."

"Charlie's wife?"

"Yeah. It happened twenty-six years ago. Six days after he opened this place. He and Julie put everything they had into it. They were living in some rat trap apartment in the Lower East Side. Charlie worked late that night. When he got home he found Julie lying on their bed, bloody and beaten. Raped. Turns out gang-raped. She lasted two days after she got out of the hospital. Then she slit her wrists."

Mabel sighed, stopped for a moment, and then continued her story. "Julie loved ceramic clocks. Every year, on her birthday, Charlie hangs another one."

"And the four o'clock?"

"The time she died."

Chapter 22

Aurora Garza walked through the door of Charlie's at exactly seven o'clock. Not earlier, not later. Exactly at seven. She acknowledged my presence with a slight nod of her head, and then strode across the diner toward my table. Her choice of dress was as it was at my apartment, all business. Black slacks and blazer, off-white blouse, black loafers. The cut of the blazer gave room to conceal a service weapon with no problem.

We greeted each other, she got a cup of coffee, and I refreshed mine. Over the top of my breakfast menu, I saw Aurora checking me out. Her eyes rested for a few seconds on my purse, then she said, "Hell. I thought I was going to like you. Now I'm going to have to put your ass in jail."

"Excuse me?"

"Your purse. There's a concealment pouch, and I'm betting it's not empty. That's an automatic year in the can. No exceptions. We don't even let Jersey detectives carry when they cross the river."

"There's something else in the purse you need to see," I said. "It'll make this all better."

"I don't know what in the hell it could be."

"Trust me," I said. "I'm going to pick up my purse now."

Aurora's hand moved under her blazer. "Very slowly."

I placed the purse on our table, retrieved the mayor's letter and handed it to Aurora.

She studied it for a few minutes, then said, "Well I'll be goddamned! First one of these I've ever seen. What'cha got on His Honor?"

I took back the letter and returned it to my purse. "Let's just say I did him a favor once."

A little smirk appeared on Aurora's face. "Must have been a hell of a favor."

"It was," I said as I put my purse back on the floor. "Let's just leave it at that." I signaled to Mabel, who came to the table and took our breakfast orders. An egg over-easy for me. Two scrambled for Aurora.

As Mabel left and headed toward the kitchen, Aurora said, "That was some performance at your place last week. Ditzy corporate broad. Very nice. My partner bought it. I didn't, Special Agent Solari."

"If you checked me out, you know it's ex-Special Agent."

"Yeah, I know. And I also know that you left the Bureau after your husband was killed. And that you were fired from InterTrans after your boss was killed. And last week your ex-husband shot your boyfriend."

The words were familiar. I'd heard them many times. In my thoughts. In my dreams. If she was trying to establish control, it wouldn't work. I'd numbed myself to their impact. Time for a counter-attack.

"I know why you wanted to meet here. But I don't understand why."

Her glance at the clocks was almost imperceptible. But I noticed. And she knew I did. She tried to recover by taking a quick sip of her coffee.

"Mabel told me the story."

Again the coffee cup to her lips. This time a longer look at the clocks. "When it gets hard. When I think I can't see any more violence, can't hear any more stories, I come here. I look at Julie's clocks. It keeps me in the game."

"Why? Her suicide was twenty-six years ago. Why keep coming to this place?"

"To remind me to never give up. My father was the detective that investigated Julie's rape. It took him five years, but he got the bastards. Every time I feel like chucking it all, I come here, remember my father, and get back in the game."

Aurora paused a second or two and said, "Who's your Julie? We all have one."

My turn to sip coffee. "Francie Marcos."

Garza leaned over the table toward me, not letting up. "Now it's your turn. Let's have it."

"Her boss at InterTrans forced her to become a corporate slut. She came to me for help. I thought I'd protected her. I hadn't. She hung herself."

Garza shook her head. "It's a fine line. The fragile ones can't handle it."

I pushed my coffee cup away. "Yeah, but for the grace of God, it's us."

I saw something soften in Garza's eyes. "Yeah, I know."

I soaked up the last bit of my over-easy egg with my last bit of toast. "An added benefit of coming here, Officer Garza. The food's great," I said as I pushed my plate away.

"And you *have* to try the tongue sandwich at lunch," she replied. "And by the way, it's Aurora."

We had spent the last twenty minutes getting to know more about each other. Gaining some trust in each other. "And it's Susan. Now, Aurora, why this meeting? But before you answer that, let's get out of here. Let's take a walk. In this city, the public places are the most private."

The edge returned to her voice. "You got it." Back to business.

We paid the check and started north on the west side of Lex. Rush hour was in full bloom. Commuters and city dwellers alike rushed up and down the Avenue's sidewalks. Corporate women in tailored suits and sneakers, their heels in a canvas bag in one hand, their briefcase in the other. Corporate men in navy suits and wing tips, their briefcase in one hand, nothing in the other. They jostled and bumped each other as they crossed against red lights in their hurry to get to the job, where every Monday morning they started the countdown to the weekend.

Aurora spoke first. "When I gave you my card at your apartment, it was because I didn't believe the corporate ditz act. I thought you knew more than you were letting on."

"But it would have been wasted on The Irish Wonder?"

"Exactly. But now it's something more. You really like this 'Ten, Nine, Eight' thing?"

"So Fitzgerald filled you in?"

"Yeah, but he thinks it's bullshit. He said he'd warn Hillary Swift, and I imagine he will, just to cover his ass. But I doubt he'll be very convincing. He'll probably dismiss the threat at the same time he warns her. But you didn't answer my question. How strong are you on this?"

We'd reached the corner of Lex and 40th Street and had paused for a red light. "I …" The siren of an EMS van on 40th drowned out my answer. I waited a few seconds and tried again. "I'm sure the same perp did both rapes. The MO's are just too similar. Mike Riley, the Dallas detective that called Fitzgerald, is working on other connections between Manion and Thompson. Looking for common enemies. But right now Ten, Nine, Eight's the best I've got."

We started up Lex again. The Chrysler Building gleamed in the sun a couple of blocks ahead. Aurora flipped open her cell phone and punched in two numbers. Her conversation was short and to the point, and she got more and more agitated as she talked. "Collin, have you seen Hillary Swift yet?…. Phone call, you warned her with a phone call? I bet that put her on high alert!…. You didn't talk to *her*? Who the hell did you talk to?…. Forget it Collin!" She snapped her phone shut and jammed it into the pocket of her blazer. "Dumb fuck. He *called* her. Then didn't even talk to her. Talked to her director of security. Some guy named John Bonnavich."

The name so startled me I grabbed Aurora's arm. "Hell, I *know* John Bonnavich."

"You do?"

"Well, at least I think I do, if it's the same guy. When I was at InterTrans, he was security director at AT&T. We talked all the time. Worked industry threats together. I'll bet this is the same guy and he's moved to Continental. Can you get me his number?"

"You bet," Aurora said as she snapped open her phone. Her conversation with Fitzgerald amounted to "Give me the fucking number." She repeated it as Fitzgerald gave it to her. I had John Bonnavich on the line in less than five minutes.

Half an hour later, Aurora and I sat in Bonnavich's office in Rockefeller Center. Aurora cut to the chase. "Did Sergeant Fitzgerald make clear the threat to Ms. Swift?"

Bonnavich looked at me. "Frankly, no. Something about a serial rapist. And the Fortune 100. Then some comment about a ditzy broad. He didn't seem very coherent. It was after five o'clock. I assumed he'd been drinking."

Aurora shot me a glance. "That ditzy broad would be me," I said. "But John, this is serious. Did you tell Ms. Swift?"

"No. I didn't take the man seriously."

Aurora left her chair and began to pace around the office. "Do you want your CEO raped?"

Bonnavich glared at her, holding back anger.

"Then you damn well better listen to Susan."

I laid out my case. When I finished Bonnavich said nothing for a few moments. Then he said, "Please excuse me. I won't be long."

He quickly disappeared through his office door. I looked at Aurora. "What'cha think?"

"I think we see the big gal. You scared the hell out of him."

"God, I hope so. She's next. I feel it."

There was nothing to do but wait. It was all up to Bonnavich. He was back in less than five minutes. "She's got a little time before her next meeting. Let's go. Take your best shot."

When we entered her office, Hillary Swift was seated in a large executive chair behind an enormous, polished mahogany desk. Through the windows at her back, I saw the tops of St. Patrick's twin spires rising up on each side of her chair. As if God was protecting her.

She stood to greet us. Her ice blue suit perfectly complimented her ash blonde hair that was sculpted into a French twist. Nothing out of place. Untouchable, unapproachable. Armor against corporate enemies? Or a shield for a wounded heart. I knew the act. I'd used it. For both reasons.

After Bonnavich made the introductions, Swift came right to the point. "John explained that you believe I'm in some danger. Frankly, it seems rather farfetched to me."

"Ask Janet Manion or Felicia Thompson if it's farfetched." Aurora's tone was angry.

A frown spread across Swift's face. CEO's aren't used to being challenged.

"Give me ten minutes to convince you," I said.

Swift glanced at her watch. "That's all you've got. Have a seat."

As I made my case, I tried to read Swift's face to see if I was getting through. Nothing. She had to be one hell of a poker player. *Time to raise the urgency ... and the fear.*

"And we think he'll strike very soon and with greater violence."

Still no change in Swift's countenance. "And why do you say that?"

"Because of two things we know about serial criminals. The time between their crimes decreases, and each event gets more violent. The time between the first two rapes was a month. And it's been over two weeks since the Manion rape. So I'd say he's ready to hit again. And more violently."

Swift looked at Aurora. "And you buy into this?"

"Yeah."

Bonnavich jumped in. "Hillary, let's play the odds on this one. There's a lot to lose. You know June Martin. She's one of my best operatives. Black belt. Ready to kick ass at the drop of a hat. Let me put her with you for a few days."

"Not gonna happen, John."

Bonnavich pounded his fist into the palm of his other hand. "Damn it, Hillary, be reasonable."

"I'm not getting any employees involved in this."

Because you can't let them see that you're afraid. "I'll do it," I said.

"You'll do *what?*"

"I'll stay with you."

A little smirk appeared on Hillary Swift's face. "Oh! I'll feel sooo much safer."

Bonnavich tried to prevent the inevitable. "Hillary, you don't know. She's ex-FBI, black belt karate. Can kick most any man's ass I know."

Swift locked her eyes on mine. There was something different there. She turned to Bonnavich. "Okay."

His relief was palpable, "Where are you staying, in the city or Westchester?"

"Westchester tonight, and then in the city Wednesday and Thursday. Ray's going to be in Los Angeles."

Alarm bells went off, clanging in my mind. "Who's Ray?" I said.

"My husband."

There was urgency in my voice. "Then it's even *more* important that I'm with you. This asshole raped Felicia and Janet while their husbands were traveling."

Swift picked up a pen and wrote something on a note pad. "Make the arrangements, John, but just while Ray's gone." Then she looked at Aurora. "But I want the real cop. Not some ex-FBI private cop."

"Probably best," Aurora replied. "Less complicated. Especially if things get a little tricky. And it just so happens my busy social calendar is open Wednesday and Thursday night."

I didn't like where this was going. "Then both of us," I insisted.

Swift shook her head. "No way in hell. Only one. And I want the real deal. See you tomorrow night, Officer Garza."

Chapter 23

I went back to my apartment, pissed off and depressed. It rained in the afternoon. The foul weather matched my mood. I was sure the rapist would attack Hillary Swift sometime during Wednesday or Thursday night, and I wanted to be there to kick his sorry ass. And I was angry at Aurora for upstaging me. I didn't know if it was intentional, but I was inclined to believe the worst.

Around four o'clock my phone rang. *Maybe Aurora asking me to join her at Hillary Swift's apartment Wednesday and Thursday night!*

"This is Susan."

"Ms. Solari, this is Victor Prieb."

I searched my memory for the name. Vaguely familiar, but still …

"We met at Cecil Boldacchio's party. My daughter said you wanted me to call. Considering what you did to that man in the hall, I dared not refuse." There was merriment in his voice. As if he saw humor in life's absurdities.

"Well, you need not fear. That treatment is reserved only for misogynists, and at the party, I could see you're about as far away from that as I can imagine. The blonde was lovely."

Once again the humor in his voice. "Your powers of observation are outstanding. Hopefully you didn't see her rejection of my proposal of how we could spend the rest of the evening."

"Her loss."

"My opinion exactly." Then his tone changed. "My daughter said you might have an employment opportunity?"

"Perhaps." I briefly explained what I had in mind. "Does this interest you?"

"Enough to suggest a breakfast meeting tomorrow morning."

It would be a late night tonight as I was meeting Lynette Mason for *The Producers*, but what the hell. "Name the place."

"Harry's Hash House. Just off of Tenth on Waverly. Nine o'clock? One of the benefits of retirement is not getting up at the crack of dawn."

"Sounds good. See you there."

✻ ✻ ✻ ✻

The St. James theatre is on 44th between Eighth Avenue and Times Square. At seven o'clock I took the 3 train and arrived at Times Square station fifteen minutes before I was to meet Lynette. As I walked down Broadway, the street music of the Theater District greeted me: the incessant honking of yellow cabs, the roar of trucks, the insistent cries of street vendors hawking their knockoffs of Rolex, Gucci, YSL.

I made my way toward 44th, remembering my wedding to Dave and the three days that followed. We had explored a world we knew well, but now saw through different eyes. From Washington Square to Midtown. From our Seventh Street walk-up to the Seventh Avenue Hilton. From Angelo's Deli to La Reserve. From our present life to visions and hopes for our future. It might as well have been from New York to Paris. It ended so badly ... so far away. I cursed myself for allowing the memories and marched on toward the St. James.

I had counted on the fact that there would be no metal detectors at the theater entrance. I was right. All was well with the .32 on my thigh. Lynette's eyes met mine the minute I entered the St. James lobby. A weak smile spread across her lips and she waved at me as I strode through the lobby toward her. Her yellow pastel shirtwaist camouflaged the knockout figure I'd seen in the deli. She had a small white clutch purse in her right hand.

"I'm so glad you could make it," she said when I reached her. "I know it was a little short notice."

The small lobby was starting to get crowded, people jostling into each other as they made their way into the theater or lined up to get their will-call tickets. I scanned the crowd. He'd tried once in Manhattan. No guarantee he wouldn't try again. But I saw no visible threats. "No problem," I said. "I've seen the movie on late night cable, and I hear this show is even better."

Lynette's hands squeezed her purse a couple of times and her eyes darted around the crowd. It was as if she, too, was looking for a threat. The hunted recognize the hunted. We know the signals, because we see them in ourselves.

"Would you like a glass of wine before the show starts?" she asked. "The bar is just downstairs."

"No thanks," I said. "Let's just get settled in the theater. I don't like to be one of those ingrates who's getting seated during the first production number." *And I don't like all these people around me!*

Lynette took the tickets out of her purse as we moved to the theater entrance. A small gray-headed granny took the tickets and pointed us to the first aisle on our left. The seats were premium, tenth row orchestra, center section. "Your boyfriend's got good connections," I whispered to Lynette as we settled in our seats.

"Apparently so," she replied. "Who'd of thought it?"

I love Broadway theaters. Each with their own charm, especially the smaller ones. Proscenium arches, velvet curtains, the rococo side balconies thrusting toward the stage. No feel like it anywhere else. The voice-of-God announcer gave the warnings about photographs and digital recordings, the orchestra began the overture, and the curtain went up. For the next two hours Terry, Janet Manion, Felicia Thompson, and Ray Swift didn't exist. My ribs hurt as I howled with laughter at "Springtime for Hitler" and reveled in the fact that at the end, Max Bialystock was off on another adventure.

As the cast took its last curtain call, Lynette turned to me and said, "Now let me buy you that glass of wine … at the Marriott Marquis bar. It's just a block or so away."

The musical must have put me in a good mood, because I surprised myself and quickly said, "That sounds great, let's go."

The Broadway Lounge at the Marriott is a popular place for theatergoers to have a late evening nightcap. True to form, the place was jammed when we arrived, but we did manage to find a small round table for two away from the large windows that overlook Times Square. No view, but at least a place to sit.

I ordered a Chardonnay, Lynette a Pinot Grigio. About the time the waitress brought the drinks, and we paid for them, my cop's instinctive curiosity about Lynette kicked in. "Do I remember correctly that you work at a bookstore?" I asked.

Lynette took a sip of her wine before she replied. "Yeah, but only until I find something else. Until a couple of months ago I was an editor at Barnhill Publishing. I was there for eight years. Then I got on the wrong side of office politics and they fired me. So I'm looking. You don't have any connections in publishing, do you?"

"Sorry, you're shit out of luck. The only thing I know about books is that I read them. And that's in a pretty narrow range ... cops, mystery, thrillers. It's like taking a busman's holiday."

Lynette's eyes widened. "You're a cop?"

"Past tense," I said, and took more than a sip of the Chardonnay.

"So what are you doing now?"

"Corporate security consulting." The evening had been a nice interlude, but Lynette's questions were quickly bringing me back to reality, thoughts of a serial rapist, and more darkly, thoughts of the last nine years. Time to cut this short. "Speaking of that," I said, "I've got a big week this week. I'd better go. Thanks for *The Producers*."

Lynette looked puzzled and hurt at the same time. "Is something wrong? Did I say something wrong?"

I touched her arm. "You did nothing wrong. It was a lovely evening. I'm suddenly just very tired, that's all."

"You sure?"

"I'm sure."

"One more thing, then. Boyfriend travels a lot. If I'm at loose ends some weekend, okay if I call you? We could do the Met or something."

I surprised myself for the second time in an hour. "Sure," I said. "I'd like that."

* * * *

The next morning *did* come early, but I dragged myself out of bed and headed to Harry's Hash House. The place was cut out of something I might have found in my days in South Texas. Blue Formica-topped chrome tables, chrome framed chairs. Glass salt and pepper shakers, a round shaker of sugar, all set in the middle of the table. Fork and knife wrapped in a paper napkin at each place setting.

As was my habit, I arrived early, got a table at the back of the place, and took a seat that faced the entrance. Prieb must have planned to arrive early also. Less than a minute after I was seated, he walked through the entrance to the café. Most of the breakfast diners were already gone, so he spotted me immediately. I stood as he darted around the empty tables and chairs. In a matter of a few seconds, he was shaking my hand.

"Good to see you again, Ms. Solari. I'm sorry we didn't get to spend some time together at Cecelia's party."

"It's Susan," I said. "And as to the party, I think you spent your time well."

A smile appeared at the corners of his mouth. "As did you, Susan. And it's Victor."

We made small talk for a few minutes, and then a pretty young waitress took our order. Victor's eyes followed her as she left to get us our coffee. "Probably an aspiring actress," he said. "It seems they all are these days."

"That or working her way through NYU. I did plenty of that when I was there," I said.

Victor cocked his head. "My daughter said you were from Texas. How'd you wind up at NYU?"

I took a few minutes to give him my background, leaving out my husbands: the murdered one and the deranged one. Then I turned to my plans for the security consulting practice. "As I said on the phone, I need a technology consultant. While I'm getting started, it'd be on a consulting basis, but if things click, who knows, it might turn out to be full time. Still interested?"

He paused a moment and pulled at his goatee. Then a big smile broke out. "You bet! Since I retired I've been going nuts. My daughter's been trying to keep me busy, but there are only so many parties she can take me to. And most times, I feel like a fifth wheel anyway. I'm ready to get back into the real world."

We spent the rest of the breakfast talking about his compensation and sketching out how he might help set up the consulting practice. As we wrapped things up, Victor said, "When do I get started?"

"Soon," I said. "I'm working on a short-term case at the moment. But that should be wrapped up, one way or another, in a couple of weeks." Then I winked at him. "But don't leave town. I've never worked a case like this one. Who knows, your talents might come in handy."

* * * *

Hillary Swift maintained a *pied-a-terre* on the thirtieth floor of the Olympic Tower condominiums. The building was located at the corner of Fifth Avenue and 51st Street, across from Rockefeller Center and next to St. Patrick's. Aurora had arranged to meet her there at eight o'clock Wednesday and Thursday night.

Wednesday evening I fussed around my apartment, irritated that I was on the sideline. *I was the one that figured this out.* Finally, at eleven o'clock, I called Aurora's cell phone.

"Anything coming down?"

"Quiet as a church mouse. She's taking a shower, getting ready to turn in. She's real pissy. Doesn't like me being here."

My frustration burst out. "Well, ain't that too fucking bad? When our boy shows up you'll be her new best friend."

"Well, he better hurry up because after she gets out of the shower, I'm locking this place down and we're *both* hitting the sack."

"How's her security system?"

"She's a CEO. Whatta you think? When I arm this thing, he couldn't slip a note under the door without me knowing it."

One last try. "You know there will probably be two of them. Our boy and the guy with the video camera. You'll need help. We haven't told her about the second guy. Talk to her."

"Sure. Uh-oh, doorbell. Gotta go." Her phone went silent.

I waited ten minutes, then fifteen. At eleven-twenty, I called. After the fourth ring, a groggy voice answered. "This is Aurora."

"All okay?"

"It was a drunk with the wrong apartment number. For God's sake, Susan, go to sleep."

Aurora called the next morning just as I was pouring my first cup of coffee. Caesar was rubbing my legs, looking for his morning treats. "She didn't buy it. It's just me tonight."

"How hard you try?"

"What the hell's that supposed to mean?"

"I can see the headlines now, 'SVU DETECTIVE CAPTURES SERIAL RAPIST.' A real rocket ride to the top."

"Is that what you think?"

"Maybe."

Aurora didn't respond. Just hung up.

I didn't hear from her Thursday night. Friday morning, I called.

She sounded pissed, "So much for Ten, Nine, Eight. Go get another theory, Susan."

"Maybe he's just waiting."

"Yeah, sure. Pursue it if you want. I've only got so much energy. I'm not going to waste it."

Saturday morning there was a knock at my door. I folded a newspaper over the Glock and went to the door, gun snuggled under the latest news from Iraq.

When I cracked it open, I saw Aurora Garza standing in the hallway. "We didn't think it through, Susan. It wasn't Hillary. Last night he raped Ray Swift."

Chapter 24

Aurora and I sat at my kitchen table, each holding a mug of steaming coffee. Outside, a cool mist fell from gray, low-hanging clouds, muting the morning noises of an awaking Greenwich Village.

"So how'd you catch the case?" I said. "I thought detectives from the local precinct would be first on the scene."

Aurora took a swig of her coffee. "They were. The guys from the 17th precinct. They found my card in the apartment and called me. As soon as I learned who the victim was, I got out of there. By the time I arrived, they'd already transported Swift to Mount Sinai."

"You said Hillary left for London yesterday morning?"

"Yeah, some big telecom show. She was pissed she was going to miss her husband. He wasn't due to be back from LA until late afternoon."

I shook my head. "Some togetherness."

"Yeah. The big bucks'll do that. She's been notified and is on her way back. Gets in late this afternoon."

I looked at Aurora. There were hints of dark circles under her eyes, and there was a slight tremor in her hand when she gripped her coffee mug. "You want a bagel?" I said. "You look like a few carbs wouldn't hurt."

Aurora ran her fingers through her tangled hair. "Got any cream cheese?"

"Done." I split the bagel and put it in the toaster. "So how'd it come down?"

"I don't know the details. Swift's security company got a panic signal from his system. When they couldn't reach him, they called 911. Building security let the patrolmen into the apartment. Swift was tied to his bed, out cold. I don't have details, but the patrolmen told me he was really mauled. The doctors say he's lucky he's not going to lose an eye. They haven't let me talk to him yet."

"So how do you know he was raped?"

"The emergency room doctors. They found rectal bleeding. Tests aren't final, but they're pretty sure."

"If our guy was true to form, they won't find any semen," I said. "He always wears a condom. He's been very careful not to leave any physical evidence at the scene."

The bagel popped up out of the toaster. I grabbed it, put it on a plate and set it and a tub of cream cheese in front of Aurora.

"Thanks." She smeared the cream cheese over the bagel and took a bite. In a few moments she said, "But about physical evidence, maybe we're about to get lucky."

"How so?"

"The apartment was really torn up. Swift must have put up one hell of a fight. This wasn't as neat as the Manion rape."

"Or Thompson's," I added.

"Exactly. So I don't think our guy could control the environment like the first two cases. I think our CSI's might find something. Fibers, some of *his* blood, maybe even a print he didn't realize he left."

"God, I hope so," I said. "We still don't have a *clue* about who this guy is ... Oh shit, have you notified number seven? And who is it?" "Done," Aurora said. "And he's Lawrence Clayton, CEO of Allied Electronics. And now that we have it together, the Feds are going to warn one through six also. You were right about this countdown stuff. I owe you an apology."

"Not to worry," I said.

"Now, I've got to go. I'm going to try to talk to Swift." Aurora left the table and turned to leave. Then she saw the look in my eyes. "Get your gun ... err, purse. You've earned this one. Clever with the newspaper, by the way."

*   *   *   *

"You can see him now, but only for a few minutes. He's lightly sedated, so don't be surprised if he rambles a bit. And I'm going in with you. When I say it's time to leave, you leave. Understand?"

Dr. John Barrett stood in the hospital corridor, between us and the door to Ray Swift's room.

"We understand," Aurora said. "We'll be as brief as we can."

Barrett shook his head. "You'll be as brief as I tell you to be. Got it?"

"Got it," I said.

The look Aurora gave me would melt cold, hard steel. "Let's go," she said. She pushed around Barrett and marched into Swift's room.

The blinds on the windows were partially cracked, admitting a soft, gray light, tinged with red from the displays of monitoring equipment attached to Swift. The spikes and valleys of his heartbeat; the flashing readout of his blood pressure; his pulse rate. Life by the numbers. As I approached his bed, the thought crossed my mind: *For all of us, it finally comes to this. One catastrophic number, a flat line, and we're done.*

Ray Swift completely filled his bed. He was a large man, but by the appearance of his arms that lay outside of his bedcovers, he was not overweight, just heavily muscled. His head was heavily bandaged, but I caught a glimpse of a deep purple bruise on his left cheek. His eyes were closed and he demonstrated no awareness of us as we came alongside his bed.

Aurora softly called his name. His eyes fluttered open and he turned his head in our direction. "Are you the police officer? They said you might come." His voice was weak and raspy. As if he were suffering from laryngitis.

Aurora produced her detective's gold shield. "Yes, I'm Detective Aurora Garza, and this is Susan Solari. She's working your case with me."

Swift looked at me, but said nothing.

"I know you're still very uncomfortable, so we really appreciate your seeing us," I said. "We'll be as brief as possible."

Swift pushed a button on the bed control lying at his side and elevated his head. "Thank you."

Aurora removed a notepad and pen from her blazer. "Let's start with your telling us what happened to you. In your own words, as you remember it."

"Okay," Swift said. "I arrived at the apartment about five-thirty. Hillary had left me a note. When is she going to be here? I know she's worried. But I'm going to be all right."

"I talked to Hillary this morning, and told her not to worry. She'll be here this afternoon," Aurora said. "Now let's get back to what happened after you arrived at the apartment."

"Oh, yes. Nothing much at first. I read the note from Hillary. She said she was fine. That this whole thing about a rapist was some stupid false alarm. That she loved me and she'd see me Wednesday. Then I made some business phone calls."

"What business are you in?" I asked.

Swift pressed his control and raised his head a little higher. "I own a construction company. We specialize in hospitals."

Aurora shot me a glance

"Can I have some water?" Swift asked.

I picked up the pitcher of ice water on Swift's bedside tray and filled a glass. As I handed it to him, I heard Dr. Barrett whisper to Aurora, "Get to your point, detective."

"Let's continue with what happened at your apartment," Aurora said.

"Around seven-thirty my doorbell rang. I was expecting a messenger service delivery. I didn't check the peephole, just unfastened the safety chains and opened the door. There were two of them. Dressed in all black and wearing ski masks. They sprayed mace or pepper spray or something in my face. Blinded me."

Swift paused and took a sip of water from his glass. "Go on," I said.

"The one of them pushed me back into the apartment and hit me hard in the face. I couldn't see, but still put up a fight. I'm a pretty big guy so when they tried to grab me, I connected with some wild punches. I knocked something out of one of their hands. I heard whatever it was hit the floor. My hand still hurts like hell.

"Finally something hit the back of my head ... real hard. I went down and I was pretty much out, but they were punching me in the head and stomach. Then I heard one of them say, 'This is for Newark.'"

Aurora looked at me, a confused expression on her face. "Does that mean anything to you?" I asked.

"Yeah. We just finished a job in Newark. Big labor problems. I guess this is to teach me a lesson."

"So after they beat you. What then?" Aurora said.

"They left. I'm getting a little tired, detective."

Dr. Barrett put his hand on my shoulder. "Time to go. It's not negotiable."

I ignored him. "One more thing, Mr. Swift. Do you know Matt Thompson or Glenn Manion?"

"Of course. My company has built a number of hospitals for Matt. And we've designed and built special facilities in those hospitals for Glenn's diagnostic machines. Why do you ask?"

"Their wives have been recently raped, too."

Swift's eyes widened and his breathing quickened. "What do you mean 'too'? Has something happened to Hillary?"

I looked at Barrett. He shook his head and quietly said, "I haven't told him."

It was as if Swift cleared all the cobwebs. "Haven't told me what?"

Barrett put his hand on Swift's arm. "The emergency room doctors think you've been raped."

Swift pushed himself into a fully erect sitting position. "They're fucking liars. All of you … get the hell out of here."

Chapter 25

John Barrett literally shoved Aurora and me out of the room. As soon as we were in the corridor, he let fly, his eyes full of rage. "Great job, Ms. Solari. We have a protocol in this hospital for dealing with rape victims. But your ham-handed questions blew all that. I had a choice of letting my patient think his wife was raped, or telling him he was."

I was having none of it. I got in his face. "You knew we were here to question him about what happened in that apartment. You knew that Detective Garza had been told of the possibility of rape. Why the hell didn't you tell us he hadn't been told? Not my mistake, Doctor."

Aurora stepped between us. Her voice sounded like a stern nun, and I felt like she was rapping our knuckles with a ruler. "Enough, both of you! We'll settle this elsewhere!" Then she marched us to a small waiting area at the end of the corridor where the three of us sat on old, uncomfortable, straight-back chairs.

Barrett spoke first, directing his question at me. "Again, how are you involved in all this?"

"I'm a private investigator," I lied.

"I have to give the police reasonable access to my patient," he replied, shaking his head. "But you, you have no official standing with me. And you're off of Ray Swift's approved visitor list as of *now*."

Aurora broke in before I could answer. "I'll decide who questions Ray Swift, doctor, not you. If I want Ms. Solari there, she'll be there. Understand?"

Barrett's face turned red as he got quickly to his feet, stethoscope jiggling in his white coat pocket. "We'll see about that, Detective." Then he turned and walked away, disappearing around a corner of the corridor.

"Thanks," I said. "I appreciate you having my back."

"Sometimes doctors can be real assholes. They think they're God," Aurora said. "I should know; I'm married to one."

"You didn't tell me that."

Aurora winked at me. "There are a lot of things I haven't told you. But that's for another time. Let's get back to Ray Swift."

Before I could answer, the public address system blared out "Code blue. Room 413. Code blue. Room 413." Two nurses at the station across from us immediately dropped what they were doing and took off running down the corridor. A man rapidly pushing a defibrillation machine was just behind them. All three rushed into a room about halfway between the nursing station and the end of the corridor.

Then all was quiet. Someone just arriving on the floor would not be aware of the desperate battle going on in room 413. Another battle flashed before my eyes. The white van has unleashed its terrible fury. My car is on the side of the road. Paramedics are working on me. Trying to stop the bleeding caused by an AK-47 bullet to my gut. Two other paramedics have pulled my husband from the passenger seat and are fighting desperately to save his life. They hit him with the paddles. Then again. Then one more time. Out of the corner of my eye, I see their shoulders slump. One paramedic speaks to the other who shakes his head.

I looked at Aurora. "Let's get the hell out of here. This place gives me the creeps."

Ten minutes later we had crossed Fifth Avenue and were walking along a path at the fringe of the East Meadow of Central Park. The morning's mist had lifted and the sun was trying to burn away the clouds. Joggers were taking advantage of the cooler-than-usual weather, pounding away along the path.

"Damn it," I said. "I thought I had it all figured out. Except that he was after spouses, not just wives. Now I'm not so sure."

Aurora took a sip from a lemonade she'd picked up at a vending cart on East 98th. "You mean the Thompson-Manion-Swift connection?"

"Yeah. There might be something in that. Maybe it's just a coincidence … the ten, nine, eight thing, I mean."

"I think you had it right," Aurora said. "I think ten, nine, eight is the deal. And I'm not buying the thing about Newark. I think that's bullshit from Swift. To cover up the rape. I don't think Swift's ego will ever let him admit he was raped. I bet the last thing he heard from our boy was 'Give my regards to Hillary.'"

The path had taken us back to Fifth Avenue. "We'll find out when we get the videotape," I said. "Did you warn Hillary about that?"

Aurora tossed her empty lemonade cup into a trash container. "Not yet. But I'll call her tonight. She gave me her cell number when I reached her in London."

"Guess that's about it for today," I said. "Call me when you get the CSI's results."

"I'll have preliminary stuff Monday afternoon ... Oh, I'd give you a lift downtown, but I'm headed to Connecticut, trying to salvage a bit of a getaway weekend."

"No problem," I said. "There's always the subway."

"Talk to you Monday, then," Aurora said. She turned and started across Fifth Avenue. Once again, I was alone in Manhattan.

* * * *

Monday morning I was about to leave my apartment to pick up a few things at the neighborhood bodega, when my phone rang. When I checked the caller ID, there was no name, just a number I didn't recognize. I let the call go to my answering machine and the caller started his message. "Ms. Solari, this is Morrie Masters with the *New York Post*. I'm working on a story..." I recognized the name. Before I left Dallas, Dom Shapiro had warned me about this guy. His byline often appeared above some of the most salacious stories in New York's most outrageous tabloid. I picked up before he could finish his sentence.

"This is Susan Solari."

The voice on the other end of the line sounded like a parrot with a bad nasal condition. "That's what I like about having my own machine. It makes a great call screener. What made you decide to pick up? Was it the mention of the *Post,* or my melodious voice?"

"Neither," I said. "When the enemy is about, I find it helpful to know their intentions."

I heard a strange sound, something between gagging and laughter, and then he said, "There's more fire to you than I was led to suspect."

"And who was doing the leading?"

"A source, Ms. Solari, a source."

"And that source is ...?"

"You know better than that."

"Then get to your point."

"Sure, sure. You're working for Glenn Manion, aren't you? About his wife's rape."

"Who I work for and the cases I work on are private matters."

Again, his strange laugh. "Not as private as you think. I know this is one weird case, lady. Wives of Fortune 10 CEO's are being raped. And now a *guy's a victim*. And it turns out he's the *husband* of a female CEO. I know you think these rapes are all connected."

I felt my face getting hot. "No comment."

"I just wanted to know if you were making any progress. You know, about to get the bad guy. The public has a right to know."

"Talk to the police. I'm sure the Special Victims Unit is investigating."

"Got another joke for me? You know they don't give out information."

One of them sure as hell did. "And neither do I."

He wouldn't let go. "You've been working the case for almost three weeks. You must have some suspects in mind. Tell me if you're getting close. It'll make the public feel safer."

"No comment."

"Can I take that to mean you, and the police, are making no progress?"

God, this guy is irritating! "You can take it however you wish. I hear that's what you usually do."

"What is that supposed to mean?"

"Your reputation is that you rarely let facts stand in the way of the story you want to write."

Now came the fake resentment. "Are you impugning my integrity?"

"This conversation is ended. And by the way, when it comes to people's private lives, the public doesn't have the right to know crap."

I slammed the receiver down and then picked it up again and called Aurora's cell phone. I heard the hitch in the ring tone when I was sent to her voice mail. I listened to her message and then said, "You've got an Irish rat in your unit. I'm gonna try to do damage control. Call me ... today!"

When I finished my last scotch Monday night, Aurora still hadn't called. Thoughts I didn't want to acknowledge crept in and troubled my sleep.

* * * *

Tuesday morning I went to the bodega early and picked up a copy of the *Post*. The headline slashed its way across the front page:

Police Track Corporate Countdown Rapist

I carried the paper back to my apartment, poured myself a cup of coffee and sat down at my breakfast table to read the article. Morrie Masters' byline was centered just below the headline. He'd put it all together. He didn't name the victims, but he didn't have to. Anyone with a Fortune 500 list and a lick of sense would quickly conclude that Felicia Thompson, Janet Manion, and Ray Swift had been raped.

He included the SVU statement that "We don't comment on continuing investigations. We don't even acknowledge there is an investigation."

He'd done his homework on me, and he took his shot. "The husband of one of the victims has hired a private detective, Susan Solari, to investigate his wife's rape. Ms. Solari also refused comment, but sources close to the police say she's yet to contribute anything useful to the investigation."

Sources close to the police, my ass. The source *is* the police. God, I hope I'm right about which one.

I finished the article and laid the paper aside. Thank God my instincts had been good. Yesterday, after my conversation with Masters, I'd called Felicia Thompson and Janet Manion and warned them what to expect. For them, a little time had passed and, ever so slightly, the healing process had begun. This would be a setback, but one I thought they could deal with.

Glenn Manion was another matter. A few minutes after I talked to Janet, he called me back, his voice loud and demanding. "How the hell could you let this happen? And why didn't you tell me about this 'countdown' theory? What the hell am I paying you for anyway?"

I was having none of it. "And why didn't you tell me about your yearly bet with Thompson? You didn't think it was important?"

We went on for a couple of minutes like that. Finally I said, "Why the hell don't you just fire me?"

"Don't tempt me. But damn it, you've brought me more than the lazy-assed cops. Just don't spring any more surprises on me."

I was calming down a little. "Glenn, I'm going to conduct this investigation the way I see fit. If it means keeping you in the dark on some things, that's the way it's going to be. Or I'm outta here."

He didn't say anything for a few moments, then he growled, "Just make 'em few and far between." Then he hung up.

I was not so sure how Ray Swift would handle the story. I hadn't tried to reach him; instead I talked to Hillary. According to her, he was still denying he was raped, although the medical evidence was very strong. Now that his violation had been revealed to the world in 20-point type, I was fearful his psyche couldn't handle it.

I was pouring myself a second cup of coffee when my phone rang. The caller ID said "Aurora Garza." She started speaking before I had a chance to say hello. "Sorry I didn't call yesterday. I've been on stakeout. Waste of time, the perp didn't show. And yes, I've seen the *Post*."

I had to contain myself to keep from screaming into the phone. "You better keep me away from that Irish sack of shit you call partner!"

"I've ripped him up one side and down the other. In English *and* Spanish. Of course he denies it. But I know he's tight with Masters. Morrie gets him into the right parties, makes sure he always has a drink in his hand."

"You gonna take this to Internal Affairs?"

"Take what? It'd just be my word against his. I've got no proof."

"Yeah, I guess you're right," I sighed. "Got any word on any evidence found at Swift's apartment?"

"Don't know about that yet. The stakeout with Shitface took all of yesterday. I'll check and call you back."

"Okay, talk to you then." I hung up and turned my attention to domestic chores: making the bed, dusting, cleaning the bathroom. At least the bathroom wouldn't take long. I didn't have a man around.

Chapter 26

I finished my domestic chores by cleaning my weapons. I knew the routine well. Swap out the ammo, exercise the spring that feeds the cartridges into the chamber, etc., etc ... I finished a few minutes before five, so I called Mike Riley in Dallas to fill him in on the attack on Ray Swift. I also wanted to know if the DPD had any new information on Terry's whereabouts.

I was lucky; Mike was still at his desk. I described the attack on Swift and Morrie Masters' story in the *Post*. When I finished, Riley said, "Well, you really figured it, Susan."

"Try telling that to Ray Swift. Besides, I'm really rethinking this 'Corporate Countdown' theory, as my friend Morrie calls it."

"Why would you do that? It looks like the attack on Swift proves it."

"We found out Ray Swift has business connections to Glenn Manion and Matt Thompson. When I was in Dallas, at the Bureau's office, you said you were going to check out the business connections between Manion and Thompson. Look for lawsuits, that sort of thing. Find anything?"

"Not yet. We're still working it. I'll ask the guys if they've seen anything involving Swift."

Another damn dead end! Time to ask my sixty-four thousand dollar question. "Anything turn up on Terry?"

"Nothing. But watch your backside, Susan. He's gotta be stalking you. First Central Park, and then here in Dallas. You still packing?"

"Sure. But if he attacks me here, and I shoot him, I've gotta hope the mayor's letter works. Otherwise, I'm the guest of New York State for a least a year."

"Another reason I don't understand why you went back."

I'll tell you why when I figure it out. "Let me know if you pick up anything."

"Instantly."

"Okay, see ya, Mike."

"See ya, Susan."

After I hung up from Mike, I popped open a bottle of iced tea I had chilling in the refrigerator. I wandered over to the living room couch and plopped myself down. The disappointment of not hearing anything new on Terry flowed over me. I'd been in Manhattan over three weeks and made no progress in opening my security consulting practice. Instead I had wasted time chasing some deranged rapist, and still didn't have a clue as to who he was. Glenn Manion's money was good, but it was time to get on with my life. I'd sleep on it, but I thought tomorrow I'd call Manion and quit. Aurora Garza was a good cop and she wouldn't let loose of this. Eventually she'd find the guy, despite having to drag Collin Fitzgerald around.

I finished my tea and was tossing the empty into the trash when there was a knock at my door. I kept the Glock at my side, kept the safety chains in place, and cracked the door open.

"We got a little something," Aurora said. She'd stepped back a couple of feet into the hallway. "I was on my way back from downtown. I thought I'd stop by to tell you personally. And from the way you look, I think you could use some good news."

I undid the safety chains and let her into the room. "You know how they say to never let the bastards get you down. Well, sometimes they do. But enough about me. What'cha got?"

Aurora sat down on the couch and looked at her watch. "Well, look at that. It's after five and I just went off duty. And I've got good news. The least you could do is get me a drink."

I smiled and shook my head. "And I thought I was getting special treatment. You're just here for my booze. Scotch or vodka is it for the hard stuff. Or I've got some Pinot Grigio or some Shiraz."

"It's been a long day. I'll take the scotch, on the rocks."

"And I'll make it two," I said as I walked into the kitchen to make the drinks.

The afternoon sun was spilling through the kitchen window, fighting the air conditioner and raising the amount I would send to Con Ed at the end of the month. I pulled the little sheer curtain across the window as I set about making the drinks. Ice in each old fashioned glass and then the scotch.

When I returned with the drinks, I found Aurora sniffing the Glock. "Just cleaned it?"

"Swabbed-out, fresh ammo," I said.

"I'm due to do that," Aurora replied. "Overdue, in fact." She had kicked off her flats. "Some days I feel like these things are just going to burn off," she said, looking at her feet which were now clad only in sheer footlets. "Boy, it feels good to get out of these shoes."

I handed her her drink. "This'll feel even better. Now, out with it."

She took a long sip of the scotch. "We've got DNA. After they stabilized Swift, they did a forensic exam. They scraped his fingernails and got some skin. From the look of the apartment, Swift put up a hell of a fight. I'll bet our perp has got some pretty fierce scratches. But probably not on his face if he wore a ski mask like the other rapes."

I was sitting in the wing chair, my hand cupped around my drink. "What else?"

"That's it."

"That's it? Nothing at the apartment?"

"Nope."

I was highly pissed and disappointed and it showed. "How the hell can that be? We got at least two men fighting in that apartment. You tell me there's broken tables, chairs, and lamps. Are you fucking telling me the fucking CSIs couldn't find one fucking thing? Is that what you're telling me?"

I was leaning out of the chair toward Aurora and realized I was jabbing my finger toward her. She let me finish my outburst, was quiet for a few seconds, and then said, "That's what I'm telling you. But at least we have the DNA. Better than the first two."

"Not by much," I said.

"You been keeping up with the FBI DNA database?" Aurora asked.

I realized I hadn't touched my scotch, made up for lost time, and set the glass on the table beside my chair. "Not really. It was pretty small when I left."

Aurora's expression was quite animated and her eyes were bright. It was as if she was trying to give me some hope. "Well, it's not so small now. It contains over a million records. And it's put almost seven thousand bad guys away. We'll run our sample through and see if we get a hit. You never know. Even if we don't, we've got the sample for comparison when we get our guy."

I was in no mood to be consoled. "You mean *if* we get him. Look, there's something you need to know. I think that tomorrow I'm going to …"

The ring of the phone on my side table interrupted me. I glanced at the caller ID and recognized the Manions' home number. "Excuse me a sec," I said as I picked up the phone.

"Hi Glenn, it's Susan."

The voice on the other end of the line was soft and reticent. "It's not Glenn. It's Janet."

"How are you doing, Janet? I'm so sorry about that *Post* story. Masters is a real asshole."

"I'm not calling about the story. Well, in a way I am. It's something *in* the story. I have to talk to you."

I glanced at Aurora and mouthed "Janet Manion."

She reached into her blazer pocket and produced her notepad and a pen.

"Talk away," I said.

"No, not on the phone. Can I see you tomorrow?"

"Sure. Want me to come to your place?" I finished off my scotch and I noticed Aurora doing the same.

"No. Do you know the restaurant called Pandora? It's on 55th between 6th and 5th Avenues."

"I know the block. That's where La Bonne Soupe is; I go there often. But I don't remember Pandora."

"It just opened a couple of weeks ago. Meet me there at one o'clock. I'll arrange a private room. Glenn's out of town."

"Sure, I'll see you then."

Aurora leaned toward me and whispered, "I want to be there."

I turned my attention back to Manion. "Janet, you know Aurora Garza, the SVU officer working your case, right?"

"Of course."

"I'd like her to be at our meeting. Okay?"

"Not okay! If you want her there, forget it."

I looked at Aurora and shook my head. "Just a thought. Not necessary. I'll see you there at one."

"Without the cop?"

"Without the cop." I heard a click and she was gone before I could say goodbye.

I looked at Aurora. "You're not invited to this party. If I had insisted, she'd have killed the meeting."

Aurora folded her notepad closed and put it and the pen back in her blazer. "What do you think she wants?"

"I'm not sure. But I don't think she wants Glenn to know she's meeting with me. She made a point of telling me he's out of town."

"I'm sure you'll handle it, and then get me on board."

"Depends," I said.

"Depends?"

"Depends on what this is about."

Aurora didn't respond and we sat staring at each other. Finally she said, "Time to go. The doctor's taking me out to dinner tonight. A rare occasion."

As I opened the door for her to leave, I asked, "You ever going to tell me about him?"

"Who?"

"The doctor."

"Depends."

"Depends on what?"

"You figure it out."

As she was about to go down the stairs, she turned to me. "Before Janet called, you said there was something I needed to know. Gonna tell me?"

"Depends."

"Depends on what?"

"Tomorrow."

* * * *

Before I went to Pandora's, I thought about the phone call. The tone of Janet Manion's voice told me something was not right. I had no idea what might be wrong, but it put me on edge. I was glad there was fresh ammo in my weapons. Fresh ammo is always good.

At noon I grabbed a cab and told the driver to take me to 5th and 55th. I figured the trip would take about twenty minutes, giving me a little time to reconnoiter the neighborhood before I was to meet Janet at one.

Traffic is never light in Manhattan, but at least we didn't encounter the police rousting street peddlers, an EMS emergency run, or any of the myriad of things that can create gridlock. The cabbie overshot 55th by one block and dropped me off at 54th by the side of the University Club. I had no objection. I love the University Club building. Designed by Sanford White and built at the turn of the twentieth century, it's probably the city's most beautiful example of Italian Renaissance palazzo-style architecture. The fact that the club, for much of its history, was for men only, I didn't hold against the building. That Sanford White was killed in a dispute over a beautiful woman gave me no small measure of satisfaction.

I walked back to 55th and leisurely strolled toward 6th Avenue, past La Bonne Soupe and a small Italian restaurant two doors down. When I spotted Pandora, I crossed the street and checked out the menu posted in the window. The entrées looked mostly New American, but they had a great selection of salads. It'd be a salad for me. I hadn't been careful lately, and the slacks I wore were a little tight around my hips.

I spent another ten minutes or so checking out the block and didn't detect anything that might be a threat. A homeless woman going through a trash bin, a street peddler with his wares spread on a blanket, a delivery truck double parked at mid-block; all familiar sights in Manhattan. Apparently, there was no need for my paranoia. But then, it only takes one mistake.

When I entered Pandora, the hostess guided me to the rear of the restaurant. The place had the faint smell of new paint, and the green and cream upholstery of the booths and chairs still looked spotless. The place was about half full. Most of the empty tables were not yet cleared as the noon lunch crowd had just left.

Janet Manion was seated at a table in a small room cut into the rear wall of the restaurant. A mural of Grecian men and women in idyllic settings decorated the wall behind her. Two place settings were laid out on the table. Janet stood as I came into the room.

"Thanks for coming, Susan. I know this was on short notice." As was the case the first time I met her, her beauty intimidated me. She wore a light blue silk top and a white skirt decorated with silk-screened pale blue and green wildflowers. She wore the outfit with a model's elegance, knowing the impression she made, but without self-consciousness when, as mine did now, glances lasted a moment too long.

"Not a problem," I said. "It's good to see you. You sounded as if you were doing better when we talked on Monday."

Janet returned to her seat and I took the other chair at the table. "I'm still trying to work things out," she said. "Some days are good, some days the tears won't stop. But there are more good days than bad."

"That's good to hear," I said.

Janet reached across the table and lightly touched the back of my left hand. "I hope you don't mind. I've already ordered for both of us. A citrus and herb salad with a poached salmon filet. It comes with a side of citrus tarragon vinaigrette dressing. Is that okay with you?"

"Sounds delicious." The words were just out of my mouth when a sturdy waitress appeared with the salads, a basket of rolls, and two bottles of sparkling water.

When she finished serving us, Janet said, "Thank you, Gretchen. As you leave, would you please close the door? And we're not to be disturbed for any reason. If we require anything we'll open the door and you can come in. Understand?"

"I understand, Ms. Manion," Gretchen said. Then she left the room, closing the door behind her.

"I apologize for all the secrecy," Janet said. "But you will soon understand why this conversation can be for no one's ears but ours."

I poured the sparkling water into the glass of ice sitting in front of me. "Then let's get started," I said.

"First I need your assurance that nothing, and I mean *nothing*, of what you learn today will be shared with the police. If what I tell you leads to suspects for these rapes, you, of course, may share those names with the police. But you are never, ever, to share the source of the information that led you to those suspects. Can I have your pledge on that?"

"Janet, before we go any further, I ought to tell you I'm thinking of quitting the case."

"Why?"

"I'm not making much progress, and I need to get on with my life."

Janet took a bite of her salmon and studied me for a few moments. "Frankly, you disappoint me. I thought there was more persistence in you. But listen to what I have to say before you make your decision."

"Of course."

"And I have your pledge regarding the police?"

"Yes."

Janet picked a roll out of the basket, broke it in half, and buttered it. When she began to speak, she studied the roll, her eyes not meeting mine. "While there were no names mentioned in the *Post* article, would I be safe in assuming that Ray Swift was the man who was raped?" She took a bite of the roll and waited for my answer.

"Janet, I'm not going to answer that. You know that I guard your privacy fiercely and I do the same for all my clients."

"No matter. It's not hard to figure out. I can't tell you the number of calls from 'friends' *I've* gotten since Tuesday morning. But back to my point; I know Ray Swift."

"That's not surprising," I said. "CEO's tend to run in packs. I imagine you and Glenn have attended some functions where you'd meet Hillary and Ray. And I know Ray and Glenn do business together. I can see how you'd know Ray."

Janet laid her fork on the table. This time she looked directly into my eyes. "There's more to it than that."

"Go on."

"Hillary and Ray, Glenn and I, we're members of an exclusive club. Takes an annual income of at least three million a year to join."

"That's some country club," I said.

Janet shook her head. "It's not a country club, Susan."

"What kind of a club is it?"

"One where the members enjoy the pleasures of each others' company. Like I told you, I *know* Ray Swift, in all possible meanings of the word."

My voice was so loud it probably carried through the door and piqued the interest of diners at nearby tables. "You're in a fucking swingers' club for millionaires?"

Janet Manion slowly nodded her head. All I could say was, "Jesus Christ!" With her looks there must have been a lot of action.

Janet pushed her salad away. "At first it was only Hillary and Ray and Glenn and I. Glenn suggested it, I was reluctant. In my modeling days, I was no saint. But this seemed so cold, so arranged."

"So why'd you go along with it?"

"Things weren't good between Glenn and me. I thought that if this was what he wanted to do, it might help."

I needed to gather my thoughts. See where to take this. I swung around and opened the door. Gretchen immediately popped into the room. "You can clear the table," I said.

While she did her work, there was no conversation between Janet and me. When she finished, I closed the door and looked at Janet. "So why are you telling me this?"

"The group has grown. Now it's eight couples. I don't know all of them well. There're whispers among the women that a couple of the guys are rough. I won't do them. Neither will Hillary. A few times they've gotten belligerent."

"So you think maybe your rape and Ray's is some sort of revenge?"

"I don't know, but I thought there might be some sort of connection."

We sat for a minute or so, saying nothing, just looking at each other. Finally I said, "Let me absorb this. Put it in context."

"So this means you're staying on the case?"

"I don't know. I'll sleep on it. If I stay, I'll need the names of the other couples in the club."

"I'll give them to you now," Janet said. She reached in her purse, pulled out a notepad and pen, and wrote down the names. She tore the page off the pad and handed it to me. "If you decide not to keep on the case, just shred this."

I looked over the names. "Which of these guys are the rough ones?"

"Bob Watson and Frank Henderson."

"Okay, I'll have Aurora Garza run a rap sheet on them, see if anything turns up. I'll need the addresses of Watson and Henderson."

A look of concern crossed Janet's face. "You have to tell the police, you know, about the club?"

"Not at first. But if there's a connection, yes."

"And then it's only a matter of time before the press knows."

I reached across the table and touched her hand. "I wish I could say no, but we both know the realities."

Janet sighed and said, "Do what you have to." She took back the notepaper, consulted a small electronic organizer, added the addresses, and returned it to me.

"Janet, I know this was hard for you. And I'll treat this information in as much confidence as is possible. Frankly, I don't think you need to worry about this leaking to the press because I don't think these guys will pan out as suspects. For one thing, I don't see any connection to Felicia or Matt Thompson. I'll check 'em out, but I doubt anything will come of it."

Janet looked down at the table. "Okay."

I waited a moment, then asked the question that was troubling me. "Why'd you stay in the club?"

Her eyes started to tear up. "With Glenn, he takes me as if I was his property. The other guys in the club flirt with me, tell me I'm beautiful, and court me. I can always say no. It was nice. But I'm out now. After the rape, I couldn't bear the thought of it. Glenn's trying to pressure me to go again. But I'm not going back. I'll divorce him first. By the way, he doesn't know I've told you any of this. Keep it that way."

A profound sadness overcame me. "Of course. This was very courageous of you. I'll call you tomorrow."

"Thank you," she said.

We left the restaurant and I couldn't help but think that one of the many troubles that escaped from Pandora's box had cursed the beautiful woman sitting across the table from me on this May afternoon.

Chapter 27

I hailed a cab heading south on 5th Avenue. As I slid into the genuine vinyl back seat the cabbie said, "So, where to?" The accent was pure Brooklyn. A throwback to the 1960s when New York cabbies made their reputation.

"Hudson and Christopher," I said. The destination was three blocks from my apartment, but there was a great deli just off the intersection and I needed to pick up something for dinner.

Thirty minutes later I had a deli bag stuffed with a half-pound of tongue, a loaf of rye, and a jar of spicy mustard. Half a salad at lunch permitted me my favorite sandwich for dinner. Tight slacks or not, after what I had heard from Janet Manion today, I needed comfort food.

When I arrived at my apartment, I checked the little piece of transparent tape I'd stuck to my front door and its frame. It was still in place. *See, you're paranoid! No, just careful, and still alive.*

When I opened the door, I saw a white envelope lying on the living room floor. From where it was positioned, I guessed someone had slipped it under the door. I set the deli bag on the breakfast table, returned to the living room and picked up the envelope. It was a standard business size, with no address on the front or return address on the back. The flap was sealed. I tore it open and pulled out a single, folded sheet of paper. The message was boldly splashed across its surface, taunting, challenging.

> You think you can catch me? You might as well try to catch the wind! Who's next? Guess! Don't be wrong. A friend won't like the consequences. Who? That's your problem. You'd better hurry. Another must pay.

I felt the hair on the back of my neck rise and a knot form in the pit of my stomach. It was as if the rapist had invaded my apartment and was threatening to make me his fourth victim. What really creeped me out was knowing that he knew where I lived and not too long ago was standing at my front door. I dropped the note on the kitchen table and went to the door, engaged the deadbolt, and slid both safety chains in place. Then professionalism kicked in.

I went to my purse and sheathed my hands in latex gloves. Then I returned to the table and studied the note. It was printed on plain white, 8 ½ X 11 paper. No watermarks, smudges, coffee rings, or other markings. I flipped it over and examined the back. Nothing there.

Still, questions roared at me. Why'd he send it to me? Didn't serial criminals usually taunt the police? Or send something to newspapers so they could see their words in headlines? How'd he get my address? It wasn't in the *Post* article, and my phone was unlisted. And why send a note at all? His crimes seemed very targeted. It didn't fit that he might be trying to frighten the general public.

But I wasn't going to get any answers by just staring at the note. I needed to get it to the police forensics lab and let those guys get to work on it. I left it on the table and called Aurora. She picked up on the first ring. "I was just about to call you. Hillary Swift got the videotape this morning."

"Just about right on schedule," I said. "How'd she take it?"

"Pretty good, since I told her to expect it. She'll be okay. She didn't look at any of it."

"You looked at it yet?"

"I started to, then this piece of shit we call a VCR jammed up. I almost ripped the tape getting it out. I was gonna call you and see if your VCR is up and running."

"Sure, bring it on over. By the way, how'd he get it to Swift, by messenger, like the last one?"

"Nope. Express Mail. Delivered to her office."

"He's getting smarter. No messenger for us to backtrack. Was there a return address?"

"Yeah, but you know it'll be fake. I'll check it out anyway. And the post office where he mailed it—the postage shows an originating ZIP code. It's a long shot, but worth a try."

"How'd he address it?" I said.

"Whatta you mean?"

"The Express Mail label. How'd he address it? Typed … handwritten?"

"Computer generated label. Virtually impossible to trace"

"Yeah," I said. "Just hoping against hope."

"Okay, I'm on my way to your place. See ya in a half-hour."

"Whoa Nellie! Before you rush out, I've got something for *you*." Then I told Aurora about the note and read it to her.

"Holy shit!" she said. "He's really escalating. And he knows your address. You gotta hire some muscle until this is over."

"I've already got my muscle," I said. "Remember Mr.Glock? Now, a question for you. Anything shown up in your mailbox?"

"Nothing as of yesterday, but I've been out of the station all day. Give me a sec, I'll check."

Aurora was off the line for a minute or so, and when she came back her answer was negative. "But it doesn't surprise me. I wasn't mentioned in the *Post* article. And that's gotta be where he got your name. The only person quoted from the unit was Wanda Peterson, our public affairs officer. But if he sent something just addressed to Special Victims Unit or to headquarters, it could still be rattling around in the central mailroom. Maybe something will show up."

"Okay," I said. "One more thing. I don't think much will come of this, but I need you to run a rap sheet on a couple of guys. A Bob Watson and a Frank Henderson."

"Wanna tell me why?"

"Can't, but cut me some slack on this."

"Sure."

I gave Aurora the address of each subject and then said, "Now get your butt over here, we need to see that tape."

* * * *

The camera was rolling, shooting the back of the head and shoulders of a ski-masked figure facing a door. The door cracked open and Ray Swift's face appeared. There was a sudden movement from the ski-masked man's arm and Swift jerked backward into his apartment, throwing his hands to his face. As

Swift staggered about, the assailant landed a punch to his jaw, but Swift didn't go down. He charged forward into the assailant, swinging his arms wildly. Then Swift and his tormentor were falling backwards toward the camera.

The scene cut abruptly to Swift lying on his back taking blows to his head and stomach. When he resisted no more, his assailant stood over him laughing. Then the ski-masked figure, voice distorted as on the first tape, said. "I think you're about ready, Mr. Swift."

Aurora made a slight motion with her hand. "Stop it a minute."

I punched the remote. "I didn't hear anything about Newark. Did you?" she asked.

"Nope, not a thing," I said. "And Jesus, this tape is different from the first one."

"I know. But let's go on and finish it."

I nodded and punched the remote again. Again the scene abruptly shifted. This time to the Swifts' bedroom. Ray Swift was standing at the foot of their king-sized bed. He was totally naked. His legs were spread and his ankles were tethered to the rollers of the footboard. He was bent at the waist, and a restraint secured his chest to the mattress, which was covered by a royal blue bedspread. His arms were stretched out above his head and tied to the posts of the headboard. There was a gag tied across his mouth.

The camera panned around the room, photographing him from every angle. His eyes were open, but were unfocused, not following the camera as it moved around him. Finally the camera returned to the foot of the bed. The man in the ski mask stood behind Swift, fully clothed. His penis, sheathed in a condom, extended from his open fly. Then in his metallic voice he said, "Tell Hillary I really enjoyed this." Then he took Ray Swift. The instant he came, the tape went black.

I looked at Aurora. "I need a drink!"

Thirty minutes later, Aurora and I were in my living room finishing our second scotches. "I still feel like I need to take a shower," I said.

Aurora set her drink down. "With industrial strength Lava soap." She raised her shoulders and gave a little shudder. "Okay, let's get into it."

I stood up out of the wing chair and rattled my ice. "I need another. How 'bout you?"

She shook her head. "I'm driving. Wouldn't be good if a cop had to be bailed out on a DUI charge. But help yourself, if I was home I'd join you."

"Permission given, permission taken," I said as I went to the kitchen and fixed the drink.

When I returned, Aurora was removing the cassette from the VCR. Her fingers were smudged with the graphite that had been used to dust the cassette for prints. She dropped the cassette back into an evidence bag. Then she slipped on her rubber gloves and produced another bag from her purse. "Give me your note," she said. "Maybe this time he's fucked up."

I slipped on my gloves and handed her the note. I watched her bag it and then sat back down in the wing chair. "Well, this time he was a lot more disorganized. Maybe because Swift fought back, but I think there's more to it than that. The way he had Swift bound to the bed; it was almost like some sort of ritual, some sort of sacrifice."

"Or hog tied." Aurora took off her gloves, picked up her glass, swished the ice around, and drained what was mostly water. "And the tape was so different from Janet Manion's tape. No fancy graphics, no pontificating at the beginning. Just raw violence and rough sex. Maybe it's because he was taking a man, but I think it's something more. But he didn't totally lose it. It was obvious he was disguising his voice."

"I think worse things are coming," I said. "He's getting more and more violent." We sat for a few minutes, not speaking. The late afternoon sun cut through my windows and splashed golden patterns on my living room walls. The breeze from my air conditioner hit my sheer curtains and caused the patterns to waver. A discontinuity. *Yes, damn it! A discontinuity.* I looked at Aurora. "Run the first two minutes again." I could hear the excitement in my voice.

Aurora looked puzzled. "Damn it, run the first two minutes of the tape again," I said. She took the tape out of the evidence bag and put it back in the VCR. I pushed the remote.

Between the opening scene of Ray Swift being maced, and the next scene of him on the floor, there was a jerk in the video. I couldn't tell what it was, but something was there. I ran the tape over and over, tried to stop on the exact point, but no luck.

"What the hell are you doing?" Aurora said.

"Looking at a mistake. This tape's been edited. Something he didn't want us to see. But he didn't quite get it all cut out. Something's there. I know it. I can't quite see it, but I know someone who can."

Chapter 28

Thursday morning I took a cab to Aurora's office and picked up a copy of the videotape of Ray Swift's rape. Late Wednesday evening I had called Victor Prieb and asked for help in trying to figure out what was in the blip on the tape. He agreed to have a go at it, so after picking up the copy, I caught another cab and was on my way to Victor's apartment.

The address was on St. Mark's Place in the East Village, an unusual place for a college professor to live. St Mark's Place was once the main street of hippie life in Manhattan. It's still the hub of the East Village youth scene. Funky shops occupy many of the basements of the apartment buildings along the street.

As my cab pulled up to Victor's building, a striking forty-something brunette wearing a deep purple Hunter College tee shirt and skin-tight jeans walked out the front door, a small overnight bag in hand. I flashed back to Cecil's party and the blonde. Victor seemed to be doing very well.

I found his apartment at the end of the first floor hallway. He answered my knock and greeted me with the same bright-eyed expression I remembered from Cecil's doorway. "Ms. Solari, welcome. Please come in."

His apartment was not what I might have expected from a widowed computer science professor. No piles of papers and printouts. No mountains of technical journals. Rather an art deco interior in soft pinks and grays, everything in its place. The look of the decor reminded me of a café I used to frequent in Piedras Negras, Mexico, El Moderno.

"Thank you, Victor," I said. "And it's Susan."

"Please have a seat at the breakfast table while I complete my domestic chores," he said. "We can talk while I work."

I took a seat at a glass-topped table while he cleared the remains of a breakfast for two. "You said you had a videotape you wanted me to look at?" he said.

"Yes." I explained what I had and what I needed from him.

"That's not really my area of expertise," he said as he stuck the last plate in the dishwasher. "But I know someone who can do it. She could find the fragrance of an aspiring actress's perfume on her audition tape."

"Then put her on it," I said as I handed Victor the tape.

"Consider it done. Now, there's still coffee in the pot. Would you like a cup?"

"Absolutely." We sipped coffee and made small talk. Finally, I could contain my curiosity no longer. "I've got a question I have to ask, Victor. What the hell is a Hunter College professor doing in the East Village? Especially on St. Mark's Place."

The twinkle in his eye got brighter. "For my salvation. When Elise died, I had two choices. Stay in our apartment on the Upper East Side and die among the memories. Or find my salvation, and vitality, among the young. What better place to be among the young?"

He paused and looked at me. "According to the Socratic method, the professor should be asking the questions. And, so, now, a question for you, Susan. How will you find your salvation?"

I didn't answer his question, but said a quick goodbye and fled his apartment. I didn't want to face my future. I didn't realize I was running headlong into my past.

* * * *

Garrett Nelson sat cross-legged in the hallway of my apartment building, his back propped up against my front door. His blue polo shirt matched his eyes. The bastard always knew how to maximize his best features. Like the way the cut of his jeans made it clear he still worked out. He saw me coming down the hallway and put down the paperback he was reading.

"Howdy, Ma'am. Greetings from Texas."

I stopped well short of him. "Get the hell out of my doorway."

He uncrossed his legs and got to his feet. He smiled. "Ah, another example of that famous New York hospitality."

I wasn't going to fall victim again. "I thought I made it clear in Dallas that we're done. I ought to file a stalking charge against you. I've got an ex-husband on my case. I don't need you." Then I made a mistake. "What the hell are you doing here, anyway?"

"Nice of you to care. Tomorrow there's a seminar on identity theft. I'm the official FBI speaker. I could have scheduled a flight back tomorrow night, but I'm leaving Saturday morning. I'm hoping we can have dinner Friday night."

"You pissed away another night in a hotel," I said. "Because there's no way I'm having dinner with you. And by the way, how the hell did you find my apartment?"

He shrugged. "I'm still FBI, Susan."

"Well, now that you've found me, you'd better forget me."

A neighbor came down the hallway, lugging two bags of groceries toward his apartment. Garrett moved closer to me to let the man get by. When my neighbor had passed, he didn't move away.

"Susan, please. There are so many things I want to tell you. Explain to you."

I shook my head. "No. A long time ago you made your choice. I moved on. Whatever was there is dead now. Been that way a long time." I took my keys out of my purse and unlocked my front door.

"Wait," he said, as he took a card out of his jeans pocket. "At least take this. My transfer to the Dallas office came through. This is my contact information."

I reached out and took the card. "Congratulations."

"I usually get what I want."

"Not this time." I went into my apartment and locked the door.

That evening there were lots of memories, scotch, and Etta James. *Damn the memories!*

Chapter 29

The next morning, I felt a tap-tap-tap on my chest. Slight but insistent pressure. Then a soft "meow" and the touch of a wet nose on mine. I opened my eyes and saw Caesar's yellow eye staring at me.

The previous evening's scotch took its revenge on my head in the form of a dull headache. I managed a quick glance at the clock: seven-thirty. The cat wanted his breakfast, and I had slept late. No harm for Caesar. But another demand I hadn't met on time.

Meanwhile, another day of waiting. Waiting on the analysis of the rapist's note. Waiting on Victor's examination of the videotape. Waiting for Terry's next move. *Waiting for my life to take some form, get some meaning.*

I threw on my robe and walked down the hallway leading to my living room and kitchen, Caesar in close pursuit. The small brown envelope lay on the floor, just inside my front door. My name was printed on a white label attached to the front. I bent down to pick it up. Then my scotch-addled brain yelled at me: *Get the gloves, stupid!* I took a few seconds to put on the gloves, picked up the envelope and tore it open. Again a single folded sheet.

> Who's Missing?

That was it, nothing else. Just "Who's Missing?" In what was now becoming routine, I laid the note on my kitchen table. The last time the bastard slipped a note under my door I'd felt a combination of energy and fear. This time, I felt a sense of defeat. This evil man was still ahead of me. Making me react to him, dance to his tune. And he was taking perverse pleasure in the dance.

* * * *

"That's all? 'Who's missing?'" Aurora asked.

I was on my wireless handset, pacing around my apartment. "Yes, that's all there was. You got any high-profile missing person cases in progress? Especially among our top seven?"

"I don't know. That's handled by the precincts. And anyway, one of them is in Texas and one's in Washington State. We'll have to check with those departments. God, this guy is a real sicko."

I couldn't deny the feeling of dread sweeping over me. "Get on it, Aurora. He's playing with us."

"Mainly, it seems he's playing with you."

Her statement hit home. "Maybe I'm just convenient. A name he picked up in the newspaper."

"Maybe. But let me off the phone. I'm going to check out the missing persons cases."

"Go to it," I said.

"Oh! One more thing. You were right. When I ran Watson and Henderson ... nothing."

Another dead end. I hung up, my sense of uselessness magnified. Waiting for someone else to take action. *Screw it!* I put on my jogging clothes and was almost out the door to do several laps around Washington Square, when the phone rang.

What the hell now? When I answered the call, the tremble in the voice of the woman on the other end of the line told me something was terribly wrong. A torrent of words spilled out of her. "Oh, thank God I got you ... This is Cecil's neighbor, Sara Grahm ... Victor Prieb's daughter ... Something awful's happened ... Cecil's been beaten ... really badly ... She wants to see you ... can you get here right away?"

I forced myself into my investigator mode, wanting to throw up in fear of what had happened to my friend. *Get the facts.* "Slow down, Sara. I need some information." My voice was quavering.

"Okay."

"When did this happen?"

"Early this morning. Two people broke into her apartment and beat her. I heard her screams and called the police. She's at St. Vincent's. She wants to see you."

"What's her condition?"

"Really bad."

"Is she in intensive care or in a room?"

"In a room."

I breathed a sigh of relief. "What's her room number?"

"It's 506."

"I'm on my way."

I didn't bother to shower, just changed out of my jogging clothes into jeans and a red knit top. But I donned a baseball cap to cover my hair. Even in crisis, vanity prevailed.

* * * *

When I walked into her room, Cecil turned her head and tried to smile. But her split and swollen lips only permitted a slight upturn at the corners of her mouth. Her black eyes and broken nose were obvious. Her other wounds were covered by her bed sheets, except for her right arm that lay on top of the sheets and was connected to an IV.

"Hi, gorgeous," I said. "What does the other guy look like?"

"Stop it," she whispered. "It hurts too much to laugh. In fact, it hurts to talk."

The bed next to Cecil was unoccupied, so we had the privacy to talk freely. I pulled a chair up to her bedside and sat down. "Can you talk a little?" Cecil nodded.

"What happened?"

"About four this morning, there was a loud knock on my front door and I heard someone shouting 'Fire ... fire!' I wasn't awake enough to think straight, so I panicked and opened the door. That's when I got a face full of pepper spray and someone shoved me back into my apartment."

"Did you get a look at him before he sprayed you?"

Cecil shook her head. "No. I hadn't turned any lights on. Besides, I think their faces were covered with something."

"There were two of them?"

"Yeah. A big one and a little one. I think it was the big one that did most of the damage, used his fists and something hard. Maybe a blackjack, but I couldn't tell for sure. I was blinded by the spray."

A nurse came into the room carrying a small white paper cup. "Excuse me a moment. I have to give Ms. Boldaccio some medication." She elevated the bed where Cecil's head rested on the pillow, took a glass of water off the nightstand, and handed it to Cecil. Then she gave her the paper cup. "This is pain medication."

Cecil dumped the pills into the palm of her hand, carefully maneuvered them into her mouth, and then took a couple of swallows of the water. "Come on babies, come on," she said.

The nurse took the water glass from her, returned it to the nightstand, and then left the room.

I put my hand on Cecil's shoulder. "Feel like visiting with me a little longer?"

She nodded her head. "Most important thing yet to come."

"And what's that?"

"Most muscle guys aren't the brightest lights in the room. Before this one left he told me who hired him."

I felt my body stiffen at the surprise. "He gave you a name?"

"No. But he might as well have." Cecil paused a moment and tried to smile again. "He said to 'tell that bitch Solari she's responsible for this.'"

It was like a knife into my heart. That an immature action on my part had caused this to happen to my friend. "Oh, Cecil! I'm so sorry, I didn't think the little twerp had the guts to come after you. And I missed that he might hire someone."

Again she tried to smile. "Not to worry. It was worth it to see you wipe up the floor with his sorry ass."

My initial pain was replaced with a cold fury. "You know, I don't even know the sorry asshole's name. Waddell something …?"

"Waddell Puggs."

"Where's he live and what's his phone number?"

She gave me an address on W. 19th and a phone number.

"Where's he work?

"He works for himself, setting up exhibitions for galleries all over the city. He offices out of his house. I gave all this information to the police. They'll get him."

I reached out and gently touched her forehead. "Not if I get there first."

Chapter 30

I spent a few more moments with Cecil, then she got a call that a pair of detectives were on the way to see her. I wanted no part of that, so we said our goodbyes and I set out on a mission.

I didn't think I'd need my weapons to handle Waddell Puggs, but it was nice to have them if I needed to put the fear of God into the little bastard. I hailed a cab and gave the driver the W. 19th Street address. The trip was a short one, and as we approached Puggs' building, I asked the cabbie to take me a couple of blocks further down the street. If, on the rare chance, Puggs saw me getting out of the cab, I figured he'd be long gone before I could get to his apartment. Also, I wanted to take some time to reconnoiter the neighborhood.

I left the cab at 19th and Seventh Avenue and slowly walked back toward Puggs' building. Though he lived within a couple of blocks of some of the finest restored townhouses in Chelsea, Puggs' building was unremarkable. Stained red brick and shutters that needed painting faced 19th Street. I found a bodega a half block away, got a cup of coffee, and killed a half-hour watching Puggs' building. A few people came and went, but none of them resembled the man I had bounced off the cement in Cecil's hallway. I finished the coffee, tossed the paper cup into the bodega's trash and started toward Puggs' building.

His apartment was a second floor walk-up, at the end of the hall. I knocked on the door and then moved to the side of the doorframe. No answer. I knocked again, with the same result. He wasn't there or somehow he had made me and wasn't answering. I turned to leave and then heard the sound of footsteps and saw Waddell Puggs in the hallway. The minute Puggs saw me, he turned and took off running down the stairs.

I charged at him and thought I'd catch his ass until a door from another apartment opened and a large, brown, scruffy dog ran into the hall. I hit it full force. The dog let out loud yelp and ran back through the door. My feet went out from under me, and I landed on my back, slid toward the stairs and stopped just before my butt was about to do a slide down the stairs to the street.

By the time I reached the street, Puggs had disappeared. But I had another plan. I went back to my apartment, and got Puggs' phone number from directory assistance. I blocked caller ID, and placed the call. I reached Puggs' voicemail.

"Mr. Puggs, this is Glenn Close. No, not that Glenn Close. I'm opening a gallery in SoHo. My exhibit designer just had a heart attack. I need someone to do the opening design. You've been highly recommended to me. I know it's short notice, but I'll pay a substantial premium. Please give me a call." I left my number and waited for the trap to close.

It didn't take long. In fifteen minutes I got the call.
"Ms. Close, this is Waddell Puggs."
"Thank you for getting back to me so quickly."
"You said you'd pay a premium."
"Yes, indeed."
"What's the job?"
"Waddell, it's somewhat complicated, being a new gallery and everything. Could you come to my apartment so we could discuss it in detail?"
"You bet!"
"Could you be here in an hour?"
"You bet!"

I gave him my address, then went to my mailbox in the entryway and replaced the "S. Solari" nametag with "G. Close." I didn't think she'd mind given the circumstances.

I went back to my apartment. To the closet in my second bedroom. I removed a metal box from the top shelf, opened it and removed a pair of handcuffs saved from my FBI days. I put the box back on the shelf, carried the handcuffs into the living room and put them on the end table by the couch. Then I went into my bathroom, took a towel out of the cabinet, carried it into the living room and laid it next to the handcuffs.

Back to my bedroom, where I took the Smith and Wesson from out of the holster on the back of my bedside table. I returned to the second bedroom closet and retrieved a box of blank cartridges I had left over from training exercises with my InterTrans security team. Back to the S&W. I swung out the cylinder, removed the live cartridges and replaced them with blanks. I was going to the edge with Mr. Puggs and didn't want an accident to make me a guest of the state of New York for the rest of my days. Blanks might injure, but they wouldn't kill. I took the gun and put it with the handcuffs and towel.

I took a chair from the kitchen and placed it the middle of the living room. Then I cut on my television and cranked the volume up. All ready for Mr. Puggs.

He was right on time. When he opened the door, I had the Smith & Wesson aimed at his heart.

The blood drained from his face and he said only one word: "You!"

He looked over his shoulder, considering his options.

"Please, come in Mr. Puggs. If you're thinking of trying to run, it'd be my great pleasure to severely wound someone who was trying to break into my apartment."

He moved through the door, shuffling his feet, in small sideways steps. I waved the revolver toward the chair in the middle of the living room.

As he moved into the room, I kept the gun aimed at his heart and my eyes glued to his.

"Sit."

Sweat broke out on his forehead as he sat in the chair. "Now put your arms behind the chair, and grasp your hands." He obeyed. I slapped the handcuffs on one wrist, then the other.

I moved in front of Puggs, stepped back, and aimed the .38 at his head. "Who'd you hire to beat Cecelia Boldaccio?"

Puggs was getting a little color back in his face. "What the hell are you talking about? I loved Cecil. You're the maniac that beat *me* up."

I cocked the hammer on the .38. "Don't fuck with me, Puggs. Again, who'd you hire?"

"Nobody. It wasn't me."

"Maybe this'll help you remember." I squeezed the trigger, aiming to the right of Puggs' head. At the sound of the blast, his face went white and he struggled to escape the chair. His words were a plea. "God, no! Believe me, please believe me! I didn't do it!"

Then he launched himself forward, charging at me, the chair still attached to his back. Before he could bowl me over, I laid the barrel of the .38 alongside his skull and he crumpled to the floor.

I knelt down beside him, grabbed his hair, jerked his head back, and shoved the barrel of the revolver into his mouth. A stain appeared on the groin area of his khakis as he wet himself. "Your dumb-ass muscle sent Cecil a message. He called my name. Tell me *his* name or you're eating this gun."

He threw his head side to side, dislodging the barrel, and screamed, "I don't even know your fucking name!"

I shoved the gun back in his mouth and screamed back at him. "The hell you don't! You were at Cecil's party. She made this big announcement of who I was."

Puggs tried to say something but couldn't manage it with the gun barrel in his mouth. I pulled it out to let him speak. His breathing was short and his words came in bursts. "Got there late. Didn't hear that. Don't know what the hell your name is."

I cocked the pistol again and pressed the barrel against his forehead. "One more time. Who'd you hire?"

His eyes darted from side to side, looking for salvation that was not going to come. "I didn't fucking do it! Don't do this, please!"

"Have it your way." I pulled the .38 away from his forehead and reached for the towel on the end table. I slowly wrapped it around the top of Puggs' head. I aimed the revolver right between his eyes and said, "I hate messes on my floor. Now, one last time, who beat Cecil?"

Tears came to his eyes, and his breath came in big gulps. "I don't know. Please believe me." His voice was now nothing more than a wail. "Oh, God. Please, please, please."

My heart sank and I knew something I didn't want to know. He was telling the truth.

Chapter 31

So, I let him go. I unwrapped the towel while his tears still flowed, the .38 constantly between his eyes. When he seemed to gain a measure of control, I took off the cuffs. He clambered to his feet and steadied himself. When he realized he would not die, his eyes were drawn to the stain on the front of his khakis. They lingered there a moment, then he slowly raised his head. When his eyes met mine, I saw shame. Then a hatred I knew would never die.

He walked to my front door and paused. "You'll pay for this, bitch. I swear." Then he was gone.

I was furious with myself. *If not him, who? And why Cecil? And why my name?* I paced around my apartment, needing to do something, anything, to prove to myself that I wasn't an irrelevancy on the periphery of events swirling around me.

I called Aurora. No reports of missing persons among our top seven CEO's. I told her about Cecil's beating and asked her to touch base with the detectives who were handling the case. "This is very personal," I said. "I want to make sure this is being done right." She promised to follow up and we rang off.

I called Victor Prieb; nothing yet from his videotape expert. He seemed puzzled that I would expect results so soon. I cursed the fact that I couldn't slam a receiver down, only hit an off button.

I went into my kitchen and poured myself a scotch. Then my fucking phone rang. "Solari," I snarled into the handset.

"Susan, it's Mike Riley."

At the sound of Mike's voice, my hostility disappeared. "Mike, good to hear from you. Thanks for letting me use your .38. How's things in Dallas?"

"Not good, Susan. Martha Kirkland is missing."

No question that I was going to Dallas. While others thought I was the traitor that almost brought down the company, Fred Kirkland had supported me in my last days at InterTrans. Now that his wife was missing, I could forgive that he was the one who'd sent Glenn Manion to me.

* * * *

The last few hours had been hectic as hell. It was get the plane tickets, pack, make an important call to a shop in the DFW airport, then call Cecil to tell her I was going to Dallas. I needed to find someone to take care of Caesar. The last item wasn't easy. Normally on short notice I'd ask Cecil to do it. But that wasn't possible. I hadn't made a connection with a vet or a kennel, and because it was a beautiful Friday afternoon, those I found in the Yellow Pages had closed their offices promptly at five.

Then I thought of Lynette Mason. Normally my paranoia wouldn't allow me to give my apartment key to a person I didn't know all that well. But I was torn. Fred needed me in Dallas, and Caesar hated flying. He didn't eat for a couple of days after a flight, even if I took him on the plane with me.

Lynette was working in a bookstore and could probably use twenty dollars a day to clean a kitty potty and put out some food and water. So I made the call. She was delighted and late Friday evening came to my apartment and got the key.

* * * *

The whine of the MD-80's engines wound down as we arrived at DFW gate C37. As I exited the ramp, Mike Riley stood about ten feet away from the gate.

"How'd the hell you get in here?" I said. "I thought you had to have a ticket."

He shook his head and opened his sports jacket to reveal his detective's badge. "Rank has privileges."

I felt myself blushing. *Six months away and you're already thinking like a civilian.* It was a long flight, with no food and too many scotches, I told myself.

He took my rolling suitcase from me. "Welcome back to Dallas. Have you checked any other baggage?"

"Yeah one other bag."

"Lead the way," he said.

As we walked up the concourse, Mike looked at me. "Why the hell did you insist on coming here, Susan?"

I knew the answer to his question, but I wasn't ready to admit it to him, or even to myself. Then the lack of food, the scotch, and the late hour gathered together and hit me hard. "You've given me the basics of Martha's disappearance. But let's fill in the rest in the morning. We're having breakfast with Fred at the hotel, right?"

"Right."

"How is he?"

"Typical CEO behavior. Demanding. Results now. Do we know what the hell we're doing? Why the hell haven't we found her?"

I looked at Mike. "That's not Fred."

"It is now."

"That's because he loves Martha."

We went through the revolving doors to the last baggage carousel in terminal C. Over the carousel American Airlines had suspended a replica of an Aspen ski lift car with a message on the side that proclaimed, "All Aspen, All the Time." Genius marketing. Days before the first day of summer! No wonder the assholes almost went bankrupt.

My bag was one of the first on the carousel. I pulled it off and extended the collapsible handle. I asked Mike to take my carry-on. "Mind taking care of this for a minute? I have an errand to run."

He took the carry-on. "Sure."

I took the bag that had come off the carousel. I walked a few yards to a sundries shop just beyond the baggage area. Mr. Yen stood behind the cash register. The routine, slightly modified, was familiar. "Good day, Mr. Yen. How is Jai-Ten?"

He bowed his head slightly. "She is becoming a young lady."

"And a beautiful one, I imagine. Did you acquire the merchandise?"

"It's in the back room." He said.

I pulled my suitcase into the room and closed the door. Two boxes of ammunition sat on a shelf. One for the .32 and one for the Glock. I opened my suitcase, removed the weapons and my thigh holster. It took just a couple of minutes to load the pistols. The .32 went into my thigh holster, easily accessible through the slit in my slacks pocket. I slipped the Glock into the hidden pocket of my purse.

All set. All legal. I'd kept my Texas carry permit current. This was so much better than sneaking my guns around New York, even with a letter from the mayor.

I was energized. Time to get to the hunt. With a nod to Mr. Yen, I returned to Mike Riley. "I'm ready!"

I'd told Mike I wanted to stay at the Adolphus in the heart of downtown Dallas. I had warned him away from the Melrose. He'd arranged for me to use one of his cars while I was in town, so I dropped him off at his home and drove on to the Adolphus. Check-in was quick.

As I slipped beneath the covers of my pillow-topped bed, I felt some of my energy slip away and I cursed the fact that I was once more drawn back to Dallas. Terry's home territory.

Chapter 32

Early the next morning I found myself in the lobby of the Adolphus. Fred had arranged a seven-thirty breakfast with Mike and me. But Mike and I had arranged to meet a half hour earlier to discuss the facts of the case. I'd dressed for Dallas weather in May: loose white cotton blouse, a pair of chinos that would accommodate the .32 on my thigh, and a pair of white sandals. I carried a modified, cocoa-colored, shoulder strap bag from Coach. The modification was panel access to my Glock.

Because it was Sunday morning, the lobby was quiet, so I took a few moments to examine the elegant surroundings. The hotel itself had been constructed in a Beaux Style in 1912 by beer baron Adolphus Busch. It's been renovated and refurbished many times. The current version of the lobby features museum-quality artwork, Flemish tapestries, red Louis XV chairs, and a Victorian Steinway once owned by the Guggenheims.

It's a very calming place. I sat in one of the chairs and closed my eyes, hoping thoughts of Terry, the rapist, Waddell Puggs, and the disappearance of Martha Kirkland would melt away for a few moments ... It was not to be.

I felt a touch on my shoulder and heard Mike say, "Wake up, Susan!" I was grabbing for the Glock, ready to draw it, when I got oriented. He was standing just a few inches away from me, beside the chair. *What if that had been Terry? I'm getting sloppy ... or maybe just tired.*

Mike watched my hand withdraw from the purse side panel. "Sorry I scared you. Wanna go get a cup while we talk?"

"I already had a pot of room service while I was getting ready to come down. Let's just stay here." I stared around the lobby, feeling an irrational threat.

My chair was one of a grouping of four that were arranged around a dark cherry circular coffee table. Mike sat in the chair directly across from me. "So do you think Martha Kirkland is the subject of your 'Who's Missing?' note?"

I had briefed Mike about the notes when he called to tell me about Martha. "I don't think so," I said. "It's probably just a coincidence. After all, it really doesn't fit the pattern. This is a missing persons case, possibly an abduction, not a rape."

Mike's tone was grim. "Not that we know of ... yet. And he's been escalating. First the videotape with Janet Manion and then the violence with Ray Swift. Who's to say he wouldn't throw in an abduction? From the last note, it sounds like he already has."

For reasons I wasn't aware of, I aggressively pressed my argument, leaning forward in my chair. "Fred *himself* doesn't fit the pattern. Sure, he's a CEO. But InterTrans is number thirteen on the *Fortune* list, and, so far, he's stayed in strict numerical order."

Mike wasn't buying it. He leaned forward too, our faces now just inches apart. "But the 'Who's Missing?' note came to you! And you're tight with Fred Kirkland. Think about that."

Then I knew why I was arguing and my heart went cold. Suddenly I didn't want breakfast, didn't want to be in Dallas, and didn't want to be involved with this case at all. I was about to protest that we might narrow the case too quickly when I heard Fred Kirkland's distinctive Kentucky accent.

"Susan!"

He was striding quickly across the lobby and was next to my chair in moments. I wrapped my arms around him and gave him a warm, friendly hug. "It's so good to see you, Fred."

When I stepped back, I saw the tall, angular frame of the man who had been so kind to me in the last year. But something had changed. Instead of the usual smile that always softened the lines on his face, I saw a brooding shadow in his eyes.

His voice had a tone of urgency. "Thanks for coming so quickly. I really need you here right now. The damn police are doing ..." At that point Fred remembered Mike was there and cut himself off in mid-sentence.

"Let me finish your sentence for you," Mike said dryly. "The damn police are doing nothing."

Fred got defensive. "Hell, it's true. All they said they could do at this point is take my report."

"True Friday," Mike said. "Not true today."

I saw a spark of hope in Fred's eyes. "You've found out something! Maybe even found Martha?"

"Not yet, but the search for her is a whole new ballgame. Let's have breakfast and I'll explain."

"Fine," I said, a delayed reaction reaching my brain. When I had tried to draw the Glock when Mike surprised me, my hand had gotten caught on the side panel. My new ring. Bought a couple of months ago as a morale booster. I pulled it off and put in my purse. No ring was worth my life.

Fred had reserved us a booth in the back corner of the restaurant, and given the hour and the day of the week, there was little chance our privacy would be disturbed. As we settled in, a middle-aged brunette waitress in a perfectly pressed yellow and white uniform brought us menus. She wore a brass nametag that said "June." She quickly took our drink orders. Coffee for the guys, iced tea for me. "I bet they have uniform inspection every morning," I said. "After all, this is the Adolphus."

A chuckle came from Mike as he unfolded his napkin, but Fred was ready to get down to business. "Okay, tell me what's changed with the investigation."

Mike took a deep breath, as if this was going to take a while. "You're right, Fred. First few days of an adult disappearance, the police don't take much action. And there's good reason for that. If there's no evidence of foul play, a person can go missing for a lot of reasons. Escape from a bad marriage, a bender, a fling, a bad argument. And that's what most of the disappearances are. The missing person is usually back in a few days."

"But this is Martha," Fred said. "We've been married thirty-five years. She'd do none of those things. She was supposed to meet me after work at our favorite restaurant. She never showed up. She wouldn't just disappear."

"I'm not saying she would," Mike said. "But you'd be surprised by what I've seen in the so-called best marriages and families."

Fred started to protest again, but Mike cut him off. "Anyway, despite how it might look to you, your case was never handled as routine. I just got the heat turned up some."

"I'm not following you," Fred said.

Before Mike could answer, June returned with our drinks and a basket of biscuits. While I doctored up my iced tea with lots of lemon, Mike changed the color of his coffee from dark brown to milk chocolate with, being that we were at the Adolphus, lots of real cream. Fred kept his coffee black and untouched, his gaze remaining on Mike. He asked June to give us a little more time before we ordered.

"Look Fred," Mike said, "the department is not blind as to who you are. CEO of one of America's largest companies. Your wife goes missing, we notice. After your report came in, two people outside the precinct were immediately notified. Officially, Chief Rumson, to make sure his ass is protected. Unofficially, me, because I used to work for you and I might come in handy if it all hits the fan."

I decided to just monitor this conversation, thinking I'd get information that would be useful later on. Little did I know how quickly.

"So?" Fred said.

Mike took a sip of his coffee. "So Chief Rumson made some calls to the precinct. He wanted to make sure they're heads-up on this. And wanted to know what detectives caught the case."

"And who did?" I asked.

Mike looked at me, and the pause before he answered told me that trouble was on the way. "Gene Wasco and Frank Balco." His eyes never left mine, waiting for my reaction.

I tried to remain disinterested. "Oh."

But Fred caught it. CEO with his antenna out. "Is there a problem, Susan?"

"No, not at all." Before Fred could press me, June was back with her order pad. It was a busy morning, and it was obvious she wanted to get the table turned. Our conversation halted while we quickly considered our menus and placed our orders. Full bacon and eggs breakfast for the guys, just a bagel and cream cheese for me. My appetite was gone.

When June left, Fred again turned his attention to me. "Once more, is there a problem, Susan?"

"Not really. When I was at InterTrans, I had some dealings with Wasco. The Waxberg murder. The Marcos suicide. I was surprised to hear his name, that's all."

Fred let it go, his eyes all shadow and speculation, and pressed on with Mike. "So, what changed in the investigation between Friday and today?"

Mike put down his biscuit. "Chief Rumson's involvement, of course. And I had a talk with Wasco ... explained a few things."

Fred's response was to Mike, but his eyes were on mine. "And those things would have to do with the Corporate Countdown Rapist?"

I was stunned. "How'd the hell you'd know about that?"

"You think I'm isolated in some ivory tower? Your successor at InterTrans put me on to what's going on after the *Post* article."

I launched into my defense. "This is not according to pattern. This is not according to the countdown. This is not according to ..." The urgent ringing of my cell phone interrupted my polemic. I fished it out of my purse, conscious of the ring on my finger that could lose me half a second and get me killed. I pulled it off before I took the call. The caller ID said 'Wireless caller" with no number. I put my phone to my ear and heard my world change.

Martha Kirkland was wailing. "Susan, Susan! He says you must come for me. Please! Please! He says it can only be you."

Then a man's voice came on the line. Metallic, heavily disguised. "You got the picture?"

I kept my response steady, Fred and Mike watching me. "Yeah, I do. You want me to come for her? Tell me where the hell she is."

Again the crackling, metallic voice. "You know Fair Park?"

"Yes."

"Go to the Swine Barn. No cops ... just you and Kirkland. Both of you must come. Got that?"

"Got it. But she better be ..."

He cut me off. "You're in no position to bargain. She'll be, shall I say, in an appropriate position. And I repeat, no cops." The line went dead.

Fred reached across the table and grabbed my arm. "What the hell's wrong, Susan?"

"Does Martha have my cell phone number?"

"No."

"Then how in hell did she just call me?"

*   *   *   *

The next hour was a blur. Mike made the phone calls necessary to get Fred and me into Fair Park. In September the park hosts the country's largest state fair. It features livestock shows, hair-raising rides on the Midway, carnies offering to guess your weight and age, the auto show, and perhaps most important, fried Twinkies. But in May the livestock barns are empty, visited only by the occasional pigeon seeking shelter from the sun.

Fred walked behind me as we approached the Swine Barn. Mike and I had had a fierce argument as to whether he should accompany me. In the end, I prevailed, convincing him that the best chance of getting Martha back alive was to meet all conditions of the caller.

I relented on one point. Fred and I were wearing bulletproof vests. I hated the damn things. They were hot, heavy, and slowed me down. As we approached the barn, I felt my sweat run between my breasts and down my back. The vests didn't protect against a headshot, anyway. And in my most recurring dream, that's how I bought the farm.

As we entered the barn, I smelled the residue of three quarters of a century of Four-H pigs and hogs. I gripped my Glock, ready for any eventuality ... except what I saw.

She was in the third pen to the right of the door, naked, lying face down in a bed of straw. A dark stain matted her blonde hair. Her arms were pulled behind her, and tied to her legs, which were arched over her back. *Hog-tied!*

With an anguished, primal cry, Fred rushed to Martha, but he could give her no comfort. She was dead.

Chapter 33

I tried to pull Fred away from Martha, but he kept pushing me away, crying and cursing while trying to embrace her, an impossibility given her grotesque position. Finally, I twisted an arm behind his back and hustled him out of the barn. I hated myself for the thought, but I feared that Martha's body was bait to draw Fred and me into a fatal trap.

I whipped out my cell phone and called Mike, who was stationed two blocks away. Then I took Fred to my car, away from the ghastly scene in the barn. Mike arrived in what seemed like seconds. As I tried to comfort Fred, I could hear the crackling of Mike's police radio as he reported Martha's murder.

Mike and I were standing just outside the Swine Barn when two blue-and-white patrol cruisers arrived. The uniformed officers went to work stretching yellow crime scene tape across the entrance to the barn. As the officers finished their task, the vans of the crime scene investigators and the medical examiner pulled up in front of the barn. They were followed immediately by the dull gray sedan of the detectives. Gene Wasco climbed out of the sedan followed by another detective I did not know, but assumed was Frank Balco.

Wasco strode toward the barn, his gold shield displayed on the breast pocket of his blue-and-white striped seersucker sport coat. As he moved up the sidewalk, he barked orders to the CSI crew, who had paused at the crime scene tape. Then he said something I didn't hear to the woman from the medical examiner's office. She rolled her eyes, gave him a "fuck you" look, and walked into the barn.

The Sunday morning sun highlighted Wasco's blond hair as he conferred with Balco and the uniformed officers. Balco left the group and went into the barn.

The officers went toward the street to control a small crowd of park workers that was starting to gather.

Wasco caught my eye and didn't divert his gaze while he walked the few feet to where Mike and I were standing. As soon as he reached us, he attacked.

"Well, I see the Angel of Death is back. Every time I see you, there's a dead body around. Solomon Waxberg, Francie Marcos, and now Martha Kirkland." Then he looked at Mike. "If I was you, Riley, I'd stay away from this broad."

I was having none of it. "You're right, Wasco. And my fondest wish is to spend the next two weeks with you. If my luck holds, you'd be the next body."

A little smirk spread across his face. "And would those two weeks include the nights?"

It was my turn to smile. "Sure. From what I've heard from the squad room, you can't get it up. I'm sure I'd get a good night's sleep."

His face turned red and he didn't respond. Instead he directed his attention to Mike Riley. "Tell me what came down here."

Mike gave him the details of what had happened this morning. When he was finished Wasco was even more agitated. "So you didn't follow procedure? You knew I had the case and didn't let me know this was coming down?" His eyes cut to me. "You let this cunt run this operation."

Mike's fist hit flush on Wasco's jaw and he went down, then Mike was on him, beating his head when the uniforms rushed up and separated the detectives. Wasco lay on the ground for maybe a minute, then staggered to his feet and wiped blood off of his chin and lower lip. When he spoke, his voice was even and measured. "You fucking mick. You'll pay for this. I'll have your ass, and your badge."

Then his burning eyes locked in on me. "You bitch! You bring nothing but trouble and death. And it's going to come down on your head. And I'll dance on your grave." He waited a moment, touching the blood at his mouth, then he headed into the barn.

"I wish he had shouted," I said. "When they go quiet, it's trouble."

Mike pushed away the officer restraining him and stood next to me. "Fucking bastard. He wasn't going to get away with talking that way about you."

I didn't know whether to be angry or grateful. "Jesus, Mike. You think I couldn't handle a yahoo like Wasco?"

I guess I was going to thank him, but I didn't get the chance. I felt a hand on my shoulder and turned around to see Frank Balco towering over me. "Despite this, uh, distraction, I need to question you and Mr. Kirkland about what happened here."

"I'm outta here, Susan," Mike said, sucking a knuckle. He walked to his car, climbed in, and drove away.

Balco and I walked to my car. Fred was pacing around the car, his hands jammed in his slacks pockets. The look on his face told me his defense mechanisms had put him in the CEO mode. When Balco told him he needed to talk to him, Fred said, "Fine. Let's get this done. I want to get this bastard."

It took a half hour to recount our experience in the Swine Barn. Before Balco left I asked him if the medical examiner had a preliminary cause of death.

"Looks obvious. Blow to the head."

Then it was over ... for the moment. I took Fred to his house in Highland Park. When I asked if I could call anyone to come stay with him, he didn't reply. He just shook his head.

As I drove to the Adolphus, I knew nothing had ended this Sunday morning but Martha's life. For the rest of the players in this drama, it was only the beginning. Especially for me.

* * * *

I was back at the Adolphus by early afternoon. The smell of the Swine Barn and death clung to my clothes and my body. I shucked the clothes, turned the shower to hot and stepped in. The water washed over me and I felt tension that I hadn't realized was there disappearing.

As I stood in the spray, I lost count of time, but I realized I had come to a decision. I would take no more of Glenn Manion's money. Now I was working for Martha Kirkland. Finally, I reached for the single handle-faucet of the shower and shut it down. I stepped out of the shower and toweled off in one of the Adolphus' wonderful bath sheets. I pulled my baby powder out of my cosmetic pouch that rested on the vanity and dusted my body. The scent brought back memories of the gentle hands of my mother and a safety that had left me long ago.

I had no agenda for the rest of the day. Fred obviously wanted to be alone to deal with his grief. Mike Riley probably didn't want to be reminded of the threat to his career. I had a brief vision of a reunion with Dom Shapiro, but chalked it up to exhaustion. A nap seemed like a wonderful idea.

I turned down the covers of my bed, put the Glock under the pillow next to me, and slipped between the butter-soft sheets. Sleep came quickly. A defense against a fear that was growing within me.

The pounding on my door woke me up. I glanced at the clock. Four p.m. My hand went under the pillow and gripped the Glock. It took me a few seconds to get oriented, then I stumbled out of the bed and walked to the closet. I slid the door of the closet open and slipped into the Adolphus' terrycloth robe.

I stayed away from the door and called out, "Who is it?"

I heard a voice that evoked memories I wanted to stay buried. "The French Room is just downstairs. I have reservations."

Chapter 34

When I opened the door, Garrett Nelson said, "I heard you were in town." He offered me a single yellow rose. "I bet you still love these."

I didn't accept his offer. "How'd the hell did you find my room?"

"I guessed you'd be in one of two places, the Melrose or the Adolphus. Given what happened the last time at the Melrose, I figured the Adolphus."

I was a little surprised that he knew about Terry's threats at the Melrose, but then all cops are connected: federal, state, local. The jurisdictional disputes are fierce, but when the subject is who's humping who or what's up with an old lover, the boundary lines melt away.

"And my room number?"

The look on his face told me I had asked a stupid question, and I knew the answer before the words were out of my mouth. In spite of myself, I felt a little smile spread across my face. "You're still FBI. Right?"

The broad smile that had so intrigued me half a decade ago appeared. A twinkle danced in his blue eyes. "And I got the badge to prove it."

I tried to recover. "You son of a bitch. Using your office to track me down. Screw you. Go away. You're the past, not the future."

He didn't retreat. "Damn shame to waste the reservations. They're hard to get on short notice. And besides, I thought maybe you could use some good wine, good food, and good company. I hear it's been a tough day. This evening, let's celebrate the past. Fuck the future."

"I doubt the future is what you want to fuck," I snarled and slammed the door in his face.

As I stood alone in the room, thoughts of Cecil Boldacchio, Waddell Puggs, Janet Manion, Martha Kirkland, and the others overwhelmed me. Too much hurt, too much hate. Suddenly I couldn't bear the thought of spending the evening alone. I needed a world beyond them. Even at great risk.

I yanked open the door to the hallway, hoping he was still there. He was in front of the elevators. I called out his name. He turned and walked toward me.

"What time are the reservations?" I asked.

"Eight."

"I'll meet you in the lobby."

He offered the rose again. This time, I took it.

*   *   *   *

Garrett was waiting next to the same grouping of chairs where I had met Mike and Fred. That meeting seemed so long ago.

He was wearing a trim cut navy pinstripe suit. The French cuffs of his white shirt were perfectly complemented by a pair of round gold cufflinks with a small diamond in the middle of each. A red silk tie and a pair of black Italian loafers completed the look. I couldn't help myself, I whistled at him.

He broke into a wide smile. "Well, after all, *it is* the French Room." Then he checked me out.

I hadn't packed anything really appropriate for dinner in the French Room. But I'd improvised as best I could. I left a few extra buttons open at the top of a tropical green silk floral blouse. *A far cry from trickling sweat behind a bulletproof vest.* I didn't bring a skirt but did have a pair of modified loosely cut blue green silk slacks that would accommodate the .32 nicely and complement the blouse. Not an ideal look but one that would do.

Apparently Garrett agreed. His eyes played over me, pausing at my cleavage. "You're not playing fair."

"You'll survive," I said. "Now, I believe you invited me to dinner. It's time for you to deliver."

We made the short walk from the lobby to the French Room. The captain seated us at a table in a far corner of the restaurant. Crystal chandeliers and gilt sconces cast a golden glow on our table. Beautiful frescos swept across the ceiling. The drapes on the tall French windows picked up the colors of the frescos, and the fabrics of the chairs in turn complemented the drapes. The room was a symphony of color, with each element hitting just the right note, all of it blending into a perfect composition.

"I love this room, it's so beautiful," I said. In our good times Terry would bring me here for my birthday. When I was trying to hold our marriage together, I clung to those memories. Tonight I pushed them away.

"There's a certain peace to this place," Garrett replied. "And I think we both can use some peace right now."

I nodded my agreement. "But there's one thing I don't understand," I said. "There aren't a lot of people here. No one's seated close to us. It's almost as if we have private dining. The place is usually full."

The twinkle in his eyes appeared again. "Well, I fibbed a bit about how hard it was to get reservations. Normally they're not open on Sunday night. But they're closed tomorrow for Memorial Day, so they opened tonight. I guess not many people knew."

I managed a smile. "You fraud ... but your taste in restaurants is still good."

Our waiter approached and offered us menus and the wine list. Garrett indicated we would be ordering wine, and in short order the sommelier appeared.

Garrett spent a few moments scanning the list, then looked at me. "Is it still the J. Lohr Chardonnay? Arroyo Vista?"

"Always."

The sommelier departed and we were alone again. Garrett spoke first. "So what did you do with the rose?"

"Put it in a vase."

"On a table, or by your bed?"

"On a table."

He looked away.

"It's a lovely rose, Garrett, and I thank you for it. And for tonight. I was in pretty bad shape when I slammed the door on you. I apologize."

He smiled. "No need. After what you've been through today, I'm surprised you didn't shoot me."

We both knew the rules ... keep it light; focus on now, not the past; keep the defenses up; and never, ever, show your hand.

We talked of our recent moves and laughed at the inevitable screw-ups. I described my apartment; he described his. He asked about my parents; I inquired about his.

The wine arrived and we went through the ritual. The presentation of the label, the uncorking, the tasting, and finally Garrett nodded. The sommelier filled my glass, then Garrett's.

We raised our glasses and Garrett said, "To the present, and the future."

I didn't respond. Instead I immediately took a sip of my wine. As the Arroyo Vista lingered on my palate, new deep, full flavors emerged moment by moment. *Fantastic!*

Garrett looked amused. "By the look on your face, I'd say that was better than sex."

"Depends."

"Depends on what?"

I put my glass down and our eyes met. "I think you know."

The rest of the meal was glorious. I had the Peking duck, he the venison steak. The waiters were solicitous, but unobtrusive. The wine began to work its magic and some of the rules began to melt away.

"You won't believe this," Garrett said. "But I'm sorry you and Terry didn't work out."

He was right. I didn't believe him. But at least he was saying the right thing. Not trying to inveigle his way back into my life. "At first, I was sorry too," I said. "I tried so hard to make it work. To make him believe in himself. That was his problem, really. Despite his bravado, he never believed he was good enough for me. He was always jealous, always suspected me of having affairs."

Garrett took a sip of his wine. "Then he got abusive."

A flash of unexpected anger swept over me. "Where'd you get that, Garrett? What was I? The subject of the daily water cooler tart tale at the Bureau?"

His head snapped up as if hit by an uppercut. "No! No! That's not what I meant at all. I kept up, that's all."

It had been going so well, and my anger was going to screw it up. I paused a moment, getting it back together. "I know you didn't mean it that way. I'm sorry, Garrett. It's just that those particular memories make me so angry, and right now, after today, I've got a low threshold."

"It was my fault. I shouldn't have brought it up. Let's let it go."

"Tell me about the current version of Garrett Nelson."

A rueful smile appeared. "Two words. Starting over. Actually, you and I are pretty much in the same boat. Starting over. Both living in new cities. Both recently divorced. Both trying new careers."

But he had suffered another loss that was beyond my experience. "What are the arrangements with Sally and Meredith?"

I knew the moment I said it, it was a cruel question to ask. The light went out of his eyes and he looked down at the tablecloth. "They're with their mother. I have visitation every other weekend, so I go to San Antonio. I'd never had made the move to Dallas if I could have seen them more. Seven-year-olds need their father. But Allison was a bitch about custody. She went by the rulebook, every other weekend only."

I reached across the table and put my hand on his. "I'm sorry."

He put his other hand on top of mine. I should have pulled my hand away, but I didn't.

"I'm sorry too," he said. "So I made the move. There were so many memories in San Antonio that haunted me. Best to start over in a new place." He gently moved his hands away.

I knew what it was like to flee from memories. "I know," I said. "I know."

We finished the meal saying little, our eyes meeting when we spoke. Occasionally Garrett took my hand, and I permitted it. The evening drew to a close and I felt something had changed between us. Whether it was forgiveness of the past, or hope for the future, I did not, dared not, know.

Garrett signed the tab. "Thanks for a lovely evening," I said. "Sorry again I was such a bitch this afternoon. I was upset about Martha Kirkland. And then there's this ... you deserved it."

He laughed at that. "Yes, I did. And by way, the evening doesn't have to end just because dinner's over."

"Oh, yes it does. I've got a noon flight out tomorrow. And because of the holiday, I imagine DFW will be extra hectic."

"There you go again; about to spoil another surprise I have for you."

"What?"

He pushed his chair back from the table. "Come on ... follow me."

I followed him out of the French Room, through the lobby, and to the bell captain's stand that was buzzing with activity from late arrivals. Garrett produced a claim check and handed it and a five-dollar bill to a bellhop, who then went into a storage room. The bellhop returned carrying a package wrapped in sparkling emerald green paper, topped by a dazzling white bow. The ribbon was like a hologram that caught all the colors of the rainbow. Garrett took the package, then handed it to me. "Something to complete the evening," he said.

I didn't know how to react. I think I mumbled something about I really shouldn't ... couldn't. But Garrett was having none of it.

"Let's open it," he said, and guided me to one of the small furniture groupings in the lobby. When we were seated, I put the package on the coffee table in front of me. "Garrett, I can't accept this. I ..."

He cut me off. "Don't jump to conclusions. Just open the package." Then he handed me a small penknife. I cut the paper off the top of the box, being careful not to touch the bow. "This is too beautiful to damage," I said as I set the bow on the table.

I cut the clear tape that sealed the top and opened the box. I saw a bottle nested in green metallic shreds. I removed the bottle, saw the label, and smiled. Glennturrett, my favorite single malt scotch.

"Thank you," I said. "You remembered the Arroyo Vista, and now this."

"I remember a lot of things about you, Susan. Especially that smile."

Against my better judgment I said, "You always knew how to make me smile."

He didn't say anything for a moment, just held my eyes with his. "Let's open the bottle," he said finally, "and make a toast to two people who are starting over."

Alarm bells went off. The evening was slipping out from under me. I didn't need another complication in my life. "Oh, Garrett ... not now. I'll save the bottle. I promise not to open it until you and I can have the first drinks. But not now. Not tonight."

He took my hand. "If not now, when? It's been a perfect evening. Let's close it in a perfect way."

I opened my mouth to say no, but the words wouldn't come out. Instead I took his hand and led him to my room, telling myself that I was still in control. "Just one drink" I said.

"Just one," he replied.

I opened the door to the room and saw that the bed had been turned down. Something I did *not* need at the moment. Garrett gave the bed a quick glance, then quickly returned his eyes to me. He opened the box and took out the bottle. "Neat or on-the-rocks?"

"Neat," I said. "You pour the drinks; I have a slight adjustment to make."

I left him, went into the bathroom and closed the door. It took me just moments to remove the thigh holster and place it and the .32 in the towel cabinet below the lavatory. When I returned to the bedroom, Garrett handed me my drink.

"Scotch, neat. In a crystal glass, no less."

When I took the drink, his hand closed over mine and stayed there a moment longer than needed. I told myself I was still in control and tried to make light of the moment. "As you said, it *is* the Adolphus."

"So it is." He released my hand and raised his glass. "To starting over."

"To starting over," I said and touched my glass to his.

He handed me his glass, took off his suit coat and tie, tossed them on a chair, and then kicked off his loafers. "That's better," he said. I gave him his drink and we sat close to each other on the light green couch that paralleled the bed.

We sipped our drinks silently for a few moments. Finally I said, "Why'd she leave?"

He didn't answer, but put his arm around my shoulders. I expected my body to stiffen. I willed it to. But instead, I leaned into him, some primal need for warmth. *I'm not as Wasco said, an Angel of Death. I'm not.*

In a couple of moments he said, "She blamed it on my work. I was away too much. I didn't have enough time for her, or the twins. She was lying."

I took his hand. "And the truth?"

"He was a rock star doctor. Working miracles every day. Only he couldn't save his wife. Ovarian cancer. Allison met him at a fund raising event."

There was nothing to say. I took a sip of my drink, then another.

He moved his arm off my shoulders and lightly touched my cheek, turning my face toward him. "And your move to Manhattan. Has it made you happy?"

I shaped my answer, remembering that the happiest time in my life was that brief, illicit year with him in San Antonio. "Define happy," I said.

He mumbled a few platitudes about family, Sunday mornings, and sunset years.

I pulled away from him, my voice as sharp as a stiletto. "You're wrong. Happiness is laughing and crying. Thrusting, parrying, always testing. Anticipating each other's thoughts. Glances that say everything, sometimes like warm oil on shattered nerve ends. Always on the edge of heaven or hell."

Tears came to his eyes. He put his arm around my waist and pulled me to him. His lips were inches from mine.

I shook my head and leaned away from him. "No, Garrett, no. This isn't right for me, for us. I'm still healing. I couldn't stand to be hurt again."

He touched his finger to my lips. "Remember San Antonio?" He pulled me to him again and I let his tongue dance across my lips, probing, testing. At that moment, I knew I had to have him. I surrendered, letting his tongue wrap around mine. Our lips lingered together, first lightly touching, then desperately pressing, as if to assure they would never part.

One of his hands stroked my hair and the back of my neck. The other tugged at my blouse. In moments, the tail was out of my slacks. Then his hands went to the buttons. But he was all thumbs.

"Here," I whispered, "let an expert do the job." I pushed his hands away, but when I attacked the buttons my hands shook so badly I wasn't much better.

When the last button was released, I shrugged the blouse off my shoulders and it fell to the floor.

He was better with my bra. It was gone in seconds. His mouth went to my breast. I moaned as I felt the teasing flicks of his tongue on my hardened nipple. His hand cupped my other breast, and he gently brushed his thumb across the nipple.

While his mouth was still on my breast, my fingers grabbed his shirt and pulled it from his trousers. He briefly pulled away from me and in seconds threw the shirt on the floor. Then he stood and said, "Come here, Susan."

I moved into him, my breath quickening as I felt my breasts flatten against his chest. I looked into his eyes and slightly opened my mouth, inviting his tongue. He made a low, deep cry.

Without ending his kiss, he slid his hands down my back, caressing every curve, exploring every hollow. When they reached my slacks, they went quickly to the button on the waistband. This time his fingers were dexterous and the button offered little resistance. I kicked off my shoes, rotated my hips and the slacks fell to the floor.

He slipped his fingers inside my panties and slid them over my hips. They joined my slacks on the floor. His hands cupped my hips and he drew me to him.

"Unfair advantage," I said. I tugged at his belt, opening the buckle. I released the button at his waistband and lowered his zipper. He quickly stepped out of his trousers, and then slid his shorts to the floor.

"That's better," I said.

"It is," he said.

He scooped me up and laid me on the bed, then lay beside me. Familiar movements, caresses from an almost forgotten time. I answered them with my own, taking in his warmth, letting go, fear and worry falling back as I found solace in his arms.

Chapter 35

I opened one eye. A shaft of light cut through the drapes and illuminated the chair that held Garrett's coat and tie. The rest of our clothes were scattered on the couch and floor. He lay in the bed beside me. I felt his breath on my back, the rhythm slow and steady. His arm rested on my side and his hand cupped my breast. I rolled over to face him and found he was awake. He didn't say anything, but pulled me to him and kissed me.

I returned his kiss and laid my arm on his shoulders. His hands began to move over me, touching all my pleasure centers. After a few ecstatic moments, we were joined, our rhythm slower than our coupling of the previous evening.

After we reached our crescendo, as we both lay quietly on the bed, I touched his face and said, "Rest awhile. I'll shower first."

After my shower, I found that he had drifted back asleep. I quietly dressed and packed my suitcase. As I zipped the bag shut, Garrett opened his eyes.

"What time is it?"

"Eight-thirty, and I have to get to DFW."

He pushed himself up on an elbow and ran a hand through his hair. "Give me a few minutes. I can take you."

"No need. I have one of Mike Riley's cars. I'm driving myself."

"Then maybe you have time for a cup of coffee before you leave."

"Garrett … it's not about the time."

He didn't reply. Just looked at me for a few moments. "I don't understand. What's wrong? I thought this was something special."

I took his coat and tie off the chair, placed them on the couch and sat down. "Oh Garrett, it was. And that's the problem."

"You're not making sense, Susan."

"After you chose Allison, I had to do something to stop the pain. So I tried to put you in a box. Convince myself I didn't love you anymore. For two years, I kept my feelings for you locked in that box. Then, after I married Terry, I thought I'd thrown away the key. I'd make love to Terry and think to myself, "See Garrett, I don't love you anymore." Now, last night, this morning, I feel like I've literally fucked up my life all over again. Allowed the box to open. Allowed much too much to escape."

I saw desperation in his eyes. "But Susan, don't you see? We're both free. We can have what we want. We can be together."

I looked at my watch. "No, we can't. Like you said last night, we're both starting over. Especially for me, emotionally. I made a decision to put Texas and all its pain and memories behind me. To build a new life in New York. I can't allow my feelings for you to come between what I might build with someone new. You understand that, don't you?"

There was a look in his eyes I had never seen before. "But we can stay in touch, can't we? An occasional phone call? Just to keep up?"

I should have ended it then. Finally. Fully. But I could not. "Of course."

A little light came back into his eyes. "If you move, change phone numbers, you'll let me know."

I grabbed the handle of my suitcase. "Sure." I moved toward the door. "When I check out, I'll make arrangements for you to have the room until noon."

There was no life in his voice. "Fine."

I fought back tears and left the room, convinced I would never see him again.

I dropped off Mike's car and he drove me to DFW. On the way to the airport, I called to check on Fred Kirkland and see if he had started to make any arrangements for Martha's funeral. I could always find a way to stay in Dallas if need be. But that turned out not to be necessary. It seemed that Martha had, for many years, expressed a desire to be buried in her family's plot in the small town of Sharpsburg, Kentucky. He'd hold a private family service there, and then arrange a public memorial service in Dallas in a couple of weeks. I assured him I'd be there.

*   *   *   *

The pilot warned that the climb out of DFW would be "a little bumpy." Late May thunderstorms boiled up around us. A large swarthy man on my left made frequent use of the barf bag and a young mother on my right couldn't quiet the screaming child on her lap. Trapped in my middle seat, I was being punished for some past or future sin.

Four hours later, I pushed open the door to my apartment. Caesar was curled up on the couch. He slowly raised his head and gave me a "meow." I gave him a few strokes and went into the kitchen to get him some treats. There was a note from Lynette on the table asking me to call her when I got home. I gave Caesar the treats and dialed Lynette's number. She answered on the first ring.

"Lynette, it's Susan. Thanks for taking care of Caesar. He seems in fine fettle."

"Hi, Susan. Thanks for the opportunity. The cash is very nice right now."

"Glad to do it. Did he behave himself?"

"He was a sweetheart. I wanted you to call to make sure you got home. Otherwise I'd have kept feeding him."

"I'm home. Can you drop my key through my mail slot sometime this week?"

There was a slight pause before her answer. "I had something more fun in mind."

"And that would be?"

"There's this restaurant, Tennessee Mountain, on Spring Street in SoHo. They specialize in ribs, brisket, and smoked chicken. It's just wonderful. I know you'd love it. Ever been there?"

I wasn't sure where this was going, but it was typical of Lynette's occasional manic enthusiasm. "Can't say I have."

"Well, let's meet there tomorrow night and I'll give you your key. Seven o'clock. Okay?"

Tomorrow night I had planned on a quiet evening with Caesar and take-in Chinese. But I had missed ribs in Dallas, and I owed Lynette for bailing me out of a tough situation. "Sure. Sounds good."

She gave me the address on Spring Street and we said our goodbyes. I unpacked my suitcase, went to the couch, and made my peace with Caesar. At six o'clock I broke out the Johnnie Black. At seven, I put the pizza in the oven. At eight, with the light still streaming in my bedroom windows, I pulled the sheet over my head and cried for Garrett Nelson one last time.

*   *   *   *

The next morning the damn phone jarred me awake. I didn't know where I was. Dallas, New York? I fumbled around, picked up the receiver, and mumbled, "This is Susan."

"Ms. Solari, did I wake you? I'm sorry, this is Victor Prieb."

I propped myself up on one elbow. "Oh. Victor. Good to hear from you." I tried to clear my thoughts. A quick glance at my bedside clock told me it was seven-thirty. "What's going on?"

"I have some results of the examination of the tape. Can you come by my place today?"

"Sure. But don't string me out. What'cha got?"

"A surprise."

I took a quick shower, threw on a pair of jeans, a tee-top and sneakers. A ball cap over my hair and a quick smear of lipstick were the only concessions I made to vanity. Caesar demanded breakfast and I, of course, complied.

As I made the cab ride to the East Village, my anticipation of what Victor might reveal mounted. Until now the rapist had been surgically perfect. The fact that we might have *something, anything*, was exciting.

When Victor opened the door, his eyes were dancing. "Come in, Susan. I have something for you to see." He led me to the glass-topped breakfast table from which I had fled when his questions demanded answers I was not prepared to give.

As I sat in one of the breakfast chairs, a tilt of his head directed my eyes toward a small combination TV/VCR player mounted on a shelf in the corner of the room. "Finding what you suspected was hard. It took my friend many hours. But in the end she was successful."

He hit a remote control and the images appeared. Ray Swift being maced. Then not accepting his fate. Attacking back at his tormentors. Then the glitch in the tape I had spotted. Victor hit the stop button on the remote. "You were correct. There is something here."

He removed a cassette from the player and inserted a silver disk into a black box sitting on the same shelf. He hit a few buttons on the remote and another image appeared on the TV. The hem of a slim-cut pair of black jeans; a delicate ankle, a slim black sneaker.

"A woman," I said.

"Yes."

I could feel the neurons and synapses firing, my brain trying to make a connection I knew was there, but couldn't yet define. More ominously, my heart told me that if I put the pieces together, the implications would be unbearable.

Victor interrupted my thoughts. "That's all we have. Swift's rapist did a good job editing the rest of the tape."

"Nothing more on the woman?"

"No. Just the ankle."

"Well," I said, "It's something. More than we had before."

Victor hit more buttons on the remote and the image disappeared. "Do you want this disk?"

"Yes."

"I fear I've disappointed you."

I stood to leave. "Not at all. Every bit of information counts." He accompanied me to the door. "Give my thanks to your technician."

A twinkle appeared in his bright eyes. "I already have."

* * * *

I returned home, still strangely unsettled by the news that a woman was involved in Ray Swift's rape. It wasn't that a woman was part of a sex crime, for in my experience in law enforcement I'd learned that some women could be as depraved as any man. Something else was bothering me, and I just couldn't put my finger on it.

I called Aurora Garza to tell her about the woman, but had to leave a message as she was out of the precinct. I'd just hung up when my phone rang. The caller ID said St. Vincent's. I cursed, realizing I hadn't checked on Cecil since my return from Dallas. When I answered, her voice came over the line much stronger than when I had last seen her in the hospital.

"Where ya been, honey? You're a hard broad to find."

"Well, you sound full of piss and vinegar."

"Yeah, I even convinced them to let me spring this joint tomorrow."

"That's great news."

"It is, but I need a favor."

I settled in on my couch. "Ask and you shall receive."

"Great, but can you hold on for a second? The Torture Fairy is here to stab me in the butt with another needle."

I heard a "clunk" as Cecil set the phone down, promptly followed by "Jesus Christ!" Then after a few moments of silence, she was back on the line. "I don't know what's in those things, but I sure feel a lot better after they've done their magic."

"Could you send some of that my way?" I said. "I could use a little separation from reality just now."

"No, no. Me weak. You strong. Now you're supposed to ask what kind of favor I need."

"Okay. What kind of favor do you need?"

"They're letting me out of here tomorrow. I've made arrangements to get home, but I'm going to need a little help after that. I ain't moving so well, sweetheart. Could you stay over the first night I'm back home? Do domestic stuff? You know, cook, clean, wash underwear? I'll offer Glennturrett as an incentive."

I couldn't keep the irony out of my voice. "Not Glenturrett, Baby Cakes. Not now."

Chapter 36

I just fiddled around my apartment for the rest of the afternoon, killing time until it was time to meet Lynette for dinner. When the phone rang, I expected Aurora Garza. Instead it was Mike Riley. I could hear the tension in his voice from the first word out of his mouth.

"I thought I'd give you an update on Martha Kirkland's case."

"What'cha got?"

"Not much. The medical examiner confirmed she was raped and also confirmed the obvious: the cause of death was a blow to the skull by some sort of blunt object. She was hog tied after she died and then left in the Swine Barn. She was killed at another location."

"Any estimate as to time of death?"

"Medical Examiner says somewhere around eight o'clock Sunday morning."

A flash of anger swept over me. "So the bastard killed her just after he talked with me. He was just playing with us."

"Sure looks that way."

"Got anything else?"

"Not yet. We're trying to trace Martha's movements last Friday. See if someone she was around might have seen something. Or if she mentioned to anyone she was meeting somebody. So far, we don't have much. She was at her hairdresser's at noon, then missed her dinner date with Fred. So we figure she was abducted sometime Friday afternoon. That's about all we've got at this point."

"Here's something new for you. Don't be surprised if there's a woman involved."

"What?"

I shared what we had found on the Ray Swift tape, then awaited Mike's reaction.

"So you think this woman's been involved in all these assaults?"

I was pacing around the apartment as we talked, the adrenaline pumping away. "Someone had to make the videotapes of the Manion and Swift rapes. But I don't think she was at the Thompson assault. Felicia only mentioned a single assailant, and there's no tape."

"Think we'll get one from Kirkland's killing?"

"I'm not sure," I said. "This guy seems to want to punish the CEOs by showing them their spouse's rape. Maybe he punished Fred by having him find Martha's body."

"So, maybe no tape."

"Maybe not. And if not, that's sort of a pattern, too."

"How's that?"

"Well, there have been four attacks. The two in Manhattan have been taped, the one in Dallas apparently wasn't. If we don't get a tape in the Kirkland murder that's some sort of a pattern."

There was silence on the line as Mike thought that over. "So, what's that mean?"

"Maybe he works with a partner in Manhattan and works alone in Dallas," I replied.

"And that tells us ..."

"Shit, Mike, I don't know, but it's *something*. Maybe it'll help make sense of something else we uncover."

"Maybe," Mike said. We were both quiet, steeped in the ugliness of it all. Mike broke the silence. "Susan, there's something going on you need to know about."

"What?"

"Gene Wasco has filed a complaint on me. Internal Affairs is investigating."

"Well, I guess that doesn't surprise me," I said. "Not only is he an asshole, he's also a wuss."

"Yeah. A wuss married to our first deputy chief's daughter. I'm a little worried about this one."

"God, Mike, I'm sorry."

"It's not your fault. I was just trying to keep you out of trouble. I could see the look in your eyes. You were just about to bust his balls, literally. Better a couple of days suspension for me than for you to be arrested for assaulting a police officer."

In spite of myself, I laughed. "You know me too well, Mike Riley."

"Look, if IAD contacts you, just tell them what happened. But you might make sure they know Wasco used the 'c' word."

"Oh, yeah. You bet I will. Look, Mike, I've got to run. I'm meeting someone for dinner."

"Who's the lucky guy?"

"No guy. Just a new girlfriend."

I could hear the smile in his voice. "What's the deal, Susan? With all your guy troubles, you trying a different route?"

I tried to sound offended. "Fuck you, Mike Riley!"

After I hung up from Mike I changed into a pair of jeans and a denim shirt. It would be a short walk to Tennessee Mountain. Seven blocks down Hudson Street, then about five blocks on Spring Street to the corner at Wooster Street.

When I left my apartment I enjoyed the mild late spring day enhanced by a gentle breeze. Many of the apartments along the way had their windows open, allowing the aromas of evening meals on the stove to waft on the breeze.

The smell of a rich Italian red sauce stirred memories of my mother's kitchen and the wonderful meals our family had shared as I grew up on the Jersey shore. That was, of course, before my father's drinking made a mockery of any family gathering. I pushed those particular memories away and took in the ambiance of the evening. An ambiance tainted by my constant awareness that Terry could spring from the next alley.

As I made my way toward the restaurant, I thought about my comment to Mike Riley about Lynette Mason. "Girlfriend" I had called her. And I supposed she was becoming that. Not in the sense that Mike had jokingly implied, but in the sense that women are permitted to have girlfriends. The friendship was just beginning, and who knew how it would mature. But it was nice to have made a new friend who had no knowledge of Tom Grant, Terry McCauley, Dom Shapiro, and Garrett Nelson. Lynette offered me a friendship grounded in the present, not the past. An opportunity to start over ... again.

The Tennessee Mountain restaurant was housed in what appeared to be an 1800's farmhouse. A surprising sight in SoHo. Lynette was waiting for me just inside the front door, dressed much as I was, in a denim skirt and a loose-fitting red-and-black-plaid blouse. She threw her arms around me and gave me a big hug.

"So good to see you. How was Dallas?"

I hadn't told her the reason for my trip and didn't want to bring her into that part of my life. "It's always good to see old friends," I said.

"I know what you mean, I miss my friends from Stanford. I keep meaning to get back there, but things keep getting in the way."

The hostess approached and said our table was ready. She led us to the back of the restaurant and seated us in a rustic booth.

"This is an unusual place for Manhattan," I said, picking up my napkin.

"Yeah," she said. "I thought you might enjoy it, what with you being from Texas. The ribs, brisket, and smoked chicken. I thought it'd be just your style."

I wanted to say my style was more lox and bagels, Reuben sandwiches, and Italian sausage and peppers. But I let it go. I wanted to find out more about her.

"Perfect," I said. A diminutive, dark-haired waitress appeared and took our drink orders. A Sam Adams for me, a Coors light for Lynette. As the waitress departed I said, "I didn't know you went to Stanford."

"English Lit." She screwed up her face. "Wonderful career move. Turns out the best subject I took was Western Civ 101. That's where I met Peter. We were an item for four years. His father was president of Barnhill Publishing. That's how I wound up in Manhattan."

"Nothing like networking," I said.

Lynette shook her head and a small smile appeared. "You mean nothing like screwing the boss's son. But when it ended with Peter, I was out on my ass at Barnhill in two days."

"After the theater the other night, you said you wound up on the wrong side of office politics."

Another little smile. "Turns out I wound up on the wrong side of the bed."

The waitress returned with our drinks, and we ordered. I got the baby back ribs fixed "Texas style" and Lynette ordered the smoked brisket. As we ate we chatted about Lynette's job prospects (she had a line on a job at an independent publisher), her family (she was from Oshkosh, Wisconsin), and finally the men in our life.

"So tell me about your current guy," I said, anxious to steer the subject away from me.

"About Bill? There's not really too much to tell. We just met a couple of months ago. He's older than me, but in really great shape. He works out every day." A blush spread across her cheeks.

I laughed and said, "It's okay, Lynette. Nothing wrong with enjoying some prime beefcake."

"I know," she said. "I thought I got over most of this at Stanford. But occasionally my Midwestern country girl background breaks out."

"Nothing wrong with that either," I said. "What's Bill do?"

"He's in insurance, a salesman. Are you involved with anyone right now?"

I deflected the question. "Who has time, what with the move and all?"

It was Lynette's turn to laugh, "Eight million people in the Naked City and almost half of them are guys. Time to get busy."

"I know, I know," I said. "Maybe Prince Charming will show up. In the meantime I've got Caesar."

"But he's just a cat."

"And like any cat, and any guy … It's all about him."

We finished the meal and said our goodbyes. Lynette returned my key and we promised to get together again soon. On the walk back to my apartment, I put Garrett Nelson back in his box. I took a break from the world of rape and death and reveled in the warm evening breezes. I had no sense of the storm that waited to engulf me.

Chapter 37

About a block before I reached my apartment, my cell phone rang. I fished it out of my purse and saw the text message on the screen. "Something's waiting 4 U at home. You'll hate it."

I felt like someone had suddenly wrapped a rope around my gut and was twisting it ... hard. I sprinted the final block to my apartment, dodging people out for a late evening walk and cursing the fact that the loafers I was wearing kept trying to slip off my feet.

When I reached my building door, I kicked off my shoes, pulled the Glock out of my purse and dashed up the stairs. A videocassette leaned against my apartment door. I scanned the hallway, but saw no immediate threat. Then, at the end of the hall, I saw the door to a maintenance closet ajar. I moved silently down the hallway, keeping the Glock leveled at the door.

But I had a problem. If I pulled the door open, he could cut me down with a couple of well-placed shots. So I decided to isolate the bastard, if he was there. From three feet away, I delivered a quick kick to the center of the door. I was rewarded by the click of a lock as it slammed into the doorjamb.

I jumped aside, putting my back to the wall of the hallway, out of the line of fire if he decided to come out blazing. But there was only silence. I waited, hoping to hear movement in the closet. Movement that could justify putting several Glock rounds through the door. But, in the end, there was nothing. I took a couple of deep breaths, approached the closet and tested the knob. It didn't budge. Then I heard a door open at the other end of the hallway and an old man wearing a stained red tee shirt and gray twill trousers emerged, carrying a hammer. I put the Glock behind my back as he approached.

"Who the hell closed the maintenance closet?" he grumbled.

"That was me, sorry," I said.

He stopped and scowled at me. "Shit. Juan left it open so I could borrow this hammer. I told him I'd return it tonight. Now he'll be pissed."

I felt relieved and foolish at the same time. "My fault," I said. "I just didn't want anyone to steal something. Let me have the hammer and I'll see that Juan gets it in the morning, along with an explanation."

He considered my offer, then declined. "Nope. I'll do it myself. That way, I'll know it's done." Then he abruptly turned and walked back to his apartment, slamming the door as he went in. I turned away and went downstairs to get my shoes. I might as well have saved the effort. They were gone.

I went backup stairs and directed my attention to the cassette at my door. I resisted the urge to pick it up. Instead, I checked my security tape at the top of the doorframe, and finding it unbroken, opened the door. The cassette clattered to the floor. I laid the Glock on an end table and slipped on a pair of latex gloves I had retrieved from my purse. I picked up the cassette, then closed and locked the door, making sure both safety chains were locked in place. Then I sat on the couch to try to get my thoughts together. But not before I'd thrown a handful of ice and two fingers of Johnnie Black into a glass.

I was sure that what I had in my possession was the videotape of Martha Kirkland's murder, but I didn't understand why the killer had sent it to me rather than Fred. And on a gut level there was something even more chilling to me. He had to be shadowing my movements to know when it was safe to deliver the tape. *And I hadn't picked up on him.*

I knew I'd have to turn the tape over to Aurora tomorrow, but before I did, I wanted to view it. *No!* I corrected myself. *You never want to view that tape. But you have to!* I took a swig of the scotch for reinforcement for what I was about to see.

The camera was shooting over the shoulder of a black-clad figure facing a door. A fist pounded on the door, waited a few seconds and pounded again. Then the door opened and I saw the figure of Cecelia Boldaccio.

"Jesus!" I shouted, and hit the stop button on the VCR. It was Cecil's beating, not Martha's murder. I was stunned by what this meant. I found it hard to catch my breath and couldn't stop my hands from shaking. I went to the kitchen and refreshed the scotch. Back on the couch, I tossed down half the drink and started the tape again.

Cecil's image. A gloved hand holding a small silver cylinder sprayed a mist into her face. She staggered back into her apartment, her hands digging into her eyes.

The tape continued to roll, shot from the hallway, through the doorframe. The assailant was on her instantly, putting her into a headlock. As Cecil tried to escape, he delivered blow after blow to her face. Blood spurted from her nose and he lost his grip. Cecil fell to the floor and the ski-masked figure buried the toe of his boot into her ribs ."Stop," she cried out. "Please stop."

I cut off the tape, unable to watch. But what I had seen confirmed my deepest fears. *This can't be! There's something I'm missing! I have to talk this out!*

I dialed Aurora's number, expecting to leave a message. I was wrong. She answered on the first ring.

"Where the hell have you been?" I demanded.

"Doing something I can't tell you about. That's why I'm here at this ungodly hour."

"Can you meet for breakfast tomorrow morning?"

"Sure. When and where?"

"Charlie's Diner, seven o'clock."

"Is something wrong?"

"Everything."

Chapter 38

When I arrived at Charlie's a little before seven, all the ceramic clocks kept their faithful time, four o'clock. The place was about half full, and I asked for a table in the back corner of the diner. I hadn't been seated five minutes when Aurora arrived. She was in her full Lady Detective outfit. Navy blazer, gray slacks, plain white blouse. The blazer was trim cut, and I saw the telltale bulge of a shoulder holster.

When she reached the table she looked me over and said, "You look like hell."

She wasn't telling me anything I didn't already know. I hadn't gotten more than a couple of hours of sleep after I cut out the light around midnight. When the alarm jarred me awake, I hit the snooze a couple of times. On the third try I finally looked at the clock. I had less than forty-five minutes to shower, dress, and get to Charlie's.

I made it a quick shower and towel-dried my hair, barely running a brush through it. Then I slipped on a pair of jeans, a long-sleeved red tee, and sneakers. A little lipstick was the only makeup.

"We have to talk," I said. "I need you to tell me I'm not crazy."

A waitress with a Brooklyn accent, a quick smile, and a nametag that said "Carol" plopped a cup of coffee down in front of both of us. She looked at me and nodded toward Aurora. "She's a regular and you look like you could use it. Ready to order?" Carol waited while we made our decisions and then was off to turn in our orders.

"Okay, let's have it," Aurora said.

"Here's the deal," I said. I told her about the text message and about finding the videotape.

"So you thought it was the tape of Martha Kirkland's murder?"

"Yeah, but it was of Cecil's beating."

Aurora took a sip of her coffee. "Have you watched it?"

"The start. But I couldn't finish it. It's different watching someone beat one of your best friends. You'd think I could take anything. After all, I watched them pry Tom Grant's body out of the trunk of a car."

A strange expression crossed Aurora's face. "I don't understand."

Of course she didn't. That was another world, another time. I thought I had buried it. "Never mind. It's just that it's hard to be professional when people we love are victims." Aurora accepted my explanation, but the look in her eyes told me I owed her a fuller accounting. It would have to wait.

"Like Don Henley's song," I said, "here's 'The Heart of the Matter.' The opening shots of the tapes of Swift's rape and Cecil's beating are almost identical. The video is shot over the shoulder of a black-clad figure who sprays something into the victim's face. Then there's the charge into the apartment. I'm sure the asshole who beat Cecil is the same guy that raped Ray Swift and Janet Manion. And most likely raped Felicia Thompson and killed Martha Kirkland, too."

Aurora's eyes were cold. "I'll give you everyone but Cecil. She doesn't fit the pattern. She's an artist, not part of the corporate world."

"But she *is* one thing," I said.

"What's that?"

"She's my friend."

Aurora nodded, waiting.

"And I may be paranoid," I said. "But try this out. After my name appears in the paper, I start getting notes, taunting me. Then my best friend is beaten. Then the bastard goes back to the corporate world and kills Martha Kirkland. Only Fred Kirkland is out of numerical order. And Fred was my mentor at InterTrans. Then I get the tape of Cecil's beating. All sounds pretty personal to me."

At that moment, Carol appeared with our breakfasts. A poached egg and link sausage for me, a waffle for Aurora. Fresh coffee for both of us.

After Carol put the food on the table and made her way to another customer, I told Aurora about Victor's revelation that a woman was on the Swift tape, and that Cecil said one of her attackers was small.

Aurora drizzled some syrup on her waffle and said, "You're making a pretty good case, but there's a hole in your theory. You had no connection to Thompson, Manion, and Swift before you took this case."

I sat with my fork poised. "That's why I think the newspaper article is so important. This didn't turn my way until then."

"And what do you make of that?"

I didn't want to admit it, but my words betrayed me. "Beats the hell out of me," I said, stabbing at my plate.

And so we were back to theories, suspicions, and maybe paranoia. But no hard evidence of anything. The realization made my heart sink, but I kept it to myself. "Any DNA evidence from the attack on Cecil?"

"Don't know. It isn't my case."

"If there was, could you have a comparison run with the DNA on the Swift rape?"

"Sure."

"Expedited?"

"Naturally." She pushed her waffle aside. "Now do you have Cecil's tape?"

I reached into my purse and pulled out the tape, enclosed in a clear plastic freezer bag. "But I need a favor."

Aurora took the tape. "I know, a copy."

"Expedited?"

"Naturally."

* * * *

We finished our breakfast and went our separate ways. Aurora to the precinct, me to my apartment. When I pushed my door open, my phone was ringing. When I answered, I was greeted by a voice that sounded like gravel going through a crushing machine.

"Is this Susan Solari?"

"Yes."

"This is Lieutenant Carl Poetschke, Internal Affairs Division, Dallas Police Department."

"Good morning, Lieutenant."

"We're investigating an incident between Detective Mike Riley and Detective Gene Wasco. We understand you were a witness to this incident."

"You mean the incident where Wasco called me a cunt."

"He denies using that word."

"And what word does he say he used?"

"He claims you were interfering with a police investigation. And that Detective Riley was complicit in your interference."

There was an edge to my voice. "Wasco couldn't conduct an investigation with a road map. And I'm confident his experience with the female anatomy is limited to an opportunistic sheep and the occasional cow."

There was a long silence at the other end of the line. Finally Poetschke said, "Did Detective Riley strike Detective Wasco?"

"Yes. He was defending my honor. I appreciated it."

Again a long silence. "Riley struck Wasco without provocation, then?"

It was too much. I took a deep breath. "Are you married?"

"Yes."

"Give her my condolences."

* * * *

Later in the afternoon, I went to Aurora's office and picked up my copy of the videotape. Then I stopped by D'Agistino's on my way to Cecil's. I purchased a pound of ground beef, an onion, a bell pepper, rice, Velveeta cheese, and a can of diced tomatoes. Comfort food for the soul.

When I reached her building, I took a chance on the elevator, not willing to shlep the food and my overnight bag up the stairs. The trip up to the third floor provided the usual jerks, bumps, and squeaks. But, at the end, I was delivered to my destination.

Cecil greeted me with her usual enthusiasm. "Hi, sweetheart. What's for dinner?"

"Ranch Hash. A Texas treat."

"Well, get with it. I've had all the hospital food I can stand."

The bruises on her face were turning green-yellow, and she walked with a noticeable limp, but her spirit was intact. "You promised me a scotch," I said.

"So I did. Glennturrett."

"Not tonight. Got any Johnnie Black?"

She cast a suspicious glance at me. "Story there?"

"None I'd care to share."

Cecil walked into her kitchen and turned to face me. "But if there comes a time, I'm always ready to listen."

I set the groceries on her kitchen counter. "I know. Now let me fix dinner."

Cecil poured me a Johnnie Black and in thirty minutes I had a Texas soul food casserole on the table. In less time than it took to make it, it was gone. "Not bad," Cecil said.

"Not bad, hell," I said. "It was wonderful."

I cleaned up the kitchen, then poured myself another Johnnie Black. Cecil sat at one end of her couch sipping a vodka and tonic; I sat at the other end. "I've got a tape," I said.

"Of what?"

"Your beating."

Cecil took a deep breath. She stared at her vodka and tonic.

"Cecil, we don't have to watch it now. I can look at it later."

She looked at me. "Yes we do, Susan. Yes we do."

"I'm not sure it's right for you," I pressed.

"I'll be the judge of that."

I put the tape into the player. I saw the spray into Cecil's face. I saw the charge into her apartment and the beating. Her fall to the floor, the kick to her ribs. Then something new. Cecil's kick to his groin. And his furious response. "You bitch."

I'd heard it time after time. When we were dating. When we were married. When he'd tried to kill me. And now he'd fucked up. He'd forgotten to disguise two words. From now on there was no doubt.

Chapter 39

The tape ended abruptly. In the final shot, Cecil's attacker delivered another vicious kick to her ribs. She gave an anguished cry and rolled on the floor, clutching her ribcage. Then the screen went black.

I looked at Cecil as I hit the remote and cut off the VCR. She shook her head. "I don't even remember kicking him in the nuts," she said. "I can't give you anything."

It no longer mattered. I'd found my answer. "Maybe the cops'll pick up something. Maybe we're both too emotionally connected to this to see everything that's there. Maybe they'll see something we couldn't."

Cecil studied me for a long moment. "Maybe." Then she picked up what was left of her drink and swished it around in the glass. "Fix me another, will you, babe? I'm not too great at moving around yet. Besides, I need to milk this, uh … infirmity, for all it's worth. And while you're at it, there's a CD on top of the Bose. It'll curl your pantyhose."

I made a face at Cecil and left my end of the couch, fixed her another vodka and tonic, splashed more scotch in my glass, and picked up the CD. *Great Women of Jazz, Songs of Heartache*. I slipped it in the player. The first cut was Ella doing "But Not For Me."

As her incredibly smooth intonations filled the room, I looked up to find Cecil studying me. "Okay," she said. "Out with it."

"Whadaya mean?"

"After fifteen years, you can't bullshit me. You saw something on that tape."

The last light of the day was fading away, and Julie London was singing, "Cry Me a River." I cut on a lamp, settled back into the couch, and admitted something I'd feared for longer than I'd cared to admit. It's Terry."

Cecil's eyes locked on mine. "I don't understand."

"It was Terry that attacked you."

"How the hell do you know?"

I took a long sip of my scotch. "When he called you 'bitch,' I recognized his voice. He called me that so often."

"You're sure?"

"I wish I wasn't. But, yeah, I'm sure."

"I don't even know the stupid fuck! Why would he attack me?"

The answer to her question was the heart of the matter. And I wasn't sure I'd ever know the full answer. So I gave her a simple one that I was sure of. "You're my friend."

* * * *

"So you're sure it's Terry." It was the next morning, and Aurora and I were in a booth at Charlie's. She had wanted to meet me at the precinct, but I had refused. I didn't want Collin Fitzgerald getting wind of anything at this point.

"I'm sure. He's called me a bitch a thousand times over the years. I couldn't mistake his voice."

Aurora hoisted her coffee mug and took a long swig. "So, according to your theory, Terry beat Boldaccio and killed Martha Kirkland as some sort of act of revenge or punishment directed at you."

I poked at the eggs on the plate in front of me. The food was a waste. I had no appetite. "That's the only way this makes any sense," I insisted.

"I know I said this yesterday," Aurora said. "But it's still true. You had no personal connection to Thompson, Manion or Swift. Those attacks don't fit your theory."

"Not necessarily. Remember, Kirkland sent Manion to me. And Swift had done business with both Manion and Thompson."

Aurora still wasn't buying it. "But if Terry was trying to send you some sort of message, why would he start with the attack on Felicia Thompson? You admit you know of no connection to Thompson. You only found out about that attack through VICAP."

"Yeah, I know. I can't explain this completely," I said. "But I do know that twisted son-of-a bitch ex-husband of mine. Look, there's one way to settle this. Did you find out if there's DNA evidence from Cecil's beating?"

Aurora pushed away a plate of half-eaten pancakes. "Well, there's good news and bad news about that." But before she could continue, Carol, who it now seemed was our personal waitress, showed up. "You done, ladies?"

We both nodded. I just wanted to get her away from the table so I could get Aurora's news about the DNA. "Yeah, you can clear the table, but we're going to stay a while longer and have a little more coffee."

"You got it." She quickly removed the remains of our breakfast. In moments, she was back refilling our coffee mugs.

When she was gone, I couldn't keep it in any longer. "What the hell do you mean … good news and bad news about the DNA?"

"The good news is that crime scene investigators recovered skin from under Boldacchio's fingernail."

"And the bad news."

"The lab lost the sample."

I lost it. "What the fuck!" The words bounced off the walls of the restaurant and the other diners snapped their heads around and stared at me.

"Calm down, Susan." Aurora had her hand on my arm. "This is no excuse, but the lab is understaffed and the people there are underpaid and overwhelmed with work. It's been that way for years."

I lowered the volume, but not my fury. "And guess what! I … don't … give … a … damn! That DNA would have been the perfect connection between the attacks on Cecil and Ray Swift. But without it, we don't have shit. All we've got is the similarity in the videotapes and my ID of Terry's voice. And I'm not stupid enough not to know what a defense will do with *that* in a courtroom. In other words, we know who our guy is, but we've got crap to prove it!"

Aurora didn't react. Just watched me for a few moments. I sank back in the booth, trying to control my anger. Finally, she said, "He'll make a mistake. In fact, he's already made one. He let you hear his voice."

"No. I thought that through last night. I've decided it wasn't a mistake. It was a message. He wanted to tell me who he was. What's the fun if I don't know it's him?"

I watched Aurora gather her thoughts. "We've got the DNA on the Swift rape. I could get a search warrant; force him to give a sample."

"And you think you've got enough probable cause to satisfy a judge? Besides, he lives in Dallas, not New York. New York warrants don't hold much water in Texas."

Anger flashed in Aurora's eyes. "You got a better idea ... Tex?"

I smiled. "You said he'd make a mistake. Well, he already did. About a year ago."

* * * *

The banker's box was jammed into the corner of my bedroom closet. The one I'd saved when I unmercifully tossed out all other evidence of my life in Texas. The words "Divorce Papers" were scrawled across the top in blood red letters.

The letter was at the back of the box. Nestled behind the thick legal records that documented the failure of love. He had written it in anger, in his own hand. Threat after threat. And the odds were he had licked the envelope.

* * * *

The next morning I put the envelope into Aurora's hands. "Here's his mistake. Let's get his ass."

Chapter 40

Later that afternoon, when I called Mike Riley, a woman answered his phone. "Detective Riley's not available," she said. "Detective Jenkins is taking his calls. I'll connect you with Detective Jenkins."

"No, wait a minute. When will Detective Riley be available? I want to talk to him, not Detective Jenkins."

Her tone was that of someone reading a script. "Detective Riley is on special assignment. His cases are being handled by Detective Jenkins. I'll connect you with Detective Jenkins."

Before I could protest again, she made a connection and a phone started ringing. I felt a knot in the pit of my stomach and slammed the phone down. "Fucking Wasco!"

I dialed Mike Riley's home phone number and my worst fears were confirmed when he answered. "Suspended?" I asked.

Surprisingly, there was a bit of humor in his voice. "Technically, no. Administrative leave with pay. What'd you do, call the office?"

"Yeah, they need better liars."

"Wasco's all they need. He claims my attack on him was unprovoked."

"What about my statement?"

"Seems you were too upset over the death of Martha Kirkland to be credible."

"Shit."

"Yeah. Looks like I'm on the fast track to the Southwest Division."

SWD, the hellhole of Dallas. Most detectives assigned there were gone in less than two years. Usually it was guys on the downside of their careers. A nudge and a message. Mike was too young. "You're probably imagining things."

"I wish. But the word's out. When I come back, that's the assignment."

"Fuck! I feel like shit. This is because of me."

"Not really. Wasco's an asshole. High time someone cleaned his clock. Now, why'd you call?"

I filled Mike in about the similarity of the videotapes, my recognition of Terry's voice, and the possibility of the DNA match. Then I asked him when he thought he might be back on duty.

"Word's out I'll be called in Monday for my reprimand and then given my new assignment."

"When you get back, could you, somehow, see that Gene Wasco is made aware of what I just told you? He still has the Kirkland case, doesn't he?"

An edge came into Mike's voice. "You ask a lot of a guy, Susan. Wasco's in the process of deep-sixing my career."

"I know. Forget it. It's just that Fred has done so much for me. I'd ask anyone to do anything to find Martha's killer."

His words softened. "I know. But you think Wasco'll listen to anything from me? Especially based on any information from you?"

"But I'm sure we're going to have a DNA match."

"Then deal with it in New York. That's where the match means something. There's nothing here. I won't even have the Thompson case after Monday. It'll be reassigned to another detective in sex crimes."

"Fuck." I knew who had committed the rapes, beat Cecil, and killed Martha Kirkland. And I couldn't do a damn thing about it! Except wait for the results of a fucking DNA match. And that would be good only if Terry had licked the envelope. The odds were good, but not one hundred percent.

I vented my frustration on Mike. "And you know what? Even if there is a DNA match, who knows if we'll ever find Terry? He could just fade away. It's not that hard to assume a new identity. This is really crap!"

Mike, as always, was optimistic. "He'll probably screw up. He seems to be getting more disorganized, more reckless."

But I was having none of it. "Maybe. Anyway, good luck Monday."

"Sunday's what I'm more worried about."

I didn't understand. "Sunday? What's happening Sunday?"

Now it was my turn to hear frustration in Mike's voice. "This morning I got a call from Randy Masden. You remember him. The asshole reporter from the *Morning News*."

"How could I ever forget that bucket of crap!"

"Well, he called and wanted some comments from me. He said he's doing a story on morale in the police department. Somehow he knows I cold cocked Wasco. Said he wanted my side of the story. I told him to go fuck off."

"Good for you."

"Maybe not so good for me. Before I hung up on him, he told me he hoped I'd enjoy seeing my name spread across page one in the Sunday edition."

Mike's words were like a bucket of cold water thrown in my face. And it all became clear. "Michael, say that again!"

"He said he hoped I'd enjoy seeing my name one page one."

If I could have crawled through the phone and kissed him, I would have. "Mike Riley you're a fucking genius!"

"What the hell do you mean?"

A few seconds to explain. Then, "I've got to go. I've got to get on page one, Sunday edition."

* * * *

My first call was to Aurora. I told her what was coming down and asked her to set up Collin Fitzgerald. "Drop the fact that I'm off the rape cases. That Glenn Manion tried to stiff me on my fee and I told him to fuck off. That I'm really pissed."

"Will do, as soon as I hang up."

"And, Aurora, sell it good, will you?"

"Don't worry, honey. I could sell that dumb mick five-dollar drafts when six packs are free."

Now it was my turn to sell. I dialed the number of the *New York Post*. "Morrie Masters, please."

A few seconds of silence. A few clicks. Then the parrot-like voice came on the line. "Morrie Masters here."

"Susan Solari here."

"I thought you didn't talk to reporters, especially reporters like me."

"Turns out maybe that was a mistake. Are you still interested in the 'Corporate Countdown' rape cases?"

"Yeah, why?"

"Never mind why. I've got information. Are you interested?"

"If it's good."

"That's never stood in your way before."

His voice went up a couple of octaves. "Look, lady, you got anything or not?"

Bitterness oozed out of my voice. "Oh yeah, I got plenty. You listening?"

When I finished, he said, "How do I know any of this is true? I'm gonna check this out. You better not be fucking with me."

I couldn't suppress a laugh. "Believe me, Morrie, fucking you is the last thing on my mind."

*   *   *   *

Saturday morning dawned bright and clear, and I figured I'd better get my morning run in early. Despite the warmth of the morning, I wore jogging slacks so I could carry the .32. The run was to be a short one. I was just getting started when I saw the *Post* headline displayed on a rack at Village Cigars on Sheridan Square.

COPS CLOSE TO CORPORATE COUNTDOWN ARREST

WOW! I thought. *Morrie really wanted to get this out.* I bought a copy, cut short my run, and hurried back home. With a cup of coffee in hand, I settled in on the couch, anxious to find out if the story had the angle I was hoping for.

Beneath Morrie's by-line, a quick scan told me the story was all I could have wanted, and more ... *A source close to the investigation has informed the* Post *that New York City police are close to an arrest in the case of the "Corporate Countdown Rapist". The same source says the evidence pointing to the identity of the rapist is strong and may even link the suspect to a murder in Dallas, Texas.*

According to the source, "This guy's really arrogant. He's even left notes taunting the police. But in reality, he's just stupid. He's made a lot of mistakes and left a lot of evidence the police have been able to tie together."

In addition, police profilers have concluded that it's likely that he's intimidated by strong women and is probably impotent in intimate situations where he doesn't have total control.

The story went on to revisit the previous accounts of the rapes and why the rapist was nicknamed the 'Corporate Countdown Rapist.' It then briefly provided information on Martha Kirkland's murder, concluding with ... *The Dallas Police confirmed that Martha Kirkland was a friend of Susan Solari, a private investigator working the rape cases. Our source confirms that Ms. Solari has been responsible for developing much of the evidence leading to the identity of the rapist and possible killer. When the* Post *contacted Ms. Solari, her only comment was, "I'm sure the rapist will be apprehended soon. Most criminals are stupid and get caught. This case is no different."*

I smiled, folded the paper, and set it on the coffee table in front of the couch. I picked up my phone and called Aurora's cell number. She answered on the first ring.

"Officially, I'm really pissed at you," she said. "Leaking information relevant to an investigation. Unconscionable! Unofficially, congratulations."

I took a sip of my coffee. "Wouldn't have happened without you. I knew Masters would call Fitzgerald for confirmation. You must have given a virtuoso performance."

"As I said, he's an easy mark."

"Now comes the hard part. Waiting."

"Watch your ass."

"You betcha."

Chapter 41

I had spoken the truth to Aurora. The hard part was waiting. Terry could be anywhere. Would he see the *Post* story? Would he react? I could control none of this. Just go on high security alert. Watch my backside.

I needed to get out of the apartment, so just after noon I put on running gear and launched myself into lower Manhattan. In the warmth of an early June afternoon, I wore a larger than usual tee to conceal the .32.

I ran down West Street, across Chambers, and back up Hudson into the Village. I'm usually charged up after a run, endorphins boosting my spirit. This time it didn't work. I looked for Terry around every corner as I approached my apartment. When I reached my door, I checked the security tape on the doorjamb and found it intact. But I still put the .32 in my hand when I put my key in the lock and walked in.

The only sign of life was Caesar wanting his afternoon treats. I tossed off my running outfit and showered, keeping the .32 folded in a towel. At four o'clock I was at loose ends and called Cecil, asking if she wanted to come meet me for an early dinner at the Leaning Power pizza parlor on Seventh Avenue, just north of Sheridan Square. I got her machine and left a message. An hour later, it had not been returned.

At five, Lynette called and suggested we meet at the deli on Varick for Sunday night dinner. About eight-thirty she said. Her boyfriend was going out with the guys. She'd be free then. I told her no. Given the gauntlet I had laid down to Terry, I wasn't ready to expose myself to the streets of Manhattan after dark. I offered an alternative. Would she like to come to my place late afternoon Sunday? I'd fix my mother's spaghetti and meatballs. She accepted and offered to bring a salad from D'Agistino's. We agreed that around four o'clock would be a good time and said our goodbyes.

But the meal with Lynette was Sunday and this was Saturday. I was on edge and in a foul mood, pacing around my apartment. I needed both company and food.

At seven, I called Cecil again ... no answer. Something tightened in my stomach. I tried again at eight, then at nine. Both times I was sent to her machine. All thoughts of food disappeared, replaced by a terrible realization. In my zeal to flush out Terry, I had put those closest to me at risk. It would be just like him to strike out at someone dear to me.

Cecil was the obvious target. He had attacked her once, but neither raped nor killed her. I could imagine he'd try to finish the job as revenge for my taunts in the *Post*.

I strapped the .32 onto my thigh and quickly changed into my black combat outfit, tee and cargo pants. I slipped the Glock into an inside my waistband holster then hurried to the street and hailed a cab to Cecil's apartment.

I left the cab on Spring Street, a couple of blocks from Cecil's place and approached her building. The street was busy with early evening traffic, complete with the obligatory sounds of impatient drivers working their horns.

The sidewalks were filled with pedestrians rushing to their destinations, but at first I saw nothing unusual. Then I spotted him. The tattered jacket, worn with no shirt; the unkempt beard; the filthy ball cap; and finally the shopping cart he pushed, all marked him as a denizen of the street.

But his shopping cart was only partially filled and looked new, as if freshly taken out of a supermarket parking lot. As I approached, I noticed his eyes were not fixed in the vacant stare so common to street people. Instead, they darted from side to side, briefly checking out the faces around him.

As I drew close to him, his eyes locked onto my face and he thrust both his hands high above his head and shouted, "I surrender, dark angel of death! You've come for me at last! I surrender! I surrender!"

Then he threw himself on the sidewalk and, writhing around, shouted, "Take me! Take me!" I jumped away, my hand firmly on my Glock. But I didn't draw.

Suddenly a man, also in tattered clothing, rushed out of the gathering crowd and knelt over the figure on the sidewalk. "Take it easy, Henry. It's okay. She's not the dark angel." Then the man looked up at me and snarled, "Get the hell out of here, lady. Get out of his sight. He thinks you're the Angel of Death. Fucking black clothes!"

I wanted to say I meant no harm. I wanted to say I was sorry. But I said nothing. Instead I thought of my dead first husband. Then of Tom Grant, of Francie Marcos, of Jim O'Brien, of Solomon Waxberg, of Jack Herndon and of Martha Kirkland. All part of my world ... all dead. As I withdrew into the crowd, the ugliness of the thought sickened me.

I was still a block and a half from Cecil's building. A long minute later, Glock in hand, I climbed the stairs of Cecil's building. When I reached the third floor, I moved down the hallway toward her door. The single incandescent bulb in the ceiling provided just enough light to find my way, but not enough to expose any threat. When I reached the door of Cecil's apartment, I paused, listening.

Silence. I tested the doorknob. Locked. I put my back to the wall of the hallway, reached out and pounded on the door. Cecil's voice broke the silence. "Jesus! What's so damn urgent? You're going to knock the damn door down!"

"Cecil, it's me!"

"Susan?"

"Yes!"

"What the hell are you doing here?"

"Let me in and I'll explain."

I heard the safety chains release and the deadbolt open. Then Cecil's ample figure was framed in the door. I pushed her back into her apartment, slammed the door shut, and threw the deadbolt closed.

Cecil stepped back, gave me the once-over and said, "You look like James fucking Bond.

I hung there, looking at her, safe and breathing. Then my tears came. I couldn't stop them. "Cecil, Cecil ..."

She came to me then, gathering me to her bosom.

Chapter 42

Later, I got it together. "Where the hell have you been? You scared me to death." I was in one of Cecil's leather chairs. She was on the couch. My Glock was resting on the coffee table between us.

"I hadn't been out of here since I came home from the hospital. It was like I was in fucking prison. So I went to the movies. Then I stopped at Billy Fats and got an early dinner." Cecil studied me over her Sam Adams. "I'm worried about you, Susan. The strain, feeling responsible for me ..."

"I'm fine. It's just seeing that you were okay." I explained about the *Post* article. "You were the most obvious and easiest target."

Cecil waved her cane in the air. "So you thought he'd come after me. He wouldn't have had a chance. I'd have beat the shit out of him with this."

I felt my face flush. "Damn it, Cecil, cut the comedy."

She studied my face. "You *are* serious, aren't you?"

I picked up my Johnnie Black and took a hit. "You bet your ass I am. Do you have anybody you could stay with for a few days?"

"How about you?"

"No. You'd just be closer to the bull's-eye. Anyone else?"

Cecil tilted her head and the hint of a smile appeared on her lips. "Remember I told you about Bill Watson? The guy that's doing a show for me next month? The one that got dumped?"

"Yeah."

"He's not hooked up with anyone yet. If I asked him if I could spend a few nights, he'd step on his tongue saying yes. Of course he'd be badly mistaken about the possibilities."

"You vixen." My brain worked on the possibilities. I needed her safe.

"We girls do what we have to do."

It was time to go, but before I left I had a question for Cecil. "What the hell's Billy Fats?"

"Oh, honey. You've been gone way too long."

*   *   *   *

The cab ride back to my apartment had me thinking. When had I cried last, especially in front of someone? Anxiety gnawed at my gut. Would Terry attack those close to me? Or would I be the primary target? I was used to being in charge. Orchestrating events. This time I'd teased a tiger I couldn't control.

*   *   *   *

The next morning a very loud boom jarred me out of my sleep. I bolted upright in the bed and pulled the sheet over my breasts. I thought maybe a car bomb until I heard the rain driving against my bedroom window. A thunderstorm! At least one had put me in fear of my life in Texas. "Frog Stranglers," they called them.

Caesar had never liked thunder anywhere, and now I could hear his complaining cries coming from under the bed. I called to him, trying to coax him out. "It's all right, baby. It's just a storm. It'll move on. Come on out. I'll get you some treats." My reassurances seemed to be working until he was halfway out from under bed and another boomer shattered the Sunday morning stillness. He scrambled back under the bed, tail whipping, and I knew all hope of getting him to come out any time soon was over. After all, I had lied to him.

I climbed out of bed, put on a tee and padded into the kitchen to start the coffee. I'd set up the pot the night before, so all I had to do was hit the brew button. While I waited, I turned on the TV tucked into the corner of my kitchen counter. Channel 4 local news was on, reporting that while the storms would soon pass, we'd likely have light rain and drizzle until sundown. I poured myself a cup of coffee and thought about the prospects for the day ahead. One being that Terry might try to kill me, and that at my invitation.

While I had made myself the cheese in the trap, I knew I wouldn't be much good sitting around waiting for the rat to show. Time to get out of the apartment. After a quick shower, I was out on Morton Street heading for the closest newsstand. I was in black cargo pants, the .32 in one pocket. The Glock was inside my waistband. A floppy yellow hat offered protection against the drizzle. Not a fashion statement, but at least I had on clean underwear. If Terry were successful, the coroner would be impressed.

I bought a *Post* and scanned the headlines for any follow-up story from Morrie Masters. Nothing. Not that that was important. I was just hoping for a little more salt in the wound. A couple of blocks down 7th, I slipped into a little deli that offered bagels, cream cheese, and lox. A table under an awning offered protection from the drizzle and I settled in to check out more of the *Post*.

I especially enjoyed the sports section's lamentations on the condition of the Mets. Some would find it unusual that I would be interested. But my father had given me the injection. He was a Mets fan, win or lose. From Casey Stengel to the miracle of '69 and beyond. There's still a cap in my closet that I can't bear to part with.

The drizzle faded away, but the sullen gray clouds to the west promised more to come. I folded my paper, tucked it under my arm and headed back to my apartment. All security measures were in place and Caesar seemed pleased to see me, having left the shelter of my bed.

I gave him his morning treats, poured cold coffee into a mug, and put it in the microwave. In forty-five seconds it was steaming and I carried it to the couch. As I settled in, I decided to cancel the dinner with Lynette. I had told Cecil not to come into the line of fire, and it should be no different with Lynette. I glanced at my watch, ten-thirty. Okay to call, even if this was the most popular morning for consensual adult activities. But there was no answer. I left a message, "Call me, about tonight."

I spent the rest of the morning reading the *Post* and doing some light housework, hoping Lynette would return my call. A few minutes after two o'clock, the phone finally rang. I answered it immediately, assuming it was Lynette. "This is Susan."

He didn't try to disguise the voice that I had both loved and feared for more than half a decade. "Hello, bitch. Time to end this. Do you love Washington Square Park? I do. Come on over. Now!"

Chapter 43

I called Aurora's cell, hoping for some backup. Her recorded message referred me to her office number, meaning she and the good doctor were probably away on a stolen weekend fucking their brains out.

Once again, I was the bait in a trap of my own creation. Like Tee Pee Hill in Dallas. There I'd had backup, and it had saved my life. This time I was on my own. But today I had the advantage of knowing my adversary. Most likely deranged, and probably not as careful as he should be.

But there was no need to stand out like a bull's eye. I ditched the red tee for one in mottled gray. The .32 stayed in my cargo pants and the Glock remained in the holster in my waistband. It was still drizzling, but I decided against rain gear. It'd slow my reactions. To keep my vision clear, I pulled on my Mets ball cap.

Just before I left the apartment, I hugged Caesar, called Cecil's number, and left her a message asking her to check on him if she hadn't heard from me by Monday. Then I set out for Washington Square Park, my senses on fire. I knew my five-year nightmare with Terry would end today, one way or the other.

He'd expect me to enter the park from the south. Instead, I walked up 7th, through Sheridan Square and down Waverly Place to where the street briefly changed its name to Washington Square North.

Once there, I hung back and scanned the northwest corner of the park. The drizzle still filtered down through the trees, but didn't discourage the chess players gathered around the stone game boards just inside the park. There were half a dozen games in progress. Chess was a favorite of Terry's, so I studied each of the players carefully. Some were quickly eliminated: too short, too tall; too thin, too heavy. Only one caught my attention. A stained, gray felt fedora pulled low on his head shielded his face. I watched the game, and when he moved his pieces on the board, his hand was quick and sure. He was about Terry's build, and the loose camouflage jacket he wore could conceal anything from a nine-millimeter to a sawed-off shotgun.

I watched the match for maybe five minutes more as the drizzle dripped off the bill of my cap. One moment I was sure he wasn't Terry, the next I was sure he was. I was about ready to take preemptive action when thoughts of the homeless man and his black angel of death told me to be sure. *You're the bait. Let him come to you.*

A few moments later, I saw his opponent pull a pint bottle from a brown bag at his feet. He took a swig and handed the bottle across the table to the man in the fedora, who took a longer drink. Problem resolved. I knew Terry's Special Forces training would never allow him to dull his reactions when a life was on the line ... his target's.

I left my corner and walked down Washington Square North and entered the park where Fifth Avenue ends at the Washington arch. I lingered under the shelter of the arch and checked out the middle of the park. Nothing unusual. A young woman in a poncho walked a reluctant blonde cocker who tried to shake itself dry every four or five steps. A teenage couple walked hand-in-hand, oblivious to what was now light rain. I glanced back toward the chess tables. The competitors had bailed out for drier quarters.

The sky suddenly darkened, lightning flashed, and thunder filled the air. Wind drove the rain in a punishing slant, and the arch offered little protection. I kept my back pressed to one of the stanchions, constantly scanning the park. I felt Terry's presence and knew one of us would never leave this place alive.

Then, as suddenly as it had come, the storm was gone. The sun broke briefly through the clouds, and a few hardy souls left what shelter they had found and ventured back into park. None of them looked like Terry.

I walked the perimeter of the park, turning 360 every twenty seconds. But no one caught my attention. Then I knew Terry wasn't coming. He was playing with me. Probably watching from a close place, laughing. Congratulating himself on pulling my chain.

One more time circulating the perimeter. I encountered a Quaker group at the arch, forming up for a peace demonstration. The chess players drifted back in to take their places at their tables. Tourists from the heartland walked and pointed. The park reestablished its weekend rhythm. Terry was not there. My watch said three-thirty. Time to go back home and meet Lynette. I'd send her away as soon as she arrived.

I made it back home with fifteen minutes to spare. I climbed the stairs and checked the security tape. In place.

When I opened the door, Terry had a nine-millimeter aimed between my eyes. A crooked smile spread over his face. "Welcome home, bitch. Come on in."

Chapter 44

Terry stood across the room, dressed entirely in black. The glare of the windows that looked out on Morton Street backlit his figure. His dark eyes were so intense they appeared crazed. He held the automatic in both hands, extended out from his chest.

I froze, convinced my life could end any second. But he didn't pull the trigger. Instead, he said, "Step into the room and close the door."

For a split-second I thought I should dive away from the door, but nine-millimeters go through dry wall with ease. So I closed the door behind me, careful not to make any sudden movement, and took a couple of steps into the room.

He wagged the gun barrel. "Hands high."

I raised my hands to shoulder level and struggled to keep my breathing under control. "How the hell did you get in here?"

He smiled again. "You'll know that soon enough." Then he glanced toward the kitchen. "Just so you know what kind of deep shit you're in, take a look."

I turned and saw the Taurus and the Smith & Wesson on the kitchen table. He must have sensed my alarm, because I heard a low laugh rumble out of his throat. "You got sloppy, sweetheart. You hid 'em in the same places you did when we were doing the mattress boogie in Dallas .The Taurus gave me a little problem, but I knew it'd be in the pantry or refrigerator. The Smith & Wesson was easy."

Though I knew it was a bad idea, I couldn't resist. "Shit. What can I say? I screwed up. But I guess I figured you'd be as inept at killing me as you were at fucking me."

His face went blank, facial muscles slack. I'd never seen a look like that in my life. He was over the edge beyond recall. He came forward and smashed his pistol across my right eye. Bright light daggered into my brain, and I heard the crack of orbital bone splitting. I collapsed and slid down the door to the floor.

He spoke quite calmly. "You've just made it worse for yourself. Now stand up." The face remained blank. "Come on, you've got one good eye. Uppsy daisy. Shit, I've got bits of bone on my gun."

I heard him, but couldn't seem to make my legs work. Finally, I got on my hands and knees, my right eye swollen closed and blind with blood. I grasped the doorknob, and pulled myself to my feet.

"There, bitch. That wasn't too hard, was it?" He smiled. "Now I need your Glock and that damn .32." He took a couple of steps toward me. "Here's what you're gonna do. First take off your tee shirt."

I didn't move, trying to buy more time to clear the daggering pain in my skull. This enraged him more. He tapped my swollen eye socket with his gun muzzle. I screamed, nearly fainting with pain; wanting to faint, to die, to just get it over with.

"Shirt off, please."

I pulled the tee off over my head. Sweat had soaked my bra and outlined my nipples.

"Raise your hands, now, like a good girl." I did as I was told and felt him take my Glock from my belt. I watched him with my one good eye as he laid the pistol on the kitchen table. "Used to wear it in the middle of your back, didn't you? That gets old real quick, doesn't it?"

He had moved away from me. "Now the .32. Where is it? In your pant's pocket or on your ankle? And don't lie to me."

"Right leg pocket. And I don't feel too good. Dizzy." I squinted at him, watching his eyes fade in and out of sanity.

"That's your fault. You didn't know a good fuck when you got one. You're probably a les ... that it? Who's your lover? That Cecelia hag? Now put your feet together."

I shifted my feet together. "Now unbutton your right pocket." He kept his weapon aimed at my heart, reached into my pants pocket, removed the .32, and put it on the table next to my other weapons. "Now, where's your cell phone?"

I patted my other pants pocket.

"Drop it on the floor and kick it toward me." I did as I was told. Terry walked to it and crushed it under his boot.

"Now spread your legs. I'm gonna pat you down. Maybe you've got something hidden in that bra."

He fondled both my breasts. Taking particular time with my nipples. Then he moved down to my waist, his thumb tracing down to the conjunction of my thighs. His lips parted and his breathing became more rapid. "Always enjoyed that."

I didn't speak as he worked his way down one leg, then the other. When he finished, I said, "I'm still dizzy. Feeling sick." I bent over at the waist, put my hand over my mouth, and made a gagging noise. Before Terry could react, I stumbled through the living room, using my good eye, but off balance. I bounced off the walls of the hallway leading to the bathroom.

Terry caught me and slammed me to the wall just before I got there. He threw open the bathroom door, shoved me inside, forced me into the shower enclosure, and slammed the door closed.

I heard him tossing the cabinet under the basin, and then held my breath when he lifted the top of the tank on the toilet. He paused a moment, looking down into the tank. I stuck my finger down my throat and forced myself to throw up into the shower.

It worked. Terry whirled around and pulled me out of the shower. "Tsk, tsk. What a mess you've made."

I called on my tears, praying they'd be there. They flowed, all salt and congealing blood. "Please, for God's sake, give me some privacy."

"No way in hell."

"You've tossed the room. There's no window. What the hell could happen? You've won."

A little smirk appeared on his lips. "Yeah, I have. So I'll give you two minutes. Throw up, piss, whatever." He threw me to the floor and pulled the door closed as he left the room.

I pulled the "Save-A-Flush" container out of the tank, broke the seal, and removed the Derringer. It was as dry as the day I had put it in the tank. I squinted at it, tears and blood blurring my vision. I cocked the hammer, moved to the right of the bathroom door, and took a few seconds to get my breathing under control. Then I let out a scream of the damned. Let out all the primal rage, terror, pain and hopelessness that I had buried so deep.

Terry rushed into the room, nine-millimeter raised toward the ceiling. I crashed into his back and shoved the barrel of the Derringer into his head, just below his left ear. "Put your weapon on the floor, asshole. It's my turn."

Chapter 45

Terry eased the nine-millimeter to the floor. I stepped away from him. "Into the hallway." For second or two he didn't move, then he slowly left the bathroom and stood in the hallway, a few feet from the bathroom door.

"Face the wall and put your hands in the air." Again he paused. I could almost hear his mind working. Desperately searching for something to put him back in control. Then, after a few moments, he followed directions.

When he was facing the wall, I picked up his automatic and put the Derringer in my pants pocket. Now I had a hell of a lot more firepower. I left the bathroom and kept away from him. Blind in one eye, I was just one of his judo twists away from him breaking my arm and regaining control. I wasn't going to give him that option. "Walk slowly toward the living room. If I see so much as a twinge, you'll be in a wheelchair the rest of your life."

He started toward the living room and I followed, keeping a safe distance between us. He reached the couch. "Sit!" This time he didn't hesitate.

I kept the automatic aimed at his heart, walked into the kitchen and reached for the phone to call 911. It was gone.

A big smile spread over Terry's face, and I stared at it, squinting then widening my good eye. "A little precaution I took." Then the smile was gone, his face slack. "You're getting no help. If you want to leave here alive, you're going to have to kill me."

I took a couple of steps out of the kitchen. "I just might do that."

"You don't have the guts, bitch. Especially since this is all on you."

Blood rushed to my face, daggering pain into my brain. "The hell it is!"

His eyes changed and he seemed to be looking at me from a different world. His words dripped with sarcasm. "These *C*... *E*... *O's*! *These captains of industry*! They're so high and mighty. They take what they want. And they get away with it. Like Tom Grant took you. And you let him. You let him fuck you."

I fought back bile rising on the agony from my damaged eye. "You're crazy as hell. He didn't take me! We didn't have ..."

"Bullshit. But I decided to take sweet fucking revenge on those high and mighty CEO's and I did. I started with the top ten and worked my way up. I shamed what they loved best. I took what belonged to them. I made them pay."

He leaned forward and his eyes darted toward the kitchen. I made a step toward him. "Come on. Try for a gun. It won't cost me much to clean up your brains."

His body seemed to contract into itself. Like a snake coiling for a strike. The end was only moments away, but I had to know. "Why Martha Kirkland? Fred didn't fit your pattern."

He smiled his big Walter Mitty smile that froze my blood. "I got lucky. The *Post* story told me you were working the rape cases. I had no idea. But how sweet this was. Now I could get two for one. A CEO's wife who was your friend. It was more than I could have hoped for. I was determined to kill you, but if I couldn't, I could kill someone you loved."

My finger tightened on the trigger. "And Cecil?"

His eyes danced the way they had when he was taking me to bed. "A chance to send you a message ... and see if you were a smart enough bitch to figure it out."

I backed toward the kitchen. Ready for his attack. Ready to put a bullet in his brain. Then I heard it. A turn of a key in my front door. The door swung open and Lynette Mason walked in.

"Get the hell out of here," I screamed.

She froze in her tracks and stared at me, then at Terry. A look of alarm spread across her face. "What ... what the hell's going on here?"

"Get the hell out," I screamed again. She didn't move.

Terry rose slightly off the couch, but I kept the automatic leveled on him. "Try that again and you're dead."

Lynette rushed to my side and cried out, "Susan, let me help you!"

I didn't take my eyes off Terry, but barked at Lynette, "You got your cell phone with you?"

"Yes!"

"Call 911. Tell them robbery in progress. Weapons discharged."

Out of the corner good of my eye, I saw Lynette pull out a revolver out of her purse. Before I could react, she smashed the gun into the side of my head. A starburst of pain flashed before my eyes, the automatic fell from my hand, and I collapsed on the floor.

Chapter 46

Terry rushed forward across the room. In one motion, he grabbed the nine-millimeter and drilled a devastating kick into my ribcage. I screamed and curled into a fetal position, steeling myself for other blows. But they did not come.

His laugh was slippery, an ululating sound of madness.

When I didn't move immediately, Lynette planted a couple of swift kicks on my shins. "Bitch, get up!"

I paused a moment more, trying to clear my head. Then I grasped the arm of the couch and pulled myself to my knees. Lynette moved away from me and stood next to Terry, her hip against his. Her right hand gripped the revolver. Her left arm lay on his shoulder, her hand massaging the back of his neck. "She ain't so tough, baby. I thought you said she was a tough little cunt."

Terry kept his weapon aimed at my heart. His free hand was wrapped around Lynette's waist, resting between her red crop-top and her low riding jeans. He watched me for a few seconds, then he said, "I used to love it when you went to your knees. Get up!"

As I struggled to my feet, I kept squinting at Lynette.

"She's always been my ace in the hole," Terry said. "I knew you couldn't resist helping a lost soul. I knew she could lead you anywhere. Even to me."

Lynette continued stroking the back of Terry's neck. "And I did, didn't I, baby?"

"You sure did."

I heard a loud meow and Caesar walked into the room. "Don't worry about him," Lynette said. "I've taken a real liking to that cat. I'll take care of him real well."

Terry took his hand off Lynette's waist. "I never liked that hellcat. But if you want him, he's all yours, baby. Get the bag."

Lynette walked down the hall and when she returned she held a dull green canvas bag. "Here it is, baby."

Terry's eyes bore into mine. "First, I'm gonna beat you the way I beat Cecil. Then I'm gonna screw you the way I screwed Ray. I'm gonna fuck you they way I fucked Felicia and Janet. Then I'm gonna kill you the way I killed Martha. And it's gonna be slow." He glanced at Lynette. "Get the camera."

Lynette opened the bag and pulled out a small video camera. "And my baby's gonna tape the whole thing. And at the end, you're going to be grateful to die."

I had always known someday it would come to this. I willed myself to stand as erect as possible. "It won't be easy, asshole. You'll kill me before you want to."

"Maybe so. But it'll be a great snuff film. And at the end, you'll still be dead." He looked at Lynette. "Get the tape."

Lynette reached into the bag and produced a roll of duct tape. Terry smiled. "Good. Wrap her hands."

I kept my hands at my sides as Lynette walked toward me, revolver in one hand, duct tape in the other. When she stopped in front of me, Lynette fumbled to peel the duct tape off the roll while still holding the revolver.

Terry saw the danger and screamed, "No, damn it, Lynette ... No!"

He was too late. Before he could move, I had Lynette's revolver. I twisted her in front of me and put the gun to her head. "She's dead." I screamed. "She's dead if you don't drop it!"

Terry leveled down the nine-millimeter and returned my scream. "She's already dead, bitch." I heard a *pop ... pop* from Terry's weapon. Lynette's head exploded, bone and brain spraying me. Her body jerked against mine.

I fired wildly, riding Lynette's body down. From some great distance, I heard Terry's automatic fire again.

Then silence. I lay still, listening for movement ... nothing. Finally, I pushed Lynette's body off of me, stood, and checked for damage.

A wound on my left arm ran blood freely. It would have to wait. Terry lay on his back, his mouth opening and closing, his eyes staring at the ceiling. An entry wound was visible on his right cheek and blood seeped from the soggy bog that had been the back of his head. The blood was dark on my carpet. His legs shook, his torso shook, then he was still. I checked for signs of life, got up, and began taking care of myself.

In the bathroom I ripped a towel into a tourniquet for my arm. I soaked a face cloth and compressed it over a tortured eye socket. Surgery would be needed to save the eye. I got a pillowcase, tore it into ribbons and bound the eye.

I heard Caesar give a couple of cries and he walked into the living room from wherever he was hiding. I bent down and picked him up, wincing as the blood went to my head, and rubbed his belly. "It's all right. We're safe, baby. We're finally safe."

Epilogue

Before I called 911, I concealed all my weapons. The only guns the cops seized for evidence were Lynette's revolver and Terry's nine-millimeter. I'll be forever grateful to Mike Riley for the gift of the Derringer. It was the second time he saved my life.

At Bellevue, I got the best of care for my eye. It could be saved. Two days later I was thoroughly interrogated about the events in my apartment. Aurora ran interference for me. A few days after that, I was allowed to leave my hospital bed. But some plastic surgery awaited me later.

In the days following, I couldn't get Lynette Mason out of my mind, so I made inquiries. It turned out Terry was right. She was a lost soul. The only true thing she'd told me was that she went to Stanford. She was the product of a broken home where both her father and stepfather sexually abused her.

Her affair at Stanford was not with a publisher's son, but with his daughter. After it ended, she went from man to man, always finding more abuse. When Terry found her and offered love, she was willing to do anything for him. It had cost her her life.

I thought about moving out of the apartment, but instead, I just had the bloodstains cleaned. I was tired of running.

On the Fourth of July, Cecil and I spent a glorious day at a celebration in Washington Square Park. When I returned home, there was a message from Garrett Nelson on my answering machine. I returned his call.

Made in the USA